THE
YEWBERRY WAY
BOOK I : PRAYER

JACK GIST

DEFIANCE PRESS
& PUBLISHING

THE YEWBERRY WAY

ISBN-13: 978-1-959677-19-2 (Paperback)
ISBN-13: 978-1-959677-18-5 (eBook)

Published by Defiance Press & Publishing, LLC

Bulk orders of this book may be obtained by contacting Defiance Press & Publishing, LLC. www.defiancepress.com.

Public Relations Dept. – Defiance Press & Publishing, LLC
281-581-9300
pr@defiancepress.com

Defiance Press & Publishing, LLC
281-581-9300
info@defiancepress.com

The happy birch-wood is a good place to wait for my day-bright girl; a place of quick paths, green tracks of lovely color, with a veil of shining leaves on the fine boughs; a sheltered place for my gold-clad lady, a lawful place for the thrush on the tree, a lovely place on the hillside, a place of green tree-tops, a place for two in spite of the Cuckold's wrath; a concealing veil for a girl and her lover, full of fame is the greenwood; a place where the slender gentle girl, my love, will come to the leafy house made by God the Father.

—Dafydd ap Gwilym

PART I
SCREENS

CHAPTER ONE

How am I supposed to know if he was telling the truth? Parts of the story could've been made-up—maybe even the whole thing. Maybe he stole some of it from somebody else and made the rest up on his own. Or maybe it's all true. I don't know.

Is he here? Can you at least tell me that? Is he alive?

Do you think my story will change if you keep asking me to retell it? Is it in your interrogation manual? How boring. Of course it'll change. It's a story. Get it? Do you think Homer's story about the Trojan War never changed? I'm alive. So is my story. Living things are always shifting.

What? I think my mother told me about Homer when I was a kid. I don't remember.

Like I said, it might be true; it might be fabricated. Is this about him or me? Why are you so desperate to find out what he told me? Is this some kind of experiment? How long are you going to keep me here? Why won't you tell me where he is?

Okay. One more time. But only if you answer this question first: Is he alive? Yes? Okay. From the beginning.

***

The glare of the sun on the sand causes him to wonder if a blind man might see light rather than darkness. When he closes his eyes, the light is still there, though dimmer, his eyelids muting the brightness. The sand is hot under his cheek. His groin feels damp. He is afraid to touch down there for fear he is bleeding. Curling into the fetal position, he wants to weep but cannot.

When he opens his eyes, he finds himself in a latticework of shade cast by a creosote bush. The sun, a white glob of brightness, vibrates at the edge of the horizon. He can't tell if it is rising or setting.

The shadows from the bush are too thin to do much good, but they soften the glare of sunlight reflecting off the sand. His tongue sticks to the top of his mouth. Black flies flit about his ears, crawl in and out of his nostrils.

He can't remember his name.

He sits up, looking at the backpack tucked under the bush. He looks at his crotch. His khaki trousers are dusty and dry. He puts a hand on his balls. They radiate heat.

Dunes of white sand dotted with creosote and mesquite roll into the distance. Peeling his tongue from the roof of his mouth, he attempts to work up a mouthful of spit. When he swallows, the pea of moisture vanishes halfway down his throat.

He unbuttons his long-sleeved cotton shirt, takes it off, and folds it. Then, he stretches out on his back in the thin shade of the bush and rests his head on the shirt. A small dust devil, as if conjured by a lesser demon, springs to life and spins into the bush. Sand skids across his chest. Later, he muses, when he is dead from exposure, the sand will swallow him up if the vultures and coyotes don't get him first. He closes his eyes and listens to the buzzing of flies.

***

The moment the door closes, the tension leaks out of my neck. There is peace in being alone. But I'm never alone.

There are no clocks. No time. Just a room with red padded walls, a floor covered with black wrestling mats, and tubes of fluorescent light set inches apart on the ceiling. The lights never go out. The hiss of electricity in the tubes erases thought, amplifying the sound of the heart beating in my chest.

I sense their return before the lock clicks and the door opens. I have no idea how long they've been gone. They wear white hazmat suits. Air pumps click on the oxygen tanks on their backs. The face shields of their helmets reflect fluorescent light like mirrors in a winter storm. I know them by the way they move. The female is shorter, lighter, the curves of her hips noticeable under the protective suit. He's heavy, older, probably bald and married to a fat lady who complains as she bakes buttery cakes in the kitchen while he drinks beer and watches his computer screen in the living room.

The female does the talking. Always. The man never says a word. He sets up the equipment and stands in a corner of the room watching. I think she outranks him. When she talks, her voice purrs from the back of her throat like a mother comforting a sick child.

But I'm no child. And I'm not sick.

***

I already told you. He couldn't remember how he got there. He couldn't even remember his name. I don't know. Maybe somebody kidnapped him. Maybe he went on a bender and the drugs and booze wiped his memory. Maybe he was looking for redemption in a drug-induced forgetting of sins. You know, maybe he took a trip to the Jungle. You can get anything you want there if you know the way—even if you don't know what you want. Maybe he OD'd. Don't you get it? He couldn't remember.

Yes, I believed him. Why wouldn't I? Because he was a stranger? Is that a crime? Maybe to you, but I wanted to help. I had to believe him if I was going to help him.

I don't know how he got out there. I guess he wandered in from the Outside.

She stands above me with her hands on her hips. A vapor of perfume trails out from underneath her protective gear. A hint of sweetwood. I want to see her eyes. I need to see her eyes.

***

The yap of coyotes awakens him. At first, he believes it's human laughter. The night is cold. A full moon hangs over the horizon like an egg ready to crack. The light is the same color as the sand. It would be beautiful if he wasn't so thirsty—if his tongue wasn't too big in his mouth.

His knees pop as he stands. He winces from a pain in his ribs. It's difficult to breathe. He knows that if he doesn't get to water, he'll die. And water isn't going to come to him. There's nothing to do but walk. He takes up the backpack and limps toward the moon.

The sun rises behind him. The light on the sand changes from moonbeam white to watermelon red. When he looks up from the sand, the moon is gone. The angular outline of a building wavers on the horizon. His head throbs. He looks at his hands, noticing the purple tint underneath his fingernails. He falls to his knees. He tries to stand but cannot.

***

That's how I found him. Kneeling in the sand, hands clasped under his chin, eyes closed. He didn't know I was there. As far as he was concerned, I was invisible.

Her shoulders tense. The man checks the gauges on the machines. This is the part of the story that interests them. I must have told it fifty times.

I noticed him when I walked out of the Outpost. I was headed to the glasshouse to get a cantaloupe from the greenhouse for my breakfast.

What?

She smells of sweetwood.

I told you. His eyes were closed. His face was dry as dust. Skin flaked from the cracks in his lips. Yes. He might have. He might have been praying. Do people still do that? He had his hands clasped under his chin. His lips were moving, his body trembling. No. No, he wasn't crying. Why do you ask? You don't know where he is, do you? What is it that you want from him? From me?

She stands. Her shoulders relax. Why would she wear perfume to an interrogation?

If you have him, you're going to need to prove to me that he's alive. I'm not taking your word for it. Not anymore. If you don't prove it by tomorrow, I won't say another word. And I'm a man of my word. You know that about me, don't you? You understand. A man of convictions. Come back tomorrow.

The man packs the electronics into cases as the woman stands, looking down on me.

I want to rip away her helmet. I need to see her eyes.

The man opens the door and carries the cases into the hallway. He's engulfed in white light. She follows him into the hall, turns, and looks at me. Then, she closes the door. The lock clicks.

How will I know when tomorrow arrives?

CHAPTER TWO

He's a boy who feels like a girl. He tells no one, not even himself. He dares not say the words, even in silence, "I am a girl."

The kids at school tease him for fussing over his clothes; the way his shirts and pants are always pressed and clean; the manner in which he carries an extra pair of shoes in case the first ones get soiled; the way his fingernails are manicured, the cuticles pushed back, the quarter moons bright under the buffed nails.

He saves the allowance he earns from tending the chickens, geese, dogs, cats, sheep, goats, horses, and cows that populate the family farm. He purchases magazines intended for teen girls while his mother cruises the aisles of the department store, pushing the hard-rubber wheels of her cart over the slick, bright floors in search of deals.

At home, the boy stashes the magazines between the mattresses of his bed. He waits for the cover of darkness, crawls under his woolen blankets, and turns on a flashlight. He smiles as light blossoms on glossies of girls sporting the latest in fashion. The girls smile back. He longs to try on their clothes, to touch up his cheeks with a hint of rouge, to paint his lips pink. For a moment, he fancies the smell of perfume, fruity and light.

***

That's how he told it most of the time, in the present tense, as if he had witnessed his father's childhood. Judging from the detail and the tone, he must have heard the story so many times that it became a part of him. It was his story as much as his father's. I believed him at first.

There were no computers back then, no cell phones—not in the nowhere where he grew up. It must have been Outside. His father's father— he never said, "my grandfather," always "my father's father"—worked the oilfields. He'd be gone for weeks at a time. It was dangerous work. Many a man lost a finger or worse in the pursuit of black gold. When Father came home, his pockets were full of money. He handed most of it to the boy's mother. He was a good provider. In the fall, he took his son deer and elk hunting and taught him how to shoot a gun and a bow. He taught him how to trap muskrats at the creek that ran through the prairie a mile west of their house.

Father believed in the old-school God, an unknowable deity entirely separate from that which it created, the God of nature and of man. He was one of the last of the Believers, or so he reckoned, and he was proud of it.

The boy loved Father. But he feared him more.

***

The raccoon hisses at the boy's approach. Her back leg is clamped between the steel jaws of a foothold muskrat trap. The trap is chained to a stake of rebar sticking out of the middle of the creek. She sits on her haunches in the shallows near the bank. Her hiss deepens into a growl as the boy approaches.

A canopy of black-bottomed clouds hangs low on the scene. A breeze snakes through sage and greasewood above the bank. The boy stands on a dirt ledge above the creek. He looks down at the moving waters. He swallows. The spit tastes metallic. The water flowing down the creek is peat moss brown.

They stand looking at one another, boy and beast, for a long moment. A tremor runs down the raccoon's back, and the spell is broken. The animal's low growl returns.

***

The first time he watched Father shoot a mule deer, he snuck away and hid behind a big greasewood. He sat on the ground and buried his face in his hands. His palms smelled of campfire smoke. Puffs of clouds wandered through the sky. A deerfly bit the back of his neck. He slapped it away. The breeze dried the tears on his cheeks. He felt as hollow as a cave.

"Hey, boy!" shouted the father. "Where you be at? Get on over here so's I can show you how to gut this thing."

The boy stood and wiped his eyes. "Okay. Comin'. Just takin' a piss."

The bullet had struck the deer in the spine. The beast lay on its side on the rocky ground, dark eyes open, paralyzed. He was a young buck, a spike, the antlers poking out of his skull like stiletto heels.

"He's alive," said the boy.

"Hold this and mind where you're pointin' it." The father shoved the 30.06 bolt action rifle at the boy and pulled a hunting knife from the sheath at his belt.

The boy stood dumbstruck as a blue bottle fly crawled over the deer's eye.

The father knelt down. He plunged the knife into the deer's neck.

The air smelled like fresh cow flop.

The deer tensed. The eye widened. The fly took flight. The deer relaxed. The fly returned. Steam rose from blood pooling in the dirt.

The boy found himself floating above the scene, the world growing small beneath him—no more than a whirl.

The father never told a soul, not even the boy's mother, that his son had fainted, collapsing to the ground next to the carcass of the deer.

The boy never got used to killing.

***

The boy wonders.

***

If he were to wade out to the stake securing the trap, the raccoon would be in a position for a desperate charge. The boy once witnessed a single coon—a big one like this—shred a bluetick hound's ears to ribbons, rip the jowls from a black lab, and blind one eye of an Irish setter before the dogs managed to drown it in the creek.

***

The boy meanders through a stand of greasewood above the moving waters.

The raccoon watches.

***

The father taught the boy where to set the traps. They placed them near muskrat dens and smeared the traps with a sweet-smelling paste. At dawn the next morning, they checked the traps. Three of the five had sprung. Drug down by the weight of the steel, the muskrats were dead at the bottom of the creek. They were bigger than the boy had imagined. He stared at the long front teeth, orange as rust, and imagined the rats coming back to life and ripping into the meat of his father's palm. Father peeled the pelts from the bodies like wet socks from feet and tossed the carcasses onto the shore.

The boy had been trapping on his own for over a month. He set the traps at what he figured to be a safe distance from the muskrat dens in the hope the poor things would have a better chance of avoiding them. Only one of his traps had ever sprung. He found the tip of a muskrat's tail in the jaws of the trap. A string of sinew floated in the water like a pink ribbon.

***

He spots it on the far side of the creek—a piece of lumber sticking out from a tangle of dead branches. Wading through the water a safe distance from the coon, the cold water rising to his crotch, he pulls the two-by-four from the branches. He tests the weight, and while stripping dried moss from the wood, a splinter pierces his palm. He drops the two-by-four, which rolls into the water.

The raccoon watches.

The boy jumps into the creek to retrieve the board. He sinks knee-deep in mud. One of his boots gets stuck. The mud smells like rotten leaves. There is nothing to do but pull his foot free. One boot off and one boot on, the boy hobbles to the bank. Mud, black as tar, smears his jeans.

The raccoon watches.

The sole of his bare foot is soft-white and sensitive. He looks at the sky and wipes sweat from his brow with the sleeve of his shirt. He wishes the black-bellied clouds would drop rain. He uses the two-by-four as a crutch and hops to the point where he first crossed the creek. He starts across the gravel bank, his foot lowering into the water, testing the bottom before pressing down. He knows what must be done. The knowledge mutes emotion. All that remains is a bright buzzing.

A carpet of brown moss covers the bank of the creek. Stepping out of the water, the boy grips the two-by-four in both hands.

The raccoon hisses.

The boy moves to a spot where he can strike the beast from a safe distance.

The raccoon snarls.

The boy swings the board. The wood smacks the top of the raccoon's skull.

The beast reels. She looks up at the boy, tongue lolling, red blood gushing from her black nostrils.

Water flows.

The boy swings again. He misses the skull and hits the coon's spine. The breath is crushed out of her lungs. She continues to look at him, her eyes narrow. He strikes again. And again. Again. Her bones break. Her guts are ruined.

Tears blur the boy's vision. Once more, he strikes her with the wood. Tossing the board into the creek, he falls to his knees. He curls into a ball on the carpet of dead moss.

Water flows. A canopy of black-bellied clouds hangs low. Breeze snakes through the branches of sage and greasewood. The water is the color of peat.

The boy bites his tongue until it bleeds.

***

He jumped at the opportunity to slop the neighbor's hogs. The job required that he feed the hogs before catching the bus to school. This meant he had to get out of bed an hour earlier and walk a mile and a half down the dirt road to the hog farm. The hour before dawn was always cold that time of year. The boy didn't mind. He no longer had time to tend the trapline in the morning and couldn't risk checking the traps in the evening because caught rats might gnaw off their legs if the water failed to drown them. Father understood. No need to cause unwarranted suffering in an already miserable world—even if there were just dumb beasts.

The boy was grateful for the hogs but sorry that he was fattening them for slaughter. He spent a portion of the money earned to purchase fashion magazines and stashed the remainder in one of his father's old cigar boxes and hid it under his bed.

He never told anyone about the raccoon. He buried the busted body under a blanket of moss and dead branches. Standing on the ledge above the creek, he looked down on the makeshift grave. He made the sign of the cross just as his father did each night before dinner.

In the name of the Father, the Son, and the Holy Ghost.

CHAPTER THREE

I already told you he didn't talk about his own childhood—just his father's. At first, I thought he was talking about himself, but it didn't add up after a while. He wasn't much older than me by the looks of it, but there was no mention of screens, not even once, in any of his stories. I can't remember a time when I wasn't surrounded by screens. TVs, phones, tablets. Everywhere. He said he didn't have any use for them. He didn't even have a wristwatch with a screen. He didn't believe in watches.

Me? No. They weren't my memories. Is that what it sounds like? They were his. Or maybe his father's. I don't know. Not mine. His.

I grew up out in the country, but it wasn't the same kind of country that was in the stories he told—like the nature of nature had changed by the time it got to me. We had screens in the country where I grew up. He must have been from Outside.

The way he talked about how his father's father—it was weird the way he never said "my grandfather"—would run horses until the air was heaving from their lungs and a froth of foam forming at their necks. It was strange the way he told it. It gave the impression that he was there . . . that he had put his hand on the horse's chest and felt the pounding of its heart against his palm. For him, or I should say his grandfather, existence was charged with an invisible current. For the grandfather, life was a beautiful and terrible buzzing. The grandfather taught him that horses running pleased God.

It wasn't like that in my family. My Dad inherited a forty-acre pecan orchard when Gramps died from a brain rupture. Dropped dead without so much as a twitch. The orchard had been in the family for something like four generations.

It was Dad who installed giant grow lights on telephone poles around the orchard. The constant cloud cover diluted the sunlight to the point it wasn't enough on its own. Never needed artificial lights before that. They turned on and off at regular intervals day and night. The cost of electricity, even with the windmills, made it impossible for Dad to make enough of a profit from the harvest to support a family of seven.

So, he took a position at the Agency of Agreement to make ends meet. He was assigned to the Compliance Department. They encouraged him to keep working the orchard so long as he donated twenty-five percent of the harvest to the Department of Common Good, a charity for people who couldn't contribute to society because, for whatever reason, they couldn't comply with the demands of the System. In other words, they either couldn't or wouldn't take the oath, so they lived in little cells at the edge of the city like lepers. They'd starve to death out there on their own, so somebody had to feed them. Good for the sake of the Common and all that. Dad didn't mind. He'd say, "Everybody's got to play their part."

I helped out with the orchard when I got old enough. I was somewhere around ten, I guess. We were required to attend school at home after the System took over. It was never the same after that. I was online for three or four hours a day for school, so I had plenty of time to tend to the trees. Dad taught me how to repair driplines and when to flood the grounds from the irrigation ditch that bordered the property. When it came to the harvest, he made a deal with the local Adult Re-Education program to borrow some of the inmates in return for ten percent of the crop. Some years, there wasn't much of a harvest. The next year a bumper crop. The next two or three not much at all. Hit and miss, but mostly miss as the seasons wore on.

Dad threw in the towel the year I turned sixteen. No matter how many times he consulted the experts from the Department of Domestic Trees, the trees did as they pleased. Sometimes they produced, sometimes they didn't. Science didn't seem to have that much of an impact. Dad got sick of it and had all the trees cut down. He sold the lumber at a profit. I can still hear the chainsaws. I remember the tears running down Momma's face as she stood on the front porch of the house watching the trees come down.

Dad sold our once-upon-a-time family orchard, and we moved into town. He didn't hear the buzz of life, I guess, not like the stranger said his father's father did. I guess we had that much in common, me and the man praying in the desert. Neither one of us could hear the buzz of being. But we wanted to. We both wanted to feel what his grandfather felt.

Our people came from two different worlds. I guess that's why I thought he was telling his own story at first, not his father's and grandfather's. Maybe he was telling his own story through theirs. Every kid's born into some kind of world, and that world shapes the kid into what he becomes. The stranger's world wasn't the same as mine. We looked at things differently. But we were both human, and so we learned from each other. Both of our worlds got bigger.

***

His mother found the girlie magazines while spring cleaning. She threw them in the garbage and didn't say a word, not to the boy and not to his father. If she had asked why he had them, he could have explained it to her, and maybe she would have understood. He wasn't like the other boys. As a woman, she must have known. But she said nothing.

When he finally worked up the nerve to ask if she had come across some magazines he was collecting for a school project, she just looked at him and shook her head. He knew she was lying. And he knew that she knew that he was lying. She was a slight woman with dark eyes and high cheekbones. Her mother was Scots-Irish, her father Irish and Shoshone. They were legendary drinkers and got killed in a car wreck the night their grandson was born. Their legacy was hidden in the dark eyes of his mother—hot eyes that flashed when she was angry and sparked when she smiled. When he asked her about the magazines, the flash in her eyes went dull. She shook her head and said, "I haven't seen any magazines." Then, she turned and walked away.

The belt whipping that would have come if his father had found out about the magazines might have prevented all that came next. Maybe it would have rid him once and for all of feeling like a girl. Or maybe it would have pushed him further into the role. Who knows? Either one would have been better than being stuck in the middle. He was too young to tune in to the throb of sexual desire but understood the girls in the magazines were beautiful while he was not. The curves of their breasts pushing against flowery blouses—the rounds of hips under denim skirts—caused a buzz in the pit of the boy's belly. He didn't know it, but he was falling in love with a dream of a girl who didn't exist. He could feel her because she was a part of him. He wasn't her, but he loved her. He didn't yet know that they weren't the same.

He didn't dare purchase another magazine after his mother found the stash. He took to trapping and hunting that fall. He rodeoed in the spring and summer. He became popular at school. The day he turned fifteen, his mother caught him in the barn drinking whiskey from the dregs of one of his father's old bottles. He was alone. She told on him for that. Whiskey, as her own parents had proven, was the sure road to Hell.

His father didn't see it that way. He liked the way the boy had turned it around in just a few years. Before that, he thought his son might be off. He kept it to himself. At night, alone at the kitchen table, he prayed to God that his only child would grow out of whatever it was that was ailing him.

Freedom is a dangerous gift. It allows a man to do away with nature if he so pleases. Like my Dad did. Like we all do, I guess, in one way or another.

God answered the prayers. It was like Paul on the road to Damascus. He never looked back. The son of the father became a crack shot with a .30-.30 Winchester rifle and a rodeo champ.

No, I didn't know who Paul was or where in the hell Damascus might be. It's just what he said. I didn't ask him about it because I didn't want to be rude. Okay? Now where was I?

A proud father tends toward mercy. A little whiskey wasn't going to hurt anything. Standing on the dirt road under a blue sky next to an old red pickup, the father told his son, "Don't let your mother catch you drinking again or I'm going to have to come down hard. She blames whiskey for everything bad. Never come around here drunk, you hear?"

The boy nodded and spit at the dirt.

"Same goes for chewin' tobacco. Not around here. I don't want to hear about it from her, so make sure you hear this from me, got it?"

"Yessir," said the boy. He spit once more.

***

Her green eyes are aflame with the light spilling from the crimson candle on the redwood bar.

His gut buzzes, and he looks away.

***

The story always started there when it came to her, with the first time their eyes met. It didn't matter what followed . . . the time he asked her out, the walks next to the cottonwood trees by the river, fishing for trout, watching movies that bored him to death, or her teaching him the two-step to the twang of country music. That first glance had in it, as far as he was concerned, everything that followed.

She worked in the hotel that housed the saloon where he drank whiskey and beer when he was in town—the same saloon where their eyes first met.

No, he didn't say where the town was. I figured it was Outside somewhere. I figure it's long gone by now. Just a memory. Will you quit interrupting me so I can tell the story? Thank you.

The bartender, who went by the name of Jack, told him as much when he walked to the bar at last call, ordered a shot of high-dollar Irish whiskey, and left a five-dollar bill on the scarred bar top. An outlaw country song played on the jukebox in a corner of the bar. He couldn't remember the lyrics, but they had to do with railroad tracks and goodbyes. Looking back, he considered it an omen. At the time, though, he didn't give it much thought. He bought the bartender a shot and found out that the woman worked the morning shift at the front desk of the hotel, 6 a.m. to 2 in the afternoon. Jack didn't know what days she had off, but she came into the saloon with her girlfriends every Thursday night. After tossing down the shot, the bartender said, "I'm pretty sure she's single. By the way, her eyes are hazel, not green. You best get that right from the get-go."

He was living on his own by then in a single-wide trailer on the prairie past the airport. Spring winds whistled through gaps between windows and window frames, under doors, through propane heater vents. He tuned it out by reading. Though he still had an interest in women's clothes, he hadn't purchased a fashion magazine since the day his mother found the stash between the mattresses of his bed.

He worked as a cowhand for Thomas Moore on the Lazy M ranch west of town. The job kept his mind off the hollowness in his chest. He spent the days repairing fences, working on tractors and balers, and tending cattle. He didn't mind shit jobs like shoveling horse manure from stables or chopping down pigweed with a gas-powered weed whacker when the need arose. By the end of the day, he was tired. That's all he wanted. His father had harped that a man was to work until he was exhausted, eat, thank God, and rest up before getting up to do it all again.

"This here's a fallen world, boy," the father said. "Best get used to it. Complaining just makes it worse."

He returned to the trailer at dusk after a hard day's work. After tuning the radio to a familiar country station, he fried up beef, potatoes, and pinto beans. He smothered everything, from scrambled eggs in the morning to hamburgers and steaks at night, in red chile sauce. His mother called it Chile Colorado. He bought the stuff by the gallon. Other than that, salt and pepper were the only spices in the cupboard above the sink.

The television reception at the trailer was poor. The shows he could tune in bored him anyway. What did he care about happenings in towns and cities he had never been to and had no desire to see? After dinner, he'd pour himself a tumbler full of whiskey and listen to music. When the glass was half-empty, he'd pull a book of poetry from a stack next to the worn leather couch and read poems. A German poet named Rilke was his favorite. When the whiskey ran out, he'd close the book and shuffle back to his bedroom. The wind whistled through a crack in the window. He'd snore through the night, dreaming dreams he couldn't remember when he woke up. He found out later he was dreaming of a girl. He was remembering a forgotten love.

***

He makes the decision while sitting in his pickup truck outside the hotel. The dawn, a pastel splash on the eastern horizon, instills courage. He rolls the window down. The air is cool. He can smell the river that flows behind the brick hotel, the same river that runs through the Lazy M some twenty miles to the west. A breeze rustles through the shiny new leaves on the row of cottonwood trees bordering the parking lot. He takes a notebook and a ballpoint pen from the dash, scribbles something on a page, tears it out, folds it in a triangle, and places it in the front pocket of his best pearl-button shirt. Stepping out of the truck, he shuts the door gently, as if not to startle the morning. Songbirds sing in the rising light.

Inside, behind the front desk in the lobby, she stands above a ledger, wearing a brown smock. Her hair, the color of pinecones, is piled on top of her head. She has eyeglasses with tortoiseshell frames and large oval lenses. Taking a yellow pencil from behind an ear, she writes something in the ledger.

Standing just inside the lobby door, he wonders if she's the same girl he saw at the saloon. Her hair had hung down well past her shoulders that night. No eyeglasses. Doubt drains the nerve from him like piss from a dying horse. Stupid idea.

As he turns to leave, she glances up. Their eyes meet. She smiles. Frozen in a half-twist—torso turned toward the door, eyes looking back at her over his shoulder—he grins. It is her. She looks down at the ledger and continues to write.

***

If he had walked out of the hotel that morning, things would've turned out differently. But he didn't. He turned around, marched to the front desk, and introduced himself. She peered at him over the rims of her glasses. He told her he couldn't help but notice her beauty from across the bar on Thursday night. He then pulled the sheet of paper from his shirt pocket and placed it on the counter.

"I'm not trying to be clever or weird or anything," he said. "I just want you to read this. You need to know."

With that, he turned and walked away. At the lobby door, he glanced back over his shoulder. She stood at the counter unfolding the triangle of paper. He opened the door and stepped outside into the birdsong light.

On the paper, hand-printed in an angular script was a poem.

The Panther

His vision, from the constantly passing bars,
has grown so weary that it cannot hold
anything else. It seems to him there are
a thousand bars; and behind the bars, no world.

As he paces in cramped circles, over and over,
the movement of his powerful soft strides
is like a ritual dance around a center
in which a mighty will stands paralyzed.

Only at times, the curtain of the pupils
lifts, quietly—. An image enters in,
rushes down through the tensed, arrested muscles,
plunges into the heart and is gone.

Below the poem, written in cursive, the script narrow and tight: *I didn't write this. It was written by a real poet. I just wanted you to know that you lifted the curtain from my pupils. Call me if you want.* He printed his name and phone number at the bottom of the page.

***

Why do you keep asking the same questions? Don't you think I don't notice the code words planted here and there to see if you can get a different response? You must think I'm stupid. Don't feel bad. I'm used to it. People have treated me like I'm an idiot ever since I took the Keeper position at the Outpost. Who'd want to work the borderlands? They'd have to be crazy, right? People assume I was put out there because I'm an imbecile. I get it. And I don't care. If the cost of keeping to myself is the whole world thinking I'm a fool, so be it. But *you* can drop the act. You know I'm as smart as the next guy. Anybody can see that you're trying to get me to change my story. I don't know why. Not yet. But I'll figure it out. Count on it.

You don't need to keep telling me to put the restraints on every time you barge in here either. Like I'm a threat. I'm sick of it. All this shit. You know I'm not dangerous. And you know that I don't know where the praying man is. Why do you pretend? And what's with those protective suits? If I've got some fatal disease, wouldn't I be dead by now? You've sucked enough blood from me to fill a bucket. If I'm a carrier of some evil parasite, why don't you just tell me? It's all this nonsensicality that bothers me the most. Things need to make sense or people go nuts. But you already know that, don't you? You're trying to get me to crack. That's it. I get it. But I won't. You'll see. You'll break before I do.

And why doesn't *he* ever say anything? It's always *you* with your butterfly voice. For all I know, it isn't even your voice at all. Maybe it's being altered by some kind of filter. Hell, for all I know you're a man and the curves under that suit are fake like everything else in this fucking world you call home. Where am I? Why are you keeping me here?

Paranoid? Who would blame me? I've been locked in here for I don't know how long, not allowed to speak to anyone but you while the goon over there watches us. You treat me like a freak from another planet. *You're* the freak, though. How do I know you're even human? I can't know, so I don't. But I'd know if you'd show me your eyes. The eyes are the giveaway. Windows to the soul and all that. You can see it in their eyes. Why won't you show me your eyes?

Now he speaks! Say it again so I can hear. Really? She promised I'd get to talk to a grievance officer, and that hasn't happened. How long's it been? Days? A week? It's hard to gauge time in this never-ending buzz of light. Anyway, I don't want to see your eyes. I want to see *hers*. We have a deal? You promise?

Good. But remember, if your word's no good, you're no good. That's the truth of a man and you've lied to me before. Or did you forget? Not me. I remember. You don't have the stranger, and you need me to find him for you. I told you I'd figure it out.

Here's another thing. I've read the old books. Yep. You didn't know *that* did you? I stashed them, lots of them. I figured the Department of Discernment was gearing up to confiscate them from the public, so I took them and I hid them and I read them. What do you think of that? Lots of people did it. Lots of people still read. The System must have known it'd be impossible to get rid of all the books. They banked on the notion we idiots would forget about the old ways in a generation or two. Am I right? We didn't. Do you still think I'm stupid?

If you break your word again, I'll never believe you. Do you hear? If I can't trust you, I've got nothing to lose. You could starve me and it wouldn't make a bit of difference. I won't talk anymore if you break your word again. You hear? I mean it.

Guess what? I don't eat that slop you give me anyway. Tastes like mildewed oats and I bet it's laced with that shit to keep dicks limp and minds numb. General Tranquility pills ground up and stirred in. You won't get me that way. But you know I haven't been eating, don't you? You're always watching. Even when I sleep.

Yes? You'll show me your eyes? I don't care about his, just yours. Okay.

***

He was young, early twenties. She was older, maybe thirty. Her biological clock was vibrating the alarm, so she chose to overlook the signs. The way he drank too much. The nervous energy leaking from his dark eyes. The way he wouldn't meet her gaze for more than a second or two. But he was a hard worker, and he was kind. He never raised his voice to her, opened doors like an old-school gentleman, brought bunches of wild sunflowers and honey from the Lazy M. And he watched her. He was always watching her. When she caught him staring, he'd turn away. But she knew.

He'd get off work at dusk, drive the twenty miles to town, and pick her up at her apartment on the east side. They'd drive to the mall and watch movies at a cineplex with six screens. Spy movies were her favorite, but she'd watch anything. He didn't see the point of it all, spending good money to watch made-up stories about made-up people. But he kept it to himself. Sometimes he'd fall asleep to the drone of the actors' voices. He took a mild interest in films based on historical events, war movies, and biopics. One film, based on the life of the FBI boss J. Edgar Hoover, intrigued him. It was the only one he remembered watching all the way through from beginning to end. He had always felt like something was watching him, maybe somebody like an obsessed FBI boss who liked to wear women's clothes.

After the movies, they'd get a drink at the hotel saloon. Jack-the-Bar-tender seemed to like him, and this eased the apprehension dripping like a slow leak from the back of her skull. She considered Jack—with his pock-marked face and stringy hair hanging in a thin ponytail at the nape of his neck—a good judge of character. She trusted him. After a drink and a bit of small talk with Jack, the two of them would move to the back of the saloon and play eight-ball. After a game or two—he let her win now and then to keep things interesting—they'd sit at a table and listen to country tunes on the jukebox. Then, he'd drive her home.

He'd walk her to the door of Apartment 307, where she'd face him and thank him for taking her to the movies, maybe recapping the parts of the film she liked best. She never had a negative thing to say about a movie, not an actor, director, writer, or even the music. The cineplex, for her, was like a church, the films gateways to magical worlds where love triumphed over logic. Sometimes, usually during a movie about a spy who fell in love with the person he or she was spying on, she experienced a holy moment. She tried to explain it, how it was like dissolving in light, but he had trouble relating. When she told him about a discovery she had made, the kinship between film and prayer, all he could think of were the fashion magazines he treasured as a kid.

She didn't invite him inside the apartment until the end of the fifth week of their courtship. When she finally did, he found her place to be as clean as bleached wool. An antique China cabinet made of mahogany dominated the living room. It had brass handles and lots of glass. It sat in the middle of the wall opposite the couch. Considering her love of film, he had expected a big-screen TV in the living room. He found out later the TV was in the bedroom.

Inside the mahogany cabinet was a collection of Hopi Kachinas arranged on glass shelves. She'd inherited them when her great-grandmother passed away years earlier. The Mudhead Kachinas were her favorites. There were three of them. Their heads were round as ping-pong balls with button ears and a horn poking out the top of the skull. All the dolls were carved from cottonwood roots, the artist's signature either burned or painted on the bottom of the base. There was a bear Kachina, a clown, a crow mother, and an Eototo. She told him the story and function of each of the figurines. He sat on the couch and listened. The stories made him uncomfortable somehow, like he was spying through a peephole into someone's bedroom.

When she finished telling him about the last of the Kachinas, the Wupamo, who served as both a chief and a guard at certain ceremonies, she led him to the door. She thanked him for the movie—he had already forgotten the title—and kissed him lightly on the lips. Opening the door, she waited for him to leave. He asked her to think about marrying him and then stepped into the hall. She shut the door and leaned against the frame, an invisible weight pressing the air from her lungs.

***

He stands in the shade of a big cottonwood. The tree marks the center of the city park across the street from the church. His gut buzzes. White butterflies flit from the yellow blossoms of dandelions. Blue bright day. Cloudless. The breeze, faint as the quietest of whispers, is cool.

The ceremony is to begin in an hour. Several guests have arrived early. A woman in a white dress and matching sunbonnet laughs along with a man wearing black jeans and a straw cowboy hat. They stand near the steps of the church. Others mingle on the sidewalk below. He doesn't recognize any of them. Having never met her parents or siblings—a sister and a brother, both younger, both attending college out of state—he's a stranger at his own wedding.

The thought of exchanging vows at the altar unnerves him. He pulls a flask of whiskey from his cowboy boot, takes a sip, returns the flask, and draws the pantleg over the shaft of the boot. He should have invited his parents, at least his mother. When she reads about the wedding in the paper, she'll be hurt. The old man will comfort her. He always does.

Jack-the-Bartender rumbles up on a Harley Sportster, purple gas tank and fenders agleam with sunlight. He parks the bike across the street from the church. He wears worn harness boots, a black leather vest, a white button-up shirt, and a bolo tie. The clasp of the tie is a silver longhorn cattle skull. His blue jeans are stiff with starch.

The bridegroom leans against the rough bark of the cottonwood. He watches Jack approach.

"Hey," calls Jack. He pauses at the boundary between sunlight and shade. Removing a pack of filtered cigarettes from his shirt pocket and a silver Zippo lighter from his vest, he lights up. "Ready for the big show?"

"For better or for worse."

"Why are you standing over here by yourself? People might get the wrong idea. Where are all your cowboy friends?"

The husband-to-be bends low, pulls the flask from the shaft of his boot, takes a drink, and offers it to Jack.

"Don't mind if I do."

"Don't have no friends left but for you." He watches Jack swallow. The whiskey warms Jack's belly. "That's sad."

"I gave up all the things that she wouldn't approve of."

Jack hands over the flask. "I tried that once. Starting over. It don't work. Past always shows back up. One way or the other."

The bridegroom stashes the flask and draws the pantleg over the shaft of his boot. "There's a bar a block over. We gotta enough time for a beer."

"Not me." Jack shakes his head. "I'm not going to be that guy."

"What guy?"

"The guy everybody blames when you leave the bride standing at the altar."

"I ain't got nowhere else to go but to that altar. I got nowhere else to run. Just need a beer to get me there is all."

***

He had dropped out of high school when he could no longer endure the boys in the locker room. In those days, all students were required to take gym classes. Team sports weren't his thing, but the coach forced him to participate—everything from badminton to basketball. It wasn't like rodeo where he rode solo on broncs and bulls. He liked it that way. Solo. Once he was done with the ride, whether he beat the buzzer or not, he could sit down and drink with the boys. They didn't give a damn if he got bucked off or not. The eight seconds to the buzzer were his and his alone. Gym class, on the other hand, was a prolonged embarrassment. Students were required to shower after class. He despised public nudity. He took it as long as he could. When he couldn't take it any longer, he quit school.

His mother never forgave him. His father told him that he'd have to fend for himself if he was in such a big hurry to be a man. He'd saved up almost two thousand dollars from working on the hog farm, even after purchasing a rusty 1948 GMC pickup, a new set of tires, and overhauling the engine. After packing some clothes, fishing gear, guns, and poetry books, he kissed his mother on the lips and said goodbye. He shook his father's hand and thanked him for providing food and shelter over the years.

Then, he climbed into his truck and drove away.

***

"We've never been together. Not like that."

He sits next to Jack at a graffiti-scarred bar a block from the church. Cigarette butts overflow from an aluminum ashtray between the two. A rerun of a college championship football game plays on the television mounted on a wall above a row of liquor bottles. An old man with a bright nose and a barrel chest sits perched on a stool at the end of the bar. He wears threadbare bib overalls and is shirtless. He talks quietly to the bartender, a big-bosomed, middle-aged woman with bleach-blonde hair.

Jack says, "Nothing wrong with that."

"I know."

Jack takes a sip from a pint of beer.

"I've never been with any woman."

Jack smiles, places his pint on the bar, and slaps the bridegroom on the back. "I guess this'll be your lucky night."

***

The foreman at the Lazy M, Cody Lannard, hired him on sight. A short man with prematurely gray hair cropped close to the skull, Lannard recognized the kid from the rodeo circuit. He twirled a tip of his gray mustache and said, "Okay, kid. I don't want to be wasting all the time it took you to drive that old '48 pickup out here. Be over there at the big barns at six o'clock tomorrow morning. If you're a minute late, don't bother showin' up at all." Lannard had been a champion team roper once upon a time and had a soft spot for rodeo cowboys looking for ranch work. Working on a ranch, to Lannard's way of thinking, was to rodeo like a street fight was to a refereed boxing match. "Just remember there ain't none of them damn rodeo clowns to jump in and save your ass out here."

The kid smiled.

The first day on the job, the kid rode with Lannard on a John Deere tractor equipped with a front-end loader over a dirt road into a prairie dotted with greasewood and sage. Lannard drove to a cattleguard designating the boundary of the Lazy M and the public land beyond. He parked the tractor. The diesel engine idled—*thump, thump, thump*. Lannard supervised as the kid unloaded two shovels, a six-foot-long pointed metal bar, and a five-gallon water jug from the bucket of the loader.

The pit below the cattleguard had filled with dirt over time, and one of the bulls had figured it out and crossed the guard into public lands. More cattle followed. After a couple of months, Lannard got bored with herding the cattle back onto the ranch in what became a weekly ritual. He aimed to put a stop to it by means of the kid.

The kid watched as Lannard climbed down from the tractor and secured a chain to the bucket and the cattle guard. Lannard then climbed back up behind the steering wheel, applied the throttle, and lifted the cattleguard with the loader's hydraulic lift.

After instructing the kid to dig out a three-foot-deep pit so that the cattleguard could do its job, Lannard pulled a paper grocery sack from behind the seat of the tractor and handed it down. Without a word, Lannard drove away. The kid stood in the middle of the prairie holding a sack of apples, beef jerky, and a can of boiled peanuts.

The silhouette of serrated mountains, dusty in the morning haze, bruised the southern horizon. The thumping of the tractor engine was swallowed by the distance.

The ground beneath the cattleguard had been compacted by rain and spring run-off. The temperatures in the summer months could climb into triple digits for weeks on end. In the fall, cooler temperatures and low humidity parched the dirt into a fine powder. Winter blizzards came sudden and swift, battered the greasewood and sage, and dumped snow that was swept by the wind into drifts that looked like white dunes undulating over a desert. Windstorms drove broken stalks of the previous year's wild wheat under the cattleguard. After the winds came the rains, remnants of southern monsoons that flooded the river and stirred the prairie into a stew of mud. The pit beneath the cattleguard was transformed into a haven for mosquito larvae. The water evaporated as the temperatures climbed. By summer, all memory of the rains receded like a dream upon waking.

The kid pulled a pair of calfskin gloves from the back pocket of his jeans and picked up the iron rod. He lifted the bar over his head and brought it down hard onto the earth. *Thump.* The reverberation penetrated his bones. The tip of the iron struck a divot in the dirt, like a dimple made by a bullet smacking a wall of granite.

***

Blue sky.
Thump. Thump. Thump.
Brown dirt.
Thump. Thump. Thump.
Raven caw.
Thump. Thump. Thump.
Yellow sun.
Thump. Thump. Thump.
Earth.

***

The rhythm absorbed him.

An ache in his shoulders brought him out of the trance. His fingers were clenched around the inch-and-a-half round of iron. He released the bar and watched it fall to the ground, a waft of dust from the concussion rising only to vanish. He pulled off the gloves and studied the blisters on the meaty pads at the base of his fingers. Tossing the gloves to the dirt, he walked to the grocery sack, plucked out an apple, and sat down on the cattleguard to take store of things.

The apple was sweet as candy. A bite of beef jerky peppered with red chile powder complemented the fruit. He balanced the five-gallon water jug on a fence post, placed his mouth under the spigot, and drank. Seized by a stomach cramp, he set the jug on the ground, walked to the pit, and pissed a brownish stream of urine. He slapped a green-eyed horsefly on his forearm with his free hand. Piss splattered his boots. The leather sucked up the moisture like sand in a drizzle. Vultures circled. The sight of them so high made him dizzy. Zipping up his jeans, he looked at his hands—at the leaking blisters where fingers met palm.

He took up the iron rod and returned to pounding. He craved the oblivion of rhythm.

***

Thump. Thump. Thump.

***

Pus wet his palms.

***

Blue sky.
Thump. Thump. Thump.
Brown dirt.
Thump. Thump. Thump.
Raven caw.
Thump. Thump. Thump.
Yellow sun.
Thump. Thump. Thump.
Earth.

***

Sweat blurred his vision. His heartbeat pulsed in his eyes. He failed to find the space that unites worker with work. Exhausted, he gave up the pounding, turned loose the rod, and fell to his knees. He whispered, "I'm sorry. I'm so fucking sorry. I thought you were a dream. It's like I've been trying to wake up and fell deeper into sleep. We'll be together again. I promise."

Sitting in the dirt, he took off his boots and socks. He wrapped his palms in the socks and pulled the boots back on. Cotton rubbed against the blisters as he snaked his fingers into the gloves. He adjusted the socks under the leather before standing and taking up the shovel. He scraped at the dirt like it was dead skin on a sunburn.

The sun moved through the sky.

The sound of the tractor's diesel—*thump, thump, thump*—drew near. He climbed out of the pit. Standing in the quarter light of the dying day, the mountains to the south as dark as night, the western sky giving way to shadow, he was relieved he was no longer alone.

***

Sunlight slices through the space between the curtains on the bedroom window. Dust floats in the light. His newly wed bride sleeps in his bed, the beam of light slashing her forehead like a wound. He stands next to her. He holds a .357 magnum, the weight of the stainless-steel revolver strengthening his resolve.

The room smells of sex and frankincense. He remembers lighting a cone of incense from the wick of a candle. A blob of hardened wax remains on the saucer sitting on the nightstand next to the bed. He remembers the taste of her mouth, her skin.

A wall of wind crashes against the trailer. She turns to her side, the bedsheet falling from her shoulder. The streak of sunlight runs vertically up her cheek, parts her hair the color of pinecones.

He looks down at the gun.

***

The cocaine was a surprise. She brought it out after the second bout of lovemaking, claimed she'd been saving it for a special occasion, that it had been stashed in a cookie jar on top of the fridge for the better part of two years. She'd given up hope that a special occasion would come. And then she met him.

They might have booked a fancy motel for the honeymoon, driven to the city, ordered lobster tail and champagne. He had money saved and was willing to blow a wad on something she could remember. But she wanted it to be out in the country, at his trailer, and convinced him he'd be more comfortable in his own bed. She wanted to hear the yapping of coyotes in the night.

***

He knows a couple of the hired hands will be coming to move cattle to the back forty. Daylight burns, and there's always more work to be done. He's not supposed to be at the trailer. He's supposed to be out of town on his honeymoon.

Unlatching the six-shooter's cylinder, he checks the load. Six hollow points. He only needs one. He spins the cylinder and clicks it shut, pulls the hammer until he hears the familiar click.

She shifts on the bed. Sunlight tattoos her shoulder.

His gut buzzes.

He turns, opens the door to the bedroom with his free hand, and slides his stocking feet over the threadbare carpet. Pausing in the hallway, he glances back at his wife. She's beautiful. He whispers, "You're not her."

He pulls the door shut and walks on down the hall.

Outside, a cool breeze cruises through a sea of wild wheat. His heart pounds. Blue sky. Thump. Thump. Thump. Yellow sun. A cow moans in the distance. Thump. Thump. Thump. He walks into the field, looks up at the sky, and places the barrel of the gun under his chin.

***

He didn't leave a note. The child was born nine months later. The mother named him Ang, a family name that reached back in time beyond reckoning.

CHAPTER FOUR

They never come right out and say it, but I know what they're thinking. They figure the Praying Man got to me, and it's clear that they consider him dangerous. Because he is, so am I. Do they really believe I'm that gullible? A stranger shows up at the Outpost, and I ditch everything I've worked so hard for? Worst-case scenario, once they figure it out: I get a year or two in Re-Ed, maybe less. Then, I'll be back on my own. They'll assign me to another Outpost because I won't fit in anywhere else. I fit the Outpost. I'm alone there. That's all I want. Like it was. I'll do whatever it takes to get back. I'll play their game.

I acted the part of the conformist to get myself assigned to an Outpost in the first place. It wasn't easy. They don't assign just anybody to those positions. You have to be a simple-minded System devotee to get an Outpost gig. They figured I'd earned it. Imagine that. Hiding in plain sight all those years, going through the motions, making them believe I was a believer. It was all an act. I never bought into the goddamn System. Not for a second. The Praying Man didn't need to convert me. I was already there.

What they don't know, what their records can't tell them, is that I knew about the Old Ones long before I found the Praying Man in the desert.

When I was growing up in the Orchard, the surveillance equipment was primitive compared to what it is today. They never suspected that the Old One might have contacted me back then. They never dreamed that I listened to any voices other than their monotone droning. They didn't believe there were any other voices. They thought they had it all figured out.

The Praying Man knew about the Old Ones. They sent him.

They first came to me in the Orchard. I used to play in the trees in the cool of the evening after dinner or in the morning before catching the bus to school. It was before the In-House Education Act forced everyone to connect to the Learning Authority so the kids could be taught on computers at home. Parents who weren't blood tied to their kids were called Guardians. I think there were more Guardians than parents by then. The I-HEA assigned screens, one screen per kid, and each kid got an implant in the back of the neck that kept track of their screen time. Not long after, the adults were required to get implants and take tests to demonstrate they understood the System at least as well as the kids. The kids had to spend a minimum of twelve hours per week on their assigned screen. Failure to comply shaved points from the parent's Model Citizen Scores and resulted in demerits or, if left unchecked, a trip to the local Re-Ed.

Thank goodness for the Old Ones. They, the One and Three, emerged from the trunks of pecan trees like whispers in a cave. I was young, living somewhere between enchantment and reality, so they didn't scare me. They liked me from the get-go. It wasn't long before I could understand the whispers. I was old enough to know better than to tell anybody what they said.

***

She took off her helmet. Her eyes are hazel. I think it was yesterday. She reminds me of somebody I met in a dream. Maybe it was last week.

***

Why would you ask *me* how *he* ate? He ate with his mouth. He was fond of oatmeal with cinnamon and apples. He ate it with a fork. Didn't like spoons for some reason. I didn't ask. What difference does it make?

I always have a good supply of apples, no matter the season. I slice them up and dry them in a dehydrator. I go ahead of the machines just before harvest and pick them green. The Praying Man appreciated that, the way I snuck them out of the orchards. I'd harvest them before dawn. There weren't any lights out there, and they hadn't installed outdoor cameras yet. Not that far out in the country. What? There *were* cameras? Is that why I'm here? For a few bushels of apples now and then? Hell, a thousand times that many rot in the warehouses before they get delivered to the commissary.

What? He told me. He was familiar with the sickening sweet perfume of rotting apples. He said he dreamed in smells. He smelled lots of things. Everything.

***

Her face is older than her voice.

He took off his helmet, too. Brown eyes. Mean eyes. Younger than her. Babyface. I imagined he was middle-aged with a potbelly and a swollen liver. That's what he will become. The System gnaws at his soul and he's learned to enjoy the pain, like getting a tattoo over bone. The pain will be a pleasure until he looks down and sees the skin of his life is a latticework of scars. Too late. All gone.

***

Okay. Okay. You kept your end. I'll keep mine.

I was boiling dried apples on the stove before adding oatmeal to the mix. The Praying Man sat at the kitchen table. I brewed coffee and was busy frying toast in melted butter in my cast-iron skillet. Dawn paled the window above the sink. By the time breakfast was ready, the light had spilled onto the table. The Praying Man had his hands palm-up in the sunshine, a gold band wrapped tight around his ring finger. His hands were long. The skin looked like sun-dried leather. His spindly fingers extended from the palm like spider legs.

The Praying Man's hands reminded me of the monkey my high school biology teacher kept in a steel cage. We saw it every other day when we turned on our screens for her class. I felt bad for that monkey. I think it was born in a cage. He was like that, the Praying Man. Freedom seemed too big for him. It was like he missed the security of his cage, wherever that was.

***

I didn't think they'd show their faces. They must've thought I really would have clammed up. They haven't figured me out—don't know what I'm capable of. They've been inside this bubble too damned long. She's old enough to remember how things used to be but probably doesn't want to bother with it. City girl, I bet. People raised in cities, even back then, were taught early on to fear Outside. They bought into the crap about subhuman outlaws roaming the wild, seeking the flesh of innocents to sacrifice on altars of demons. I'm a country boy. I know. Lies. All of it. She bought into it, though. I can see it in her eyes. She's been afraid for as long as she can remember. She's afraid that nature's a riddle that the System can never solve. She should be on her knees and praying that the mystery always remains. Praying like he was when I found him in the desert.

***

He drank his coffee black for over a week before asking if I had any tea. I don't drink tea. It's not like I was expecting visitors. He smiled when I apologized, stood up, and walked to the storage room. I'd set up a cot for him back there. Threw together some shelves for his things. He came back to the kitchen carrying a leather pouch. He stood, looking at me like I was supposed to read his mind.

"You want me to boil some water?" I asked.

"That would be splendid."

He talked like a foreigner minus the accent, if that makes sense. Do you remember all the different countries before Unification? Seems like another life. But it wasn't that long ago. Some of my teachers had accents, but they tried to cover them up. They didn't want to be different. Not him. He said he was Gaelic and he was damn proud of it. I didn't know what that was, never heard of it before, but I didn't press him. I don't know why.

He reminded me of the white-haired Hispanic guy who used to come to the orchard looking for work. The poor old guy didn't even know how to log on to a screen. He didn't have one. But he had an accent. A thick one. Mom said he was Puerto Rican. I didn't know what that was. When I asked her about it, she changed the subject.

Dad let him sleep in the barn for a few weeks at a time before sending him on his way. He was too old to work the trees, so he helped Mom around the house. Washed clothes and hung them on the clothesline in the backyard, peeled potatoes, and whatnot. It was like he walked out of a history book. It seemed that way with the Praying Man too, but it didn't make sense in his case. Like I said, he wasn't much older than me. He just *seemed* old. You know, an old soul. You ever heard that before? An old soul. That was him.

***

Her hair is the color of pinecones on the floor of a forest. There are lines on her face. She hadn't had an operation to make herself look younger. The people that have operations don't think anybody can tell they went under the laser. You can tell a person's age by the skin at their throat. Everybody knows. They just don't say anything. They're not being nice, either—not most of them anyway. They're afraid of demerits for offending a fellow citizen. Nice has nothing to do with it.

The crow's feet at the corners of her eyes spread out like finger canyons into the hollows of her temples. They might have come from laughter, but the creases on her forehead look to be from worry. I can't imagine her laughing. But at least she hasn't been machined. I can tell from her eyes. Hazel eyes. She's human. That's enough.

***

What? The tea? He didn't offer me any, and I didn't ask. I don't drink tea, remember? It smelled kind of like cat piss. He got quiet after he drank a cup. Sat at the table staring out the window. He picked a piece of apple out of his bowl and sucked at it. Didn't touch the oatmeal. Rude. Rather than waste it, I set the oatmeal out for the cats when he went back to his room.

***

She must have been a real looker ten years ago. Still is in her own way. She's been ground up and spit out by the System, weighed down with responsibilities and paperwork, more bureaucrat than anything else. Worn out and ready for pasture. Not him, though. Mean Eyes is the System. Without the System, he wouldn't know who he is. He wouldn't be anybody. One day, he'll figure out that none of this shit is real. I'd like to be there to see it.

***

After breakfast, we'd walk through the orchard checking driplines and irrigation gates. He was at peace outdoors. Not that he acted any different—not really—but there was an ease about him when we were outside. In the Outpost, he was calm enough, but he was always looking out the window, even at night, like he was waiting for a knock at the door. You know how it is with people waiting: sometimes you can't tell if they're dreading what's coming or looking forward to it—just that they're anxious. He was like that.

Sometimes, he'd go out by himself. Mostly at night. Might be gone a few minutes or a couple of hours. When he came back, he wouldn't say where he'd been. I didn't ask. Figured he wanted to be alone. I can appreciate that.

He was good with the trees. Almost like he could talk to them. He didn't say anything—not out loud. He'd put his palms on the trunks and stand still as a stone. Like he was listening with his hands. Like he was praying. The apple trees were his favorite. He'd stand with his hands on the trunks while I metered the soil pH or repaired a dripline. He'd go to a tree every time I brought out a meter. Like he was trying to tell them to calm down, that everything was going to be fine. Some kind of aversion to measurements, I guess. I didn't press him on it. He seemed content standing with his palms on the trees. Why bother a man with questions you might not want to know the answers to?

He always seemed like he was waking up from a dream.

$$***$$

She thinks she can tell when I'm lying. I saw it in her eyes when she took off the helmet. She thinks she's smarter than me with all her psychology and neuroscience bullshit. But I never lie. At least not all the way.

$$***$$

Yes. I'm supposed to report when an unauthorized stranger shows up at the Outpost. You want to know why I didn't? Why I broke the rules? I'm not hiding anything. Not like you think. I didn't ask him where he was from or where he was going because I didn't want to break him open like an egg and have the yolk spill out. You know what I mean? I didn't know what he'd been through. He'd seen things. I didn't want to know what he'd seen. I didn't want to know his secrets. There's more to respecting a person's privacy than being polite.

Listen, I've had about enough for today. When are you going to let me talk to somebody who can get me out of here?

CHAPTER FIVE

The sun peeks over the mountain.

Morning birds flitter and chirp, alighting on bare branches of oak and cottonwood trees. A heron stands long-legged on a rock at the edge of a river, water lapping against the stone.

The boy casts. The fly line arcs through the rising light, the tip descending feather-like. A fly he tied out of elk hair rides the current.

***

Daisy kept the child for more than a year. The booze and cocaine had worked into her by then, opening the door to other things—harder things. Jack-the-Bartender hired her as a barmaid two months after she had the baby.

Emily was Daisy's younger sister, a registered nurse. She babysat while Daisy worked. Emily was a stout girl with tawny hair and green eyes. She married a Mexican man named Francisco Juarez the day she graduated from school. A quiet, steady man, Francisco had worked at a local oil refinery since graduating from high school. He was ten years older than Emily and maintained a small ranch he had inherited to the east of town.

Nobody would have guessed that Francisco was religious, but Emily knew. That's why she married him. Francisco fell in love with the child.

Emily took note of her sister's decline, the haggard expression on her face, the skin hanging from her face like a costume worn too long. She noticed the slouch in Daisy's shoulders. She didn't dare come right out and say it but hinted as best she could: "You look exhausted," or "Are you feeling ok?" Most women are sensitive about their looks. Not Daisy. Not after what had happened. Emily understood. What would cause a man to put a bullet through his brain the morning after his own wedding? She knew that working the bar was the only thing keeping Daisy from sinking completely into a mire of despair. Emily was happy to help until Daisy came to terms with things. She hoped it was soon. Emily had children of her own to raise—a two-year-old girl and another on the way.

Emily loathed Jack-the-Bartender. He was polite enough. That wasn't it. There was something about his face, the pock-marked cheeks, the stringy hair tied in a ponytail at the nape of his neck, the deep-set eyes. Jack made Emily uneasy.

Emily belonged to a women's group that held weekly meetings at Jack's saloon on Friday nights. There were five of them in the group, all graduates from the same school. The group had failed to meet only once in three years.

Jack-the-Bartender wore the same leather vest, no matter the season. If it was cold, he'd wear the vest over a sweater. When it was warm, he opted for a white t-shirt under the black leather. And then there were the boots. Worn black harness boots. Emily imagined they smelled like rotting potatoes when he bothered pulling them off. The heels of the boots had been ground down, and Jack's greasy gait verged on a limp. Emily had never seen him wear anything other than faded jeans. And then there was the cologne. Cheap and heavy. It made her sick to her stomach.

Daisy disappeared a year after Jack-the-Bartender re-hired her at the bar. She vanished on the eve of her marriage anniversary. Jack-the-Bartender went missing too.

***

The tip of the flyrod twitches before bending sharply. The elk-hair fly disappears into the current. Pulling the rod up and then back—gentle, no yanking, as Francisco had taught him—the boy grins. He can feel life at the end of the line. He slowly reels in the taut line, taking in slack as the fish comes upstream. The boy knows by the way the fish swims beneath the surface that it's big. And then, in one glorious instant, globules of water burst from the river as if the fish has been hurled through a window into an alien world. Sunlight ricochets off fish scales in a rainbow blast. The next instant, it's gone, the rainbow and the trout. The line slack. The boy looks at the sky.

"Shit," he says. "He ain't gonna believe it. May as well not even bother telling."

The boy is called Ang. He can't remember his mother, though every now and then, he dreams of a woman who smells of tequila and perfume holding a baby close to her chest. The baby finds his mother's milk sour and refuses the nipple. The baby cries. The boy awakens. The dream sinks into darkness. He fights going back to sleep for fear that the dream will return.

Ang knows that Emily and Francisco are his aunt and uncle, but he calls them Mom and Pops. They don't mind. They treat him as one of their own. Leah is his cousin. The kids at school think she's his sister. Neither Ang nor Leah attempt to dispel the myth. The same goes for his baby cousin, Frank. Born with Down syndrome, Frank is good-natured. Ang is quick to introduce him as his brother to anyone who asks.

It's Emily who explains to Ang that his father killed himself. Not the manner—the gun and the gaping wound, the brain matter splattered over the field, the blue bright sky—but the fact that he took his own life. She tells him nobody knows why. She tells him on an afternoon during the winter of his tenth year. She sits next to the boy on the worn leather couch in the living room of the ranch-style home. An explosion of pitch in the fireplace sends a red ember onto the tiled floor. Francisco, sitting in a wooden chair to one side of the fire, takes up the ash shovel next to the hearth, kicks the ember into it with the tip of a boot, and tosses it to the flames. He sits down in the chair and watches the fire dance.

"I told you: nobody knows why. He didn't leave a note. He didn't tell your mother. It's one of those mysteries you learn to live with." *Reaching out to the boy, she brushes a lock of hair from his brow.*

"Like God?" *asks the boy.*

"Yes."

Afternoon light streams through a south-facing bay window onto the tiled floor.

The boy glances at Emily. "Did he know about me?" *He looks at his cowboy boots.*

"Your mother didn't even know. It was too early."

"Do you think he would have changed his mind if he did?"

"I don't know."

"My mom knew."

"I'm sorry."

"Do you think she thinks about me?"

"Yes."

The boy looks at Emily and then at his boots. His leg trembles. Flakes of dried mud have fallen from his boot onto the floor.

"You think she's dead?"

"Your mother? I don't know. Listen, my love, we decided to tell you because you're getting older. That's all. It doesn't change anything. We love you. You're just like Frank and Leah—one of our own."

He knows he's not just like them. He knows he's different. "Do you think she'll come back?"

Francisco stands, takes a log from a rack near the hearth, and stokes the fire. He says, "He wouldn't have done it."

Emily looks to Francisco who crouches in front of the flames.

The boy stands. "What?"

"If he knew about you, he wouldn't have done it."

The boy walks to the fireplace. He places a palm on Francisco's shoulder.

Emily stands and smooths her skirt. "It's getting late. I'll call the others in to wash up."

"I'll do it," says the boy. "I have to check the traps."

"Hurry," says Emily. "It'll be dark soon." She notices the flakes of dried mud on the floor.

The boy exits the room.

Francisco gets to his feet slowly, knees popping. The cold weather causes his hip to ache. He takes up the broom and the ash pan next to the hearth. He delivers the tools to Emily. "Don't worry," he says. "The river will take his mind off of things."

***

The sound of the door unlatching snatches me from the electric buzz of the lights. She walks into the room. Alone. She wears the usual hazmat suit minus the oxygen tank. After locking the door behind her, she removes her helmet. Her hair is tied in a bun on top of her head. Lipstick the color of living coral stains her lips. Black eyeliner. Walking to the bed, she sits on the floor and looks up at me. She smells of sweetwood.

"You're an experiment."

I rise to awareness like a stunned boxer to a referee's count. I'm not sure where I am. Sitting up on the bed, I plop my feet on the cement floor. The room is hot. The floor is cool.

"What?"

"They've been pumping drugs into this room for days. They cause you to experience the memories of others as if they're your own. At least that's what they're hoping. They hope you remember where the Praying Man is going."

The makeup makes her look younger than she is. Even so, she looks tired, like a woman afraid of sleep.

"It's okay," she says. "I stopped it. At least for now."

"Stopped what?"

"The experiment."

"That's why you're not wearing a helmet?"

She nods.

We sit in silence. The buzz from the fluorescent lights gets louder. I place my palms over my ears and rock back and forth on the bed.

"Withdrawal," she tells me. "They cut you off of the drugs last night. Don't be afraid. You'll be okay."

I lift my head to look at her. The buzzing subsides. Her forehead is moist with sweat. "Who are you?" I ask.

She stands and holds out a hand in offering. "Doctor Uket."

I take her hand. Her palm is warm and moist.

"I'm a neuroconsciousness specialist. You can call me Yew."

"That's your name?"

She smiles. Light glances off her teeth like tiny projectiles.

I press my fingertips to my temples.

"No, I just like it."

I don't know if she's teasing or not.

The pain dims like an outgoing tide. I open my eyes and find her sitting on the floor at the foot of the bed. Hazel eyes.

"It's okay," she says.

"Why?"

"Why what?"

"Why are you here?"

"I convinced them to stop." Her forehead creases. "You were forgetting yourself."

An explosion of light. No pain, just buzzing brightness.

"They were erasing you. I pleaded with them, but they wouldn't listen."

Her voice sounds like flowers blooming.

"I invoked the Declaration of Dignity."

She's nothing but light.

"They weren't even aware of it. Somebody forgot to strike it from the lawbooks. There was nothing they could do."

The air moves as she stands. She smells of sweetwood. I remember Mean Eyes. I fear for her.

"I didn't know it existed until last week. I was searching for something, anything, to stop them. I found a clue in the appendix of the Human Nature Initiative. Can you imagine that?"

I feel her smiling.

"I followed the trail and ended up at the Declaration of Dignity, a leftover concession to the Daughters of the Habit before they were labeled as enemies of the System."

The throbbing at the center of my brain syncs with my heartbeat. I open my eyes and watch her pacing the length of the bed, up and back, hands clasped behind her back. With each of her words, the throbbing gets closer.

"Where is he?"

"Who?"

"Your sidekick."

"Sergeant Krassmore? Don't worry."

Mean Eyes.

"He's in training. The latest in security trends." She continues to pace. "The key," she says, "was in Section One, Paragraphs 3–4." She stops pacing and recites the words, " 'Although a shared human essence does not exist, human beings are self-conscious and must be treated with dignity. Acute self-awareness frequently results in a distortion of reality. Certain individuals, despite attempts to mitigate by means of education and/or other regimens, perceive themselves as autonomous. They fail to recognize the authority of the System. Those inflicted with the condition possess inflated notions of free will. Though delusional, these individuals, with few exceptions, pose little danger to the public when subjected to chemical correctives and intensive counseling. Nevertheless, the afflicted are to be assigned to occupations that require little to no contact with the public. They are to be confined to residences when not performing official duties. Provisions will be made for the afflicted to refurbish and/or procure essential items, comply with regulatory appointments, and visit relatives at prescribed intervals.

'It is hereby declared that, because the afflicted are human beings, they are not to be subjected to Erasure. Erasure, as has been documented in all cases heretofore recorded, reduces patients to a vegetative state and so violates the dignity inherent to the concept of the human being. Subjects who undergo Erasure are rendered useless to society. This is a miscarriage of justice. As evinced by the mass graves of days past, Erasure procedures are in violation of the Doctrine of Societal Norms, which makes clear each citizen must contribute to the greater good. Human vegetables devour resources and do not reciprocate. Therefore, Erasure is prohibited unless justified by extraordinary circumstances.' "

I don't know where I am.

"Well?" she asks.

I look at her. A bead of sweat rolls down her cheek and clings to her chin. She smiles, and the droplet falls.

"I memorized it. Do you understand what it means?"

"Yes." I don't know who she is or what she's talking about.

"They called me to the Chamber this morning, and I recited it just like I did here."

She paces the length of the bed. Her protective suit is the color and intensity of the fluorescent light. She glows.

"The full cohort of the Council, all eleven of them, sat in high-backed wooden chairs behind the bench. The bench looked like a giant horseshoe of polished obsidian. They wore dark glasses with mirrored lenses and were dressed in white jumpsuits with gold stars the size of platters embroidered on the chests. They had identical hair—platinum, straight, and stiff—falling to their shoulders. Their bangs looked like wire. I'd never been called to the Chamber before, but I wasn't afraid. It's their law, not mine."

It's her eyes that bring me back. Hazel.

"Why?"

Her hands fall to her sides. The floor is now hot under my feet.

"They were erasing you. Don't you understand? To get to him. They don't care about you. He's their white whale. Not you. They'll do anything to get to him."

"White whale?"

She smiles. "Nothing. Just a story."

"A story?"

She clasps her hands behind her back and returns to pacing. "They were in violation of the Declaration of Dignity. I don't think they were aware of it before I told them. One of them took the dark glasses off and ordered me to the center of the horseshoe. I was alone, but I felt someone at my side. I don't know who it was. A friendly ghost or something—a spirit. Because of it, my voice didn't shake. The Council members all took off their dark glasses. They were trying to intimidate me. But I wasn't afraid to look directly into their albino eyes . . . eyes allergic to sunlight. I was wearing my dress reds, full regalia, the only time I had worn them since graduating from the Academy of Neuroconsciousness. I had them dead to rights. I knew it. So did they."

"Did you read it?"

She stops and looks at me.

I repeat, "Did you read about the white whale, or did somebody tell you?"

She mouths the words but doesn't say them out loud. "I read it."

CHAPTER SIX

Ang disappeared on his sixteenth birthday. He went night fishing for walleye at Lake Antonio and never returned. The authorities called in divers and dredged areas of the lake he was known to favor. They found his fishing skiff but no sign of the teen. The boat was tied to a dock owned by an old man who had built a cabin next to the lake when his wife died a decade earlier. One day when Ang was fishing, he saw the old man sitting on the dock in a wooden rocker holding a fishing pole and a can of beer. The old man waved the young man over. The old man's long, grey beard and beat-up, wide-brimmed, oilskin hat put the teen at ease. The two of them struck up a friendship on the spot.

The old man told the deputies that he hadn't seen Ang for over a week. He went on to say that the kid sometimes tied his boat to the dock and went hunting for arrowheads on the red dirt ridge above the cabin. The ridge had been owned by the Lazy M ranch before the old man bought it. The Lazy M didn't have much use for the lakeshore property or the barren ridge. They couldn't graze cattle where there was no grass. NO TRESPASSING signs mounted on posts near the shore of the lake had kept unwelcome visitors away for the better part of fifty years. The old man, after buying the property, left the signs in place.

The founder of the Lazy M, Cotton Mather the Fourth, claimed the land in the 1880s. Prior to that, the Shoshone, Crow, and Arapahoe tribes had pitched seasonal camps on the ridge. Native craftsmen chipped arrowheads, scrapers, and stone knives while sitting around campfires. They could see for miles in every direction. Each of the tribes considered the ridge sacred. Remnants of arrowheads, scrapers, and broken blades marked their passing.

A couple of cowhands had taken a passing interest in the artifacts years earlier, but it was Ang who figured out the ridge once served as a burial ground. He sometimes sat on a flat rock on top of the ridge, watching the sunset, the sky a deep orange over a crimson horizon. He daydreamed about life before there were schools made of concrete that felt like cages. Sometimes he stretched out on the red dirt and looked at the sky. And sometimes he fell asleep there, the slow rhythm of the waves on the lakeshore below whispering a dream.

***

A buffalo scratches the earth with a hoof. The beast snorts. Its hide is pinkish, the mane blood-red in the light of the setting sun.

The buffalo is dying.

Crouching behind a shelf of red sandstone at the edge of the ridge, Ang swallows the fear that constricts his throat. He closes his eyes and hopes he's dreaming.

When he opens his eyes, the buffalo is gone.

In its stead stands a thin woman with dark hair. She wears white buckskins. Her hair is the color of pinecones. She whispers something but he can't make out the words.

***

Ang fell in love with the buckskin woman over the course of the autumn. She appeared both day and night, at school and at home, while he was doing chores or taking a shower, driving his truck or fishing the river. She was everywhere and nowhere at once. She was silent as the dead, forever standing at the corners of his perception.

One day, after scribbling a note to Francisco (he had grown distant from Emily over the years, resenting her without knowing why), he drove to the lake and hauled a backpack to the top of the ridge. He was determined to find either the buffalo, the woman, or the peace of a dreamless slumber after a week of tossing and turning in his bed. He set up camp where the buffalo and the woman once stood, built a small fire, and warmed a can of pinto beans on a slab of slate next to the flames. Streaks of the auburn sunset pierced the clouds and spread over the lake. Ang prayed the white buffalo would once again herald the arrival of his newly beloved. He couldn't know that the buffalo and the woman would never again return to the ridge or that a seed had been planted. He couldn't know that the seed would germinate, take root, and call him homeward.

Darkness fell and Ang opened a pint bottle of whiskey he had purchased at school from a ne'er-do-well kid with a blockhead and a wall-eye. The kid warned him to be careful because evil spirits that had been trapped for years in barrels of bourbon longed to be free to claim their revenge. Ang drank the whiskey, hoping that the freed spirits, instead of being angry, might call out to the woman on his behalf. He drank half a pint and stretched out on the spot where she once stood. Interlacing his fingers behind his head, he looked to the stars.

A cool breeze swept over the lake, onto the shore, and up the ridge. Ang traced the outline of the woman in the stars, a figure of light stitched onto a canvas of night. A shooting star coursed through the darkness.

***

From the blackness of space, a form takes shape. Two eyes, like blue pulsars, flicker. Below the blue, a curve of starlight shimmers like a bright smile. A hint of light from stars long dead pale the brow above the eyes. The cheeks take on the rosy colors of Mars. On top of the head sits a diadem of jewels resembling galaxies.

***

It took several moments for Ang to realize the throbbing in his body wasn't from the beating of his heart but from the marrow in his bones. He rubbed his eyes and shivered in the dawn.

He had fallen asleep on top of his sleeping bag. The whiskey bottle, empty, lay on the red dirt next to him. He got to his feet and searched the area for something, not knowing what that something was. He found no trace of the woman, no footprint, no sign she existed outside of his imagination. Crawling inside the sleeping bag, he covered his head. The sun rose over the eastern horizon.

***

What was it that she had whispered? Where am I to go? I'll do any-thing. Please. Don't leave me here. Don't leave me alone.

***

He avoided the ridge for the next month. The longing for the woman wasn't his own. It was bigger than him, a myth come to life. It threatened to absorb him.

He no longer bothered with trapping or fishing. He gifted his collection of arrowheads and stone tools to the old man at the cabin near the lake. He tried to act normal, attending classes at the high school that felt like a prison, tended to chores, fed the livestock. He knew he was being watched. He knew that they knew that he had witnessed a Holy One. And he knew that such knowledge was forbidden. They were waiting to punish him. Everyone. His teachers and classmates, Emily and Francisco, Frank and Leah, even the horses and the dog. They all knew.

When he couldn't take it any longer, he climbed the hill to the red ridge. Numbed by the presence of people who would call him crazy if he told them about the spirit woman, who laughed behind his back, he felt he had nothing to lose. The stars in the night sky understood him more than "society" ever would. And maybe the woman would take pity and come back to him. Maybe she would speak to him in the night.

***

What was it she had whispered?

***

Halfway up the ridge, his bowels cramped. The thought of shitting on the ground like a mindless animal brought the bile to his mouth. He scrambled for something to use as a shovel. He found a large scraper chipped from a hunk of chert sitting on the ground next to an outcropping of granite. He scraped a shallow hole with the rock. The edge of the chert was sharp against his palm. Two inches into the earth, he dug up six buffalo hooves tied to a rib bone. He recognized the bone. Deer. He tossed it aside and squatted over the hole. He listened to waves lapping against the shore of the lake below. Relieved, he pulled up his jeans. He noticed the blood on his palm. He picked up the scraper and threw it down the hill.

Don't leave me alone.

The stone skidded to a stop on the slope. The lake sparked with remnants of sunlight.

He took up the hooves and bone. They were well-preserved. He stuffed the find in his backpack, picked up his gear, and continued the climb to the top of the ridge.

CHAPTER SEVEN

Mean Eyes is back. He saunters into the room, wearing protective gear, complete with helmet and oxygen tank. I know his walk. There's someone with him—a face hidden by a reflective shield attached to the helmet. The soft step of the newcomer and the roundness of the gait puts me in mind of a woman. Unless it's a man acting like a woman. They'll try anything. Confuse me enough, they figure, and I'll break. That's what they think. That's what their books and manuals tell them. But I'm no theory. I'm real.

They figure I'm soft on women. That's why Yew's gone. They want to use her as leverage. Hold her back because they know I like her. She's probably in on it. Even if she's not, it's best not to trust her. I'd be a fool to trust anybody in this place. Anyone who takes the oath and is serious about it is a sell-out. And every yahoo that works in this hellhole takes the oath seriously, or once did.

I took the oath. We all did. Back in school. But it didn't count. Not with me. It's like the way the old Puerto Rican said they used to baptize babies. The babies never agreed to it. Us students were just doing what we were told, going through the motions like good little citizens. I never agreed to anything, just moved my lips. The words were stillborn. I've never been a citizen of the System. Not really.

The Puerto Rican stopped coming around the orchard a few years before I took the oath. When I asked Mom about him, she said he might have gotten sick and been put in the Haven for the Wayward Old. That made me sad. I don't know why. I didn't know him—not really. He'd stay around for a few weeks, and then he'd be gone like he was never there. I missed the way he talked. He had a thick accent. His presence broke up the monotony of attending school on the computer, doing chores, eating, sleeping, brushing my teeth, doing it all over again, day in and day out. It was like I was inside a computer program in a virtual reality machine. When the Puerto Rican came around, it seemed like there was more to the world than the sun going up and down—up and down, up and down.

I figured the Puerto Rican knew about the Old Ones. I figured he knew lots of things they didn't teach on screens, things I was afraid to ask because I was too much the coward. I liked being bored. And I was ashamed that I liked it.

That's why the Old Ones stopped whispering. It was my fault. They hadn't come around in years. Not since Dad caught me with them in the orchard one morning.

I remember the sun wasn't up yet—not quite—and the eastern horizon looked like a blood blister ready to pop. A couple of robins were singing in the day. The trees were in full leaf. They stood straight and tall like sentinels. A breeze fluttered through the leaves of the trees, coming in from the fields to the south of the orchard. The air smelled of alfalfa.

I'd been going out to the orchard most mornings, sometimes when it was still dark, in the hopes of coming across the Old Ones. Some mornings, they were out there waiting. Others, when they weren't, they'd leave signs, shapes carved in the bark of pecan trees or built out of branches woven into rings just big enough to fit over my head like a crown. I didn't know what the symbols stood for. They were stick figures—some four-legged, some with two. Stick birds. Stick spears. It's a blur now, but I bet I'd recognize those shapes if I saw them again.

The Old Ones didn't speak in words—not like us—and it wasn't like what they call telepathy. It was something in-between . . . like the symbols on the trunks of the trees, more image than word. They sounded kind of like drunks humming the lyrics of a forgotten song. The meaning wasn't really in the words. They're not like us that way. The meaning was in the music behind them. Pipe music I guess you'd call it—flutes and the like. But you couldn't actually hear the music. It was more like remembering a melody to an old song. A piper's song. That's it. Like that story the Puerto Rican told me each year when he came around . . . a story about a piper who lured children away from their parents with a magic pipe. It was a song like that.

Dad caught notice I was leaving the house before the sun came up. I don't know how. Chores had to be done before breakfast and after dinner. The trees had to be tended and the animals fed. Dad didn't usually get up until Mom had coffee made and was busy with breakfast. He'd be sitting at the kitchen table sipping from a steaming black mug waiting for his eggs and ham when I came in after chores. I didn't give it a lot of thought. I didn't figure he'd be up at the crack of dawn checking on me. But he was.

*** *

They're harder on me now that Yew's gone. Mean Eyes likes to watch me squirm. I don't think the new attendant cares one way or the other whether I'm in pain or not. I'm just an object. They need to extract something from me like syrup from a maple tree. It's that simple. It's like Dad with the trees. He was after the pecans. That's all. He didn't give two shits about the orchard itself: the birds and bees and trees and earth and water and sky—everything working together to give Dad his pecans. Product was all that mattered to Dad. Product and numbers.

I'm more pecan tree than maple. And this season isn't going to produce much of a crop. The two System flunkies—neither one of them is a real doctor, not like Yew—are desperate. Like they're afraid of being starved or something if they don't get what they came for. Dad wasn't worried about starving. He had his System job to keep his gut full. He wanted control over the trees. That's what he was after. He wanted them to do what he told them to do—produce a bumper crop year after year. Yet, the trees refused to accommodate. I'm like those pecan trees. They may just have to cut me down.

***

Dad rarely talked to me about anything other than chores. I was practically running the orchard by then. Had been for a couple of years, ever since I got into the Virtual High School for Agricultural Vocations. Maybe Dad wanted me to be something other than an orchard keeper. I don't know. He never said. My plan was to finish school and take a position at the Orchard Institute. I wanted to be a grower. I'd keep the family orchard and pass it down to my own kids once I settled in and found a wife. I wasn't asking for the world. I'm not proud. I just wanted to fit in so I could be left alone. Fitting in was my way of getting what I wanted. I didn't believe very many people bought into the whole System thing anyway. Most of them were like me. They just wanted to be left alone. Simple peace. That's what I wanted. To be left alone with the Old Ones.

***

I had no idea Dad was planning on having all the trees cut down and selling them off like so much scrap. He could've at least said something—given me a chance to talk him out of it. Just because he didn't have any luck with the trees didn't mean shit. Things had been looking better since I took over. Maybe he was jealous. I don't know. He never said. He just gave the order and all the trees were cut down. No more orchard. Just like that.

***

"Yes, yes, I understand."

His body moves, a herky-jerky jig in rhythm with the water rumbling down the irrigation ditch bordering the orchard. His head tilts back. His eyes close. Morning light the color of peaches splashes his cheeks. He grins. His teeth gleam, moist. His back arches as his arms stretch outwards like thunderbird wings. Energy oozes from the earth, flowing into the soles of his feet, moving up through his legs, surging into his torso, and gathering in his heart. His body moves off-time.

His father watches from the edge of the trees.

***

The Puerto Rican showed up a few weeks before I took the oath before graduating from the Virtual School. He didn't look any worse for wear, really—maybe a few more wrinkles in his leathery jowls, the shock of straight white hair a little thinner, the hunch in his back a little more pronounced. But his eyes were the same. Black eyes that smiled when he talked. Mom said he had a Puerto Rican accent. Looking back, I wonder how she would have known what a Puerto Rican accent sounded like.

Mom had never been more than fifty miles from the orchard, so far as I know. She didn't talk much about her past, her childhood, her parents. Dad said Mom's mom, my grandmother, was a Welsh looker, a real movie star type. She got seduced by an older man when she was a teen. She got pregnant and gave birth to a baby, who happened to be Mom. After a couple of years, still practically a kid herself, she met an Indian guy nearer her own age. Not an Indian from across the ocean. An Indian from here. A Navajo. He introduced her to whiskey. She left the baby with her parents and ran off with her new love, booze. The two of them died from alcohol poisoning a few years later. Their livers couldn't take it.

Maybe Mom knew the Puerto Rican from her past. I never asked.

Mom's past was off-limits somehow. The two of them, Mom and the Puerto Rican, never talked much, but she seemed at ease around him, more so than with me or Dad. It made me wonder.

Dad didn't seem to mind. He went about his business. Off to work and back home to the orchard. Mom had dinner on the table at the same time each day, except for weekends when we had it an hour earlier. Us kids couldn't talk at dinner while Dad ate. We had to eat a portion of everything on the table even if we hated it. I hated beef liver. I ate it anyway. One of my sisters almost puked when it came to rice. It reminded her of maggots. She had to sit at the table until she could choke down at least a few bites. One of my brothers was good at folding broccoli in a napkin and slipping it into his pocket. None of us kids told on him. Neither did Mom.

After dinner, Dad sat in the living room drinking a bottle of red wine while listening to New History podcasts. Us kids tended to the evening chores. The girls helped Mom in the kitchen doing dishes and mopping and whatnot. The boys went outside to tend to the animals and water the garden if the season was right. I made my way to the orchard to check on the trees.

The sound of dishes clinking in the sink irritated Dad. So did the sound of the vacuum cleaner. Even the sound of the broom sweeping the floor frayed his nerves. I think kids irritated him in general. I don't know why he and Mom had so many. You think he would have known kids annoyed the shit out of him after the first one or two popped onto the scene. He was all into math and measuring, but he never did measure that.

Not a whole lot makes sense in this world. I understood that earlier than most. I didn't know how to say it out loud back then, but I knew. I don't think Dad understood. Most people don't. They rely on the System to make sense of things for them. But it doesn't. It's just wishful thinking. The System isn't designed to make sense. It's designed to control.

***

The father watches his son sway in the dawn light. He blames the boy's madness on the trees. He blames it on the earth and the water and the sun that spawned them.

He stands and watches. He cannot move.

A cadence of tides lapping faraway shores summons the rising light. The crescent moon fades. Stars pulse, invisible in the darkness behind the light.

The father watches.

A gushing, like the rush of a swollen mountain stream, tumbles through the trees.

The father cannot move.

The earth heaves as night crawlers make their way upward into the light. They emerge from the dark soil. The boy stands with his back arched, arms extended, his face turned to the sky. The procession of worms, prodded by an instinct birthing intuition, converge behind the boy and ball up into a writhing mass.

A murder of crows descends into the trees. Dawn gives way to day. A murmuration of starlings appears on the southern horizon, thousands of the birds looping and swirling in a living wave of flight. Then, as one, they descend to the alfalfa field behind the orchard. There, they break into a chorus of song.

The boy opens his mouth. His arms, sticking out from his sides like airplane wings, rotate in tight circles. The trill of birdsong intensifies. The sun blossoms ever brighter. And then the trilling is gone. The starlings rise. Breeze flows. Water trickles through the irrigation ditch. The boy closes his mouth. He collapses onto the mound of worms.

The crows caw.

Water trickles down the ditch.

"Your way," mumbles the boy. "Not mine."

***

Dad never said a word about what he witnessed in the orchard until the day I asked him why he was cutting down the trees. I didn't know if he was making it up or not. I didn't know what he was talking about—couldn't remember any of what he said had happened—but that didn't mean it didn't happen. Communicating with the Old Ones came at a price. I couldn't remember what they looked like. I couldn't remember what they sang. All I knew was that I went out to the orchard and listened until I heard a high, faint sound like a person whistling. Then, everything went fuzzy, and there were moving colors, like a far-off kaleidoscope moving closer. A warmness washed over me, but it wasn't heat, it was feeling. Emotion. It felt safe. I didn't want to leave. The Old Ones whispered things to me—secrets—and they knew I wouldn't reveal them because I wouldn't remember when I found myself curled in a ball on the ground. I'd look to the sky to gauge how much time had passed. Twenty or thirty minutes. My shirt was always wet with sweat. My heart always sank when I realized they were gone.

Was it my fault the orchard was destroyed? Dad wanted me to think so. He feared the Old Ones. It was his fear that destroyed the trees. When he told me I was screaming about worms coming up out of the ground and birds singing, I believed him, but I couldn't remember. Dad knew he'd never be able to control them. I knew it too. He was right to be afraid.

Dad lived in a world made out of numbers. The world he saw that morning threatened the notion that numbers held the power to subdue the world. I didn't know much about religion back then—I still don't—but I knew enough to realize that the world Dad lived in was void of gods and at the mercy of men. He couldn't handle what he had witnessed, so he swept his one shot at redemption under the rug. No miracles allowed.

"It was all in your head," he finally said. It was his way of putting the whole matter to rest. "Some kind of dream. You fell on the ground and started yammering about eruptions of worms, clouds of starlings, and something about crows. Don't you see? None of it happened. It was all in your head. Like those imaginary friends of yours. You don't think anyone sees you out here in the goddamn trees talking to shadows? I do. I've had my eye on you. There's something wrong with you, kid. Something out of whack. I should've reported it the first time I saw it, but I hoped you'd grow out of it. You're my son. Maybe you *have* grown out of it. I don't know. It's hard to tell with you anymore, the way you keep to yourself. Cutting down the orchard will put an end to it once and for all. None of it's real. You see that don't you?" Dad didn't care whether what he was saying was true or not. He just wanted it over and done. "I'm doing it for you, kid."

Dad was a liar.

When Dad claimed he was destroying the orchard to help me, I remembered the starlings moving through the sky like a thought finding form. I remembered falling on the mound of worms, their bodies sliding over my face like the moist fingers of a lover. I remembered the scream of crows. It was real. All of it. Dad was lying. He'd seen it all happen. He was a witness. In the days and weeks that followed, he convinced himself that his lie was the truth. To maintain faith in the System, Dad buried the mystery. They all did. They still do. They call it a rite of passage, a putting away of childish things. They have it ass-backward.

Dad had me committed to the Dissociative Identity Unit after the trees were cut down. He claimed that I'd had a psychotic break. Once you get put in there, you never really get out. That's what they say. They do whatever it takes to make you Reality Compliant. The head doctors probe your brain with tendrils of electricity while nurses shoot the latest concoctions of chemical cures into your veins. And then there's hour after hour of therapy, talking and talking until a kind of damp gray blanket falls over your thoughts and you're comfortably numb. Then they send you to a vocational school. Branded a head-case, you're assigned a job cleaning toilets or the like. If you're really, really, lucky, you might get assigned to an Outpost. That's what happened to me.

I got assigned to an Outpost.

That's when I started to believe again.

*****

I can't be the only one. I'm not saying that every kid has the privilege of coming face-to-face with Old Ones. But I can't be the only one.

I'll bet lots of kids catch a glimpse of the otherworld. They just don't tell anybody. If they were stupid enough to tell their parents or teachers, they'd just be told the same lie I was. "It's all in your head." They'd be told the same thing over and over, and it wouldn't take long for most of them to believe it. They'd do what they had to do to be a good citizen. They'd put away childish things. Most of them. But not all.

I can't be the only one.

CHAPTER EIGHT

They weren't trying to erase me. That wasn't the goal. But they didn't care if it happened to happen, as they tried to extract whatever they thought the Praying Man had stashed in my brain. In order to get to it, they had to get past me. If that meant eliminating my personality altogether, so be it. They didn't give a damn.

I can't remember much. Probably never will. It comes in snippets. Memories I guess you'd call them. But they're not in order. I don't even know if they're mine. I don't know how long I was with the System doctors, how many times they came to my room, how many days passed. For all I know, it might have been years. The rows of fluorescent lights surged until I thought the tubes would burst from the buzzing. Sometimes they wore black hazmat suits instead of the usual white. The game kept changing.

I remember two of the attendants. I figured the one replacing Yew might be female by the way she walked, but I couldn't be sure. I suspected it might be a man posing as a woman. I couldn't make up my mind. The familiar one, Mean Eyes, didn't bother disguising the way he walked. He wanted me to know it was him. They may have wanted me to think the new attendant was Yew. I couldn't tell one way or the other. The whole scheme was designed to confuse. They were feeding me conflicting information so I wouldn't know what or who to believe. That's the game. When you can't trust anything, you break.

I said, "That's not Yew."

"Sit on the bed and put on your restraints," said Mean Eyes. "You know the drill. Let me hear them click."

I sat up. "Where is she? What did they do with her?"

"Get the restraints on. Now."

The lights dimmed. The buzzing receded. The room was still bright but not to the point of pain. I took up a restraint, looped it over my wrist, and squeezed until it clicked. The new attendant stood still as a statue next to the room's lone door. Fluorescence slid off his hazmat suit like water off waxed glass. Or maybe it was a her. I couldn't be sure.

"Now the feet."

"Where's Yew?"

"I won't ask again."

Mean Eyes pulled a metal baton from a sheath at his back. A Snake Stick. He'd pulled it before. Yew never let him go so far as to use it. But he *wanted* to use it. I clicked the restraints around my ankles.

"Good," said Mean Eyes. "That's good. Now let me introduce you to my new friend. You're right, it's not Yew." He pointed the baton at the door. "This is Attendant *Ra-shay*. He spells it R-a-c-h-e-t but it's pronounced *Ra-shay*. Understand? You and I are going to talk. *Ra-shay* is here to observe. Play it straight and it'll go easy. Make it tough and you'll pay."

"Where's Yew?"

Mean Eyes tightened his grip on the Snake Stick before jamming it into my shoulder. A shock of electricity zagged through my body.

Mean Eyes pulled the stick away. I could feel him smiling from behind his mask.

"Hurts, don't it?" he asked. "I got bit by this thing for certification training. Hurts bad."

"You're to use it only when necessary," said Rachet. The voice wasn't male or female. It was somewhere in between.

"And who gets to say when it's necessary?" asked Mean Eyes. "You? You ain't even been through certification yet. So, no. Not you. Me. That's who. I've got seniority here, and I'm no believer in that 'be nice' bullshit. Not like Doc Uket. Nope. I'm after results. Yew Uket was an idealist, a fucking martyr—that's what she was."

Pain, like a tumble of red-hot pennies, dropped from my shoulder into my arm. I watched as my palm turned red.

"Uket can't protect you. Not no more. They moved her over to Admin. Desk job. Your precious Yew won't be working with patients no more. She was too soft—too much the dreamer. Always talkin' about how things should be and shit. This here ain't how it should be. It's the way it is. I ain't no dreamer. I'm a realist. That's me. The real thing."

The pain moved into my chest. "You mean prisoners, not patients, right?"

"It's all a matter of perspective," said Mean Eyes. "Right, *Ra-shay*?"

"Right," said Rachet. "If you cooperate and tell us what we need to know, you'll heal yourself. Do you understand? We're not here to hurt you. You're hurting yourself."

"Yeah," said Mean Eyes. "I'm not the one hurting you. You're hurting yourself."

He stepped closer, and his presence weighed down like darkness. My chest tightened.

"But it's me that can make the pain go away. Do you hear? All you gotta do is say the word. If you can't talk, nod."

"Looks like he's going to explode," said Rachet.

I still couldn't tell if Rachet was male or female. The fact presented itself like an itch at the back of my brain. I fastened onto that itch like it was a candle burning in a dark room.

Mean Eyes patted me on the back, and my shoulder muscles clenched.

"Don't worry, *Ra-shay*. He might go unconscious, but he won't die. A Snake Stick ain't lethal. What would be the point? Right now, he feels like he's suffocating. But he ain't. I know the feeling. You'll know it too when you go through certification. But they won't tell you that it won't kill you. You'll feel like you're dying but you're not. Get it?"

"Yes," said Rachet.

"Remember it and remember who told you."

"I will. Thank you."

Mean Eyes stepped away. My brain buzzed white. Inside the buzz was an echo, and inside the echo was a voice.

"I gotta recommend you for certification, *Ra-shay*. You know that, right?"

"Yes," said Rachet.

"How about a yessir, then?"

"Yessir."

"Come over here, *Ra-shay*."

"Yessir."

"Now, take this and jam it in his neck."

"I'm not certified, sir."

"Don't worry. It won't kill him. You want the recommendation?"

"Yessir."

"Then jam the damn thing in his neck."

The echo was like waves slapping up against a beach.

"It's an order, *Ra-shay*. I ain't going to ask you again."

***

"Yes, I hear you."

***

"Yessir."

Rachet is a boy who thinks he's a girl.

✳✳✳

"I understand."

✳✳✳

They came every day, Mean Eyes and Rachet. I *think* it was every day. I had no way of knowing. There was nothing to indicate the passing of minutes or hours. The dull buzz of the fluorescent lights paralyzed me. I couldn't move. Red walls. White light. Black floor. White light. Black mood. White light. I was the buzz. The contrast allowed me to exist. Without it, there would have been nobody to hear the buzzing. At least I could hear the buzzing. That meant that I was more than the buzz. It meant that I was real.

Their coming and going made time out of the light. Mean Eyes would open the door and walk through. He'd draw the Snake Stick from the sheath on his belt and stand by the door. Rachet stepped into the room next, as if on cue, turned and closed the door. He stood facing me with his hands clasped behind his back. It wasn't like the first day—chatty, chatty, chum. They didn't talk at all. It felt rehearsed. Official. The two of them stood motionless on either side of the door. They stared at me through the mirrored lens of their face shields.

The tick of a metronome. I thought it was my heart, but it was too steady, too machine-like. I didn't know where it was coming from. It grew louder by degrees. *Tick. Tock. Tick.* Mean Eyes and Rachet stared at me. *Tick. Tock. Tick.*

I waited for Mean Eyes to say it.

He wanted me to click on the restraints without being told. He wanted me to do it automatically. But I wouldn't—not even if Mean Eyes bit me with the Snake Stick. The pain let me know I was real.

I'm not a machine. I am real.

"Restrain yourself."

Tick. Tock. Tick.

Mean Eyes pointed the Snake Stick at my face. He did it every time. The same gesture, the same threat. "I won't say it again."

Tick. Tock. Tick.

Looping the restraints over my ankles, I'd squeeze them until they clicked. Then, I'd sit waiting for the next command. It was the same every time. A ritual.

"Now your wrists."

Tick. Tock. Tick.

Click.

"Next time, do it without me telling you to. Understand?"

I knew what was coming next. Always the same.

Without word or gesture, Rachet walked over to Mean Eyes. His movements were practiced. Mean Eyes handed the Snake Stick to Rachet. Rachet then jammed it in my neck.

I fell in love with the pain. It was the only way to beat it.

Tick. Tock. Tick.

***

The Snake Stick made me see everything at once. I watched *the man kneeling in the sand that first time I found him in the desert; Francisco at the fireplace as Aunt Emily told me about Daisy; Yew Uket removing her helmet for the first time; Daisy finding the body of her newly consummated husband dead outside the trailer, his head a red mess on the ground; the two-by-four bludgeoning the raccoon.* I watched it all at once. *Horses galloping under a sky the color of rust. Doc Uket and Mean Eyes. Rachet with the Snake Stick.* Everything. *I saw myself at the edge of the orchard. The Old Ones.* All at once.

It was like being a god.

But there is no such thing. There are no gods. That's what they keep telling me. They say, "It's all in your head."

***

The beast is dying.
Bile burns the boy's throat.
A thin woman with dark hair stands before him. She wears a dress of white buckskin.
Her skin is bloody with sunset.
What was it she whispered?
Please.
Don't leave me.
Don't leave me alone.

***

The sun peeks over the mountain like the eye of a waking child.
A trout rises.

***

Her hair is the color of pinecones on a forest floor.
She's been afraid for as long as she can remember.
She can't remember.

***

The room smells of sex and frankincense.
Outside, a cool breeze cruises through a sea of wild wheat.
Blue sky. Bright sun.
His heart pounds.
Thump. Thump. Thump.

***

Her face is older than her voice.

***

The boy strips dried moss from the two-by-four.
A splinter pierces his palm.
The raccoon watches.

***

He is a boy who feels like a girl.

***

He looks at the gun in his hand.

***

"I understand."

***

"Follow my voice. Understand? Follow me."

***

"Yes. Yes. I hear you."

***

"I'm giving you something to help. Concentrate on my voice."

***

"Yes."
Fire clutches my chest.

***

"You'll feel a burning sensation in your lungs. Don't be afraid."

***

Red dragon rising.
We rise together.
Black sun.

***

"The things you're seeing aren't real. They're all in your head."

***

Her voice flutters past like a leaf falling from a dying tree.

***

"Come back. Fight it."

***

Bright sky. Black sun. White ash.

***

"Don't go. It's not you. It's him. He's in your head."

***

"*Yes.*"

***

"He'll kill you."

***

Ashes fall from the sky like snow.

***

"Come back. Don't leave me here."

***

I can fly.

***

"Can you hear me? Come back to the light."

"Yes."

"I thought you were gone."

"I hear you. I'm here."

"Thank goodness."

"Thank God."

***

The hiss of electricity amplifies the sound of my heart.

"Open your eyes."

A woman's face takes shape in a glaring ripple of fluorescent light. Doctor Uket. Yew. Her face is older than her voice. I remember.

"Good. You're back," she says. "You almost went too far."

I try to speak. My tongue is like a cold stone.

"Here," says Yew.

She takes a bottle with a plastic straw from the table at my side.

"Drink this."

I sip from the bottle.

"Easy," says Yew. "Not too much."

"They want him," I whisper. "Not me."

"I know. I'm here now. I'm going to get you away from this place. We're going to find him."

"Who?"

"Remember. The Praying Man. We have to find him. You have to remember."

***

She got me on a stretcher somehow, strapped me down on my back so I wouldn't roll off, and wheeled me out of the room. We traveled through corridors of light, all of them the same, tubes of fluorescence passing over me like white lines on an electric highway. The wheels of the stretcher squealed as she rounded corners. When the cart started to tip, she brought it back into balance as if she had been practicing for a race. I felt sick. My head reeled.

"I'm gonna be sick."

"Don't. They're watching."

The stretcher slowed. We turned a corner smoothly, the sound of the rubber wheels on the tiled floor producing a rhythmic whiz.

"Better?"

I didn't answer for fear of vomiting.

"Nod if you can. Don't talk. We're being watched."

I nodded.

CHAPTER NINE

I read in a book, when there were still books—the kind of books you hold in your hands and turn the pages—that God is omniscient. That means God knows everything all at once, the past, present, and future, the number of hairs on your head and your great, great grandfather's head the day he died, even the ones on the little girl who shares a bit of your DNA a thousand years from now, assuming there are still people and a world to house them that far down the line. Everything all at once. That's the main reason the System targeted God for Erasure. That's what it said in the book. If there was a God, the System couldn't control It because they couldn't know all at once like It did. The System couldn't know God; therefore—so the argument went—there was no God because God would know the System but the System would not know God. Something like that. It was confusing. We never read anything like that book in school. It was contraband. Those caught with it would be subject to Erasure.

It's plain enough to see that people experience things successively, one moment after the next, not all at once. It doesn't take a genius, or even a book, to figure that out. The System was created by people, so it's situated in time. It has a past and a future, just like people do. It will die one day, just like people do. The System can't see the past and the future at once. It can't see the future at all because the future's a probability, because it doesn't actually exist. For God, there wouldn't be a past and a future—just a Now. It's a hard thing to wrap your head around. For the System, the Now is in the collection of data they use to project a future. The past is gone. It can't be changed, but it can be erased. The future is malleable. The System wants to control the future by manipulating probabilities. Something like that.

For God—if I understood the book correctly—the past and future are contained in the Now, and that's why God knows everything at once. For God, there's no future, so it can't be changed. The System can't have that. So, there is no God. Bottom line: there are things about the System that don't make any more sense than God does, but the System has to make sense of them or it won't work. God is a mystery and must remain a mystery or it won't work. The System thinks stifling mystery fixes everything. But it just makes things worse. If there's no mystery, nothing makes sense.

***

I remember learning about baseball when I was a kid. We watched games on screens in school. A female computer voice explained how the game was played while I watched my screen alone in my room. The batter had to keep their eye on the ball. The "coach"—that's what they called the voice—kept saying over and over, "You have to keep your eye on the ball. Whether you're fielding or batting, you have to keep your eye on the ball. If you don't keep your eye on the ball, you'll miss your swing or drop the ball. It's that simple. Keep your eye on the ball."

My brothers and sisters didn't like baseball, so I played on my own. They didn't like much of anything when I think back on it. Except for screens. They were always on screens. Even when they were free to go outside and play, they'd stay in the house glued to screens. One of my sisters loved music. Another fashion. My brothers were secretive about what they liked. I don't know what they watched on their screens. I guess they loved their privacy. But there was no privacy. The screens were watching them too.

I was bored by it all. There's nothing real about a screen except the smart glass collecting signals. The games were fun for a while—fighting giant insects with lasers . . . they even had a baseball game—but a time always came when I couldn't get around the fact that it was all make-believe. The Old Ones, the One and Three, were real. The screens weren't. But I couldn't tell anybody. If I did, they'd say I was crazy. It wasn't me who was crazy, though. It was them.

One day, I went out behind the orchard, found a good straight branch to use as a bat, and a round rock. The rock was a lot smaller than a baseball, but I figured it weighed about the same—maybe a little less. I imagined a crowd cheering me on as I stepped up to the plate. I'd toss the rock straight up, watch it come down, and take a swing. *WHOOSH.* I missed a lot at first. So, I followed the coach's advice and concentrated on watching the rock. Soon enough, *CRACK!* The rock flew a little way into the field behind the orchard and thunked into the weeds. My hands stung from the impact of wood on rock. I'd drop the branch and run around the field. Homerun! The crowd roared. I was a hero. I knew it was make-believe. But at least the branch and the rock were real. And the big puffs of clouds in the sky. The sound of water in the irrigation ditch. The whine of mosquito wings in my ear and the feel of a fly landing on my forearm. Brown stubble in the field. That was all real. Much better than a projection.

The coach was right. You can either focus on the ball being thrown or the bat in your hands, but not both at once. You have to keep your eye on the ball if you hope to hit it. If you think about the bat, you'll miss the ball. But who's thinking about the bat as it swings? Who's swinging the bat if your attention is on the ball? It's still you. You know it all at once. You just have to concentrate hard on one thing for it all to come together into the now—all of it at once. I imagine God would be something like that. Only bigger. Much, much bigger. Too big.

✳✳✳

The angel hovers, a band of light encircling her head.

"Don't be afraid."

Her face is older than her voice.

"I'm here."

Her hair is the color of pinecones.

"Don't be afraid."

The angel is absorbed in a cone of descending light.

"You're burning up."

A cool cloth slides over my brow.

"Stay with me."

I recognize the voice.

"I'm here."

The cone of light falls from a surgical lamp hanging from a metal arm over the bed. My arms are strapped at my sides. My ankles are secured to the bed posts. A machine beeps near my ear.

"Yew?"

"Yes, I'm here."

You are not him.

"Am I a prisoner?"

"Try not to move. You'll tear the stitches."

"Where are we?"

"We're safe."

You are not him. You are not safe.

"Where are we? Who are you?"

She steps into the light, smelling of sweetwood.

"It's me. Doctor Uket. Yew." She wipes the cool cloth over my brow. "It was touch and go for a while, but Doctor Waters was successful. He detached the MIU from your brainstem. The operation sparked a fever, but the worst of it seems to be over. They won't be able to track you now. They won't know where you are."

"Who's Doctor Waters?"

You are not who she thinks you are.

A man steps into the light. He is tall. His face is hidden in a tangle of beard the color of seagulls, gray and white at once.

"It's Doc Waters to you, kid."

The creased skin on his brow is the color of rosewood. Eyes the color of used oil.

"I was confident my method would work, but I wasn't certain." His voice is deep and warm. "Nothing is certain, you know. Nothing at all. It took months to map out a pathway to circumvent the neural implosion monitoring protocols. The thing with theories is . . . well, they're just theories. I couldn't be sure until I actually got into your brainstem. It appears to be a success, though."

Doc Waters smiles at Yew.

"In other words," he continues, "the fact that you're not a vegetable is a miracle. That's why I'm a bona fide genius."

Yew smiles.

You are not him.

A machine beeps as Yew wipes the cloth over my brow.

"He needs rest."

"Let it be so. You're next, Doctor Uket. But don't worry. Yours will come out much smoother now that I know what I'm doing."

"You should have done mine first."

"Too risky. I didn't know if it would work. I couldn't risk losing you."

"He's more important."

"Not to me."

"To us all. He's important to us all."

***

Light flickers, near and warm. It comes from inside my head.

"Is it really him?" asks a voice that sounds like tin scraping against concrete.

"They say so," says a voice sounding like air bubbling up through mud.

"Do you believe them?" asks the tinny voice.

"Why not?" returns the muddy one.

"If it *is* him, he looks more puppet than man."

"Maybe he's both."

The voices are muffled but distinct. Whispers at twilight.

"Really?" asks a third man in a wheezy voice. "Don't you feel just a little silly? Believing in something because you can't find anything else to believe in?"

"I don't need to believe it," says Tinny. "I believe in getting rich. There's treasure out there, and I'm going to find it."

Mud says, "What good would it do if you did find it? This treasure of yours. They'd just take it away. Nobody gets more than they're allotted. Even you know that."

"They've gotta catch me first. Imagine it. Gold and silver. Rubies and emeralds. But it's not money I'm after. It's beauty. Beauty is wealth."

"And you think I'm crazy? He's right here. Look at him. The Seven Cities of Gold are a myth, but he's right here."

"He looks more puppet than man."

Light flickers. The smell of sweetwood.

"And what about you?" asks Tinny. "Why are you here?"

"I'm bored," answers Wheeze.

"Bored? You know what they'll do if they catch us, right?"

"Yes. That's why they can't catch us."

"You're ready to risk it all because you're bored?"

"I want to go Outside."

"You don't care if it's really him or not?"

"Not really."

"He's like me. Puppet man doesn't matter one way or the other. I'm after beauty, not truth."

"That's crazy."

"No crazier than believing in something just because there's nothing else to believe in."

"Quiet. Here he comes."

My eyes open. Light wavers from the flame of a candle sitting on the table beside the bed. My arms are still strapped at my sides. They must have moved the bed to a different room. My vision clears, and I see what I thought was a flame is really an electrical current pulsing through a coiled filament inside a lightbulb mounted on a lamp. The lamp is designed to look like a real candle, the bulb a real flame, but it's not.

"How you boys holding up?" says a new voice.

Mud says, "Good enough. Ready to go."

"Fine, I guess," answers Tinny.

"I'm bored," wheezes the third.

"When are we headed out, Doc?" asks Tinny.

The voice is familiar. I remember. It's Doc Waters. I try to close my eyes but can't.

"He'll be ready soon. He can probably hear us right now. We'll head out in a day or two."

"Thank the stars. If I had to sit around this shithole doing nothing much longer, I'd turn to stone."

"It's only been a couple of months," says Doc Waters. "That's not a lifetime. They won't be hunting you now—not like before."

"You think they'll be looking for us Outside?" asks Wheeze.

"Maybe," says Doc Waters. "But they never go far even when they do go out. They're afraid to."

"Afraid of what?" asks Mud. "There ain't no rules to be broken out there. They'd be free. They afraid of that?"

"I don't know. Maybe. Maybe you should be too."

"What about Doc Uket?" asks Tinny.

"What about her?" returns Doc Waters.

"Is she going with us?" asks Wheeze.

"We wouldn't have made it this far without her. They'll figure out that much. They'll erase her if they find her. They'll erase us all. I won't let that happen."

"It went okay with her?"

"Perfect," says Doc Waters. "They won't be able to track her now. We're ghosts. All of us."

Mud smiles.

Tinny says, "Do they believe in ghosts?"

"No," says Doc Waters. "But you've been scrubbed from the System"

"Who scrubbed you?" asks Wheeze.

"Yeah," said Tinny. "What about you?"

"I did," says Doc Waters. "Don't look at me like that. Once I understood how to do it, it was easy. Doctor Uket assisted."

"If you say so," says Mud.

"Yeah," says Tinny. "If you say so. You must be real good. A do-it-yourself brain surgeon. Think of that."

"I can't take the waiting around much longer," complains Wheeze.

"He needs more time. They were hard on him. The attendant who replaced Yew was just following orders. The other one, though, that son-of-a-bitch, is mean for the sake of it."

"Well, since we got to wait longer, can you get us a bottle or two and a new deck of cards?" asks Mud. "We're out of drink. And I like them real cards, not the kind on screens."

"But you knew how to cheat on screens," says Wheeze. "I don't play cards, real or not, with cheaters."

"I'll play," says Tinny. "And bring some of that hard cider, okay?"

"Okay," says Doc Waters. "Just make sure you stay away from all screens. Do you understand? Do *not* engage with a screen. They'll find us if you do."

"We understand," the three say as one. "No screens."

PART II

JORNADA DEL MUERTO

CHAPTER ONE

G o and get some mesquite so we can get a fire going. I don't think he'll make it through another night if we don't keep him warm."

"How come we do all the work while you bark orders?"

"Yeah. Who made you boss?"

"I'm a medical doctor. Without me, he won't be the only one dying out here. Get it? Get some wood. I saw some dry mesquite back there around the bend."

"Fine."

"Yeah, fine."

"In the meantime, you keep an eye on the legend there. We don't want him to get snatched away like she did."

"Why not? *He's* a nobody. *He* don't even know who he is."

"Go on now, before it gets dark."

The talk of fire lured me to the scene. I had no idea where we were, how long we'd been there, or how we got there. For all I knew, we could've been wherever we were for a day, a week, even longer. I'd been floating in and out of consciousness, days and nights passing like seasons contained in the blink of an eye. The thought of fire caused an ache to clamp onto my bones. Thank goodness. Pain is clarity.

It was Doc Waters giving the orders. Mud and Tinny did the complaining. I opened my eyes. A couple of wayward stars—planets maybe—poked through the twilight. I tried to sit up but didn't have the strength. I turned my head in the direction of the voices. Doc Waters sat a few feet away from where I was stretched out on the ground. He was barefoot, his unlaced System-issue boots sitting in the sand next to him. The air was dry as a sun-bleached bone. Doc Waters rubbed his feet between his hands. He was cold, too.

Doc Waters said, "We have to risk it."

I couldn't tell if he was talking to me or a ghost. Mud and Tinny were gone.

"I'm no good to you dead, and he's not going to make it without me. We've got no choice. There's a good chance they won't see us down here in the arroyo, and we'll keep the fire small—just big enough to warm up. And then we'll get on with it. I'll find you. I promise. I'll find you. Just hang on."

He was talking to Yew. I don't know how I knew but I did. When I tried to say her name, my voice lodged in my throat.

Doc Waters turned to me and smiled. His big front teeth shone in the dusk. The rest of his face looked like a shadow in the failing light.

"You're awake, are you?" He pushed his feet into the boots, and his smile drooped. "Good. Glad to see it. We'll get a fire going. I'll brew some hot tea. I slipped some into my bag before we left. Yes. That'll warm you up."

He got to his feet and limped over to me. "Don't worry." He knelt down and put a hand on my forehead. His palm was cold, like river water in winter.

A coyote yapped. It was close.

"Let me do the worrying." He smiled and his big teeth lightened the darkness of his face. "It's my job. Did you know I couldn't get you to wake up last night? No. How could you?"

He was afraid. I could see it in his eyes—the dark orbs that shone like oil above the tangle of his beard.

"Hear that?" he asked. "It's them. They're coming back with wood."

I heard voices, far off, like two men talking in a boat in the center of a pond. I looked to the sky once more. Billions of stars pulsed and whirled in the darkness.

"No," said Doc Waters. "Don't you go back to sleep. Understand?" He grabbed me by the shoulders and shook me. "Stay awake! You have to stay awake!"

I couldn't think. Time lurched.

"What the hell you doing?" Mud's voice was near and far at once. "You'll kill the bastard."

"Yeah" chimed Tinny, "you'll kill him. Then we got nothing to bargain with."

Doc Waters shook my shoulders. There wasn't a single thought rattling in my head. Empty as a drum.

CHAPTER TWO

Yew's grandmother told her the story about her ancestors. The grandmother said it was her sacred duty to hand the story down to Yew, the same story her own grandmother had handed down to her, the same way Yew would hand it down to her granddaughter if there happened to be any grandchildren left in a world gone mad. Nobody knew for sure how far back the tradition went—the handing down of stories—but it was the girl's turn to memorize the story in order to keep the past alive so the future wouldn't arrive stillborn in the present.

Yew told me her story as I slipped in and out of consciousness in the desert. She didn't think I was listening. But I was. When I could. It went something like this:

Yew's great-great-great-great-great-great-grandfather lived for half a year after being mauled by the mountain lion. His hair was straight and black and hung to his shoulders. His oval eyes were the color of his hair. Strangers often asked if he was Sioux or Apache. Rather than answering, he'd wink and walk away or spit at the ground before looking at the sky. He was a thin, tall man with a jagged white scar on his forehead. The rhythm of his gait concealed a springy cat-like strength.

As a grandfather—who knew not of Yew but knew of the story—he invited his grandson to the mountains to hunt grouse. The grandson was thrilled. They dressed in buckskins and rode horseback out of hill country dotted with juniper, scrub oak, and cholla cactus into mountains of pinyon and ponderosa pine. The summer had been long, and the grandfather yearned for cooler climes where he could soak his feet in the icy waters of a mountain stream. He was tasked with teaching his grandson to hunt grouse with a bow and arrow and how to fish for Gila trout. The grandfather, in his own manner, was preparing his grandson for the approaching coming-of-age ceremony. Like his grandfather before him, it was his duty to make sure his grandson was tuned into the rhythms of nature before the story of his people was put into his care.

They camped the first night near a cluster of rock columns held sacred by the Apache, Navajo, and Pueblo tribes. The columns stood forty feet tall and were composed of ash spewed from a volcano in a time before human reckoning. The ash was hot and welded together as it fell in heaps on the ground. The ash heaps turned into rock. The cooling of the rock caused vertical cracks in the columns. Rain, wind, ice, and heat worked on the cracks to create sculptures that ranged from phallic to pious (namely, one column resembling a nun kneeling in prayer). The sculptor of the statues, claimed the grandfather, the mind behind the design, was older than the mystery of being.

The grandfather was friendly with the local Apache tribe and had married the daughter of a cousin of a prominent chief from a neighboring band. He wasn't worried about the horses staked out in the desert getting stolen or unwelcome eyes spotting the small campfire that crackled brightly in the night. Because the grandfather wasn't worried, the grandson was at ease. The two of them filled their bellies with salt pork and the grandmother's special frybread and drank water out of leather skins. They checked on the horses before stretching out to look at the night sky.

The grandfather pointed out constellations, calling to them with words that sounded strange in the grandson's ears. The grandfather explained that the sky was Father and the Earth was Mother. The boy listened.

***

Because of the Father and Mother, there are fish and buffalo and deer and grouse, woods and water and grasses. Air to breathe and fire to ward off darkness. The stars are made of fire.

Because of these things, there is People. People is the keeper of the story. Without People, the Father and Mother would be forgotten. It is People's job to hand the story down through generations in honor of the Father and Mother.

***

The grandson listened. He believed.

The grandfather smiled.

The rock monoliths stood as sentinels throughout the night. Coyotes yipped and yowled at the coming of dawn. The grandfather rekindled the fire by adding dry pine needles to the bed of warm ash in the shallow pit. He bent low to blow flames out of the ash. He attached a metal pot to a pine branch with a metal wire produced from a saddlebag. He propped the branch against a wall of stacked stones at the edge of the fire. Flames licked the bottom of the pot. Water sizzled and hissed as the grandfather poured it from his waterskin into the pot. The boy, his eyes sticky with sleep, watched as the grandfather added coffee to the water. The two of them went to tend to the horses while the coffee brewed.

After a breakfast of pinyon nuts and the grandmother's spiced pemmican, the grandfather and grandson walked the horses under a bright blue sky through a maze of stone columns. Somewhere near the center of the maze, they spotted a horned owl spying from its nest built in a depression near the top of a twenty-foot-tall pillar of stone. The pillar had been shaped by the elements over centuries, and it looked to the man and the boy like a woman holding a baby to her breast. They filled the waterskins from two rainwater cisterns at the heart of the maze. The monsoons had arrived late that summer and the cisterns—one carved by wind, rain, and ice, the other by ancient Puebloans grinding corn and acorns—were full of water. They watered the horses before returning to camp.

This is the first of the secrets the grandfather would share with the boy: the secret of water.

The second night found them in the mountains. They camped next to a creek. Pockets of pine pitch exploded in the campfire. It was different from the crackling of mesquite, louder, more urgent. The air was cool, and the creek chattered down the slope. Sparks from the campfire fire floated upwards, beyond the swaying limbs of pines.

The grandfather told his grandson about the story he was to be entrusted with, not the story itself, for it wasn't yet time, but about the tradition of storytelling that reached beyond memory. The old man told the boy that everything had begun in Red Canyon.

∗∗∗

The story was birthed by People Who Knew Not Words who wandered existence and witnessed the unfolding of creation. One summer People was driven into Red Canyon by Demon Horse, a cavernous spirit the color of rust and wild as the wind. Blood frothed from the demon's mouth. Its mane was thick with flames. Each of the four hooves dripped tar. Demon Horse feared Red Canyon for it was haunted by the last of the One in Three who bore Loneliness. The Old One was said to ride through the canyon nights on banshee winds.

There was no rain that summer. The sun weighed down like a spiteful god's unblinking eye. Sand pink as blanched rose petals burned the soles of People's feet as they wandered the canyon. People huddled in caves carved into the canyon walls by the Old One when One was Three. People came out from the caves under the cover of night to forage for scorpions and rattlesnakes. They harvested prickly pear and fishhook barrel cactus, sucked moisture from pulp, and spit it into clay pots. People cherished the pots and carried them on the tops of their skulls back to the caves. They dug at low points in the arroyo, searching for water, at the base of scrub oaks at the bottom of sloping rock formations. People worked through the night.

The world turned. The moon budded bright and round and then withered and budded again. People absorbed the rhythms of Red Canyon. The high-pitched howling of the scorpion mouse, the X-shaped tracks of the Snake-Killer Bird, the shadows of buzzards on the desert floor as they skated across the sky during the bright hot days.

Days were spent in the shade of the caves, away from the withering gaze of the sun. People slept or carved animal figurines from the roots of cottonwood trees, looked out into the bright hot canyon or shooed away black flies. One drew runes on the canyon walls—stick figures of men with bows and spears chasing buffalo and deer, the X-shaped tracks of the Snake-Killer Bird, and stick buzzards flying above the outlines of puffy clouds.

One morning at dawn, a Snake-Killer Bird stepped into a spot of sun at the mouth of a cave and stood watching a little girl play with a doll made from sticks and wild gourds. The air was already hot. Dry. The little girl noticed the bird and smiled. The Snake-Killer Bird clicked and clacked its long beak. It hopped up and down, the blue-black crown on top of its head standing at attention, the long tail feathers fanned out. The little girl approached the bird. The bird continued to click and clack and dance in the spot of sunlight. The girl stepped into the light and began to hum.

People had never hummed before. People had always been silent. When the old woman with the broom looked at the little girl standing next to the Snake-Killer Bird in the light, she could no longer see the girl's thoughts. The hum was too loud. The old woman walked to the mouth of the cave and shooed the bird with the broom. The bird toppled from the mouth of the cave like a stone. The little girl cried, "Na!" She kicked the old woman in the shin. The Snake-Killer Bird, at the same moment, opened its wings and glided to the floor of Red Canyon. The little girl, seeing the bird was safe, shouted, "Yi." And that is how Snake-Killer Bird stole People's silence.

That night, when banshee winds rolled through the canyon, the women burned bundles of sage and marked the firelit walls of the cave with ash.

There was no rain that summer.

***

The grandfather paused. He looked down at his grandson, who was resting on his back near the fire. The grandson watched a star twinkling above the swaying boughs of pine. The grandfather asked the grandson if he understood that People was dying.

The grandson sat up and looked at his grandfather. "But they don't have the story yet."

***

A dream of Red Canyon winds woke the boy in the deep of night and he had huddled under a woolen blanket for what seemed like forever trembling from an incomprehensible fear. He then fell into a dreamless slumber while listening to the song of a whippoorwill. His consciousness rose once more to the aroma of salt pork and coffee, and he was able to shake off the clinging dread that had followed him from dream into wakefulness.

The grandson gulped down a cup of lukewarm coffee and devoured a slice of salt pork as the grandfather instructed him on how to spot dusky-colored grouse that blended into the mountain landscape like gray lichen on slate. He told him where to look and how to listen. After washing down the meat with a pull from a waterskin, the grandson armed himself with the bow and quiver of arrows presented to him by his grandfather. Then, he walked into the forest alone.

The grandson searched for grouse until his stomach started to rumble. Looking up, he found the sun staring down. He hadn't seen anything but some dusty blue pinyon jays swooping through the trees cackling among themselves. He was about to head back to camp for a lunch of pemmican and coffee when he heard a woodpecker pecking the trunk of a pine. The bird noticed the boy noticing him and took to the wing. The grandson followed the bird into the trees. The woodpecker flew a few yards, landed on a tree, and pecked at the bark as if to signal the boy. The boy followed. The bird then flew ahead and found a new tree to peck. The boy continued to follow.

The woodpecker flew farther and farther ahead of the boy until the sound of the pecking was lost in the trees. The grandson stood still. He waited for the knocking of a woodpecker pecking. The forest was silent. Only the sound of a breeze in the top of the trees. A spate of panic belted the boy like a blast of the Red Canyon winds of his dream. He dropped the bow and quiver, sat on the forest floor, and placed his face in his palms. He was lost.

The forest breathed. The boy fancied he heard the burble of faraway water, a hiss of movement, a creek. Standing, he picked up the bow and quiver of arrows and walked toward the sound. When he found the creek, he followed it upstream.

The boy began jogging as he approached camp. He was excited to tell his grandfather about the woodpecker—how it had flown from tree to tree just ahead of him stopping to peck at the pines. He wanted to tell the old man how the bird had tricked him, leading him deeper into the woods only to disappear. It was the water that saved him. The sound of the creek coming through the trees. The secret of water.

When the boy saw the mountain lion, his heart leaped. It took a space of seconds for him to realize that his grandfather's legs were sticking out from under the beast. In a single motion, the boy notched an arrow and loosed it. The arrow struck home, the obsidian point thumping into the cat's side just behind a front leg. Not a twitch from the beast. A woodpecker began pecking the trunk of a nearby pine.

The grandson notched a fresh arrow. He aimed for the same spot. The arrow arced and fell. The arrowhead, chipped from chert, was heavier than the obsidian. The arrow descended into the space between the lion and the old man.

The grandfather groaned.

***

The valley was cast in a half-light that could have passed as either dusk or dawn. Water burbled down a creek. A column of pine smoke rose like a white rope from the campfire. The grandfather had been washing the pot in which he had first boiled coffee and then fried salt pork. Catching the scent of the fried meat on the thin air, the mountain lion crept up on the old man as he hunched over the fire. The grandfather didn't hear the cat's approach. He felt it.

The lion ripped half of the grandfather's scalp from his skull with a single swipe of a paw. The claws of the other paw dug into the old man's guts as the beast made ready to sink its teeth into the meat of the old man's neck.

The grandfather yanked the hunting knife from the sheath at his belt at the same moment the sun peeked into the valley. The glint of sun on metal caused the lion to hesitate. That proved enough for the grandfather to plunge the knife to the hilt into the back of the lion's neck. The sharpened metal severed the lion's spinal cord at the base of the skull. The beast collapsed into a heap on top of the grandfather. The old man, trapped under the cat, rested his head on the forest floor. He peered into the beast's gaping mouth. The lion lay paralyzed. Its breath smelled of peat. The old man and the lion looked at one another. For the space of a breath, there was no fear.

The moment passed. The cat died. The old man looked past the lion's shoulder into the sky above the swaying tops of the pines.

He thanked the sun for saving him.

***

The fire crackled and popped. The grandson wasn't sure if his tears were from the wood smoke or sorrow. He had managed to roll the lion off of his grandfather. The grandfather wouldn't allow the boy to pull the arrow from his gut, so the boy dabbed the gash on the old man's skull with a wet rag. The grandfather instructed his grandson to build up the fire, and as the boy gathered wood, the old man gripped the shaft of the arrow in both hands and snapped it in two. The boy heard his grandfather's groan, dropped the armload of wood he had gathered, and ran back to camp. The boy's eyes fixated on the burgundy blood soaking the front of his grandfather's muslin shirt.

The grandson realized his grandfather would die if he failed to act. He built up the fire and watched as his grandfather seared the slash in his gut with a smoldering tip of a pine branch. The smell of burning flesh made the grandson's knees go weak, but he willed himself to stand tall. The grandfather instructed his grandson to chop down aspen saplings— straight trunks six feet or more in length. By the time the boy completed the task, the light in the valley had been replaced by shadow.

The grandfather watched as his grandson notched the ends of the saplings and wrapped them with strips of woven aspen bark.

"That's it," whispered the grandfather. "Tie 'em tight. Good, good."

The sky was neither light nor dark—neither blue nor black. There was no sky.

The grandfather said, "Have to wait for morning."

The boy couldn't bring himself to ask if the old man would last that long.

"Where were we?" asked the grandfather. "Wait. I remember . . ."

***

There was no rain that summer.

People panicked because they could no longer see thoughts. They abandoned the caves and fled headlong into Red Canyon. The moment the sun sank behind the canyon's red rim, a thunder of hooves echoed from the walls. Demon Horse smelled People's fear, and the fear filled him with craving. The demon thirsted for souls.

Demon Horse, the color of rust, ran wild through the canyon, blood frothing from his mouth, his mane thick with flame. The eastern wall of the canyon burned crimson in the dying light. The hooves of the horse kicked up a cloud of red dust. People, dizzy with thirst, the cheeks of her crying children dry as baked sand, stumbled and staggered over the canyon floor. Sensing that the safety of the caves was too far, a young girl, holding a doll made of gourds and sticks, turned to face Demon Horse. The girl began to hum, a whisper of life in the descending darkness. The thunder of hooves pounding the earth lent rhythm to the girl's tune. Her humming grew louder. People heard the hum and formed a circle around the girl. Soon, they joined her, and the humming became a chant. And the chant became a song, "Yi, yi, ya, ya, yi, yi, ya!"

The hooves of Demon Horse skidded and sparked on the canyon floor, the dust igniting in a burst of light that was immediately swallowed by the devouring night. Gnashing his teeth and snorting, Demon Horse bit his tongue. Blood drooled into the froth on the horse's heaving chest as the horse bucked and kicked. A rumble of faraway thunder whipped the demon further into a frenzy. The beast slashed the air with its hooves—kicked and screamed and whirled. Rage and desire roiled into poison, and the horse burst into a stampede of devils that then rushed People.

The Old One listened to People's song as she sat cross-legged on top of a pillar of sandstone. "Yi, yi, ya, ya, yi, yi, ya!" She hadn't heard singing since her mother abandoned her to Red Canyon—taken up in a fog, never to return, leaving her child alone. That was long ago. Another age. Another story. The Old One found the song beautiful in the devouring night, a hint of forever light in the darkness. And then she heard the scream.

The Old One leaped down from the pillar of sandstone and mounted a banshee wind. Hushing its wail with a whisper, she rode the wind through the twists and turns of Red Canyon. She spotted People standing still as a statue in the path of the Demon Horse devils' juggernaut rush. The Old One dismounted the banshee, sprouted a set of raven wings, and flew into the night sky.

People watched the Old One. She came to them as a ship of light descending from the heavens. She landed on the crown of an ancient oak on the floor of Red Canyon. And then, as if summoned, Buffalo emerged from the canyon floor. He stood as big as an ark on the far side of the oak. He shook dust from a mane the color of burnt milk. Buffalo stood between People and the Demon Horse devils. He snorted and pawed at the ground.

The People took up the song.

"Yi, yi, ya, ya, yi, yi, ya!"

Demon Horse gathered his devils and charged. Buffalo charged to meet them. Buffalo and Demon Horse collided. Thunder ignited lightning. The earth teetered.

People sang.

"Yi, yi, ya, ya, yi, yi, ya!"

Rain fell.

"Yi, yi, ya, ya, yi, yi, ya!"

The battle raged.

"Yi, yi, ya, ya, yi, yi, ya!"

Dawn blushed and a river gushed down Red Canyon, the water a glutinous red. Demon Horse was gone. Buffalo stood chest-deep in the flood.

People, exhausted, stood at the edge of the water. They collapsed onto the earth and fell into sleep.

The Old One came down from her perch in the tree. She sang into People's dreaming—a song for them to remember. Buffalo fell to his knees in the river. He bowed his head low and became one with the mud.

When People awoke, the river ran clear. People remembered.

They remembered the song of the Old One.

***

The grandson listened to the story of People and Demon Horse as he built the makeshift travois. When he was finished with the job, dawn paled the sky. He lifted his grandfather under the armpits and pulled him onto the sled. The grandfather moaned.

"I'm sorry," said the grandson.

"Why?" whispered the old man.

"For killing you."

The grandfather smiled. "Dead men don't talk."

The grandson tied a length of rope between the handles of the travois and looped it over his horse's saddle horn. The handles of the travois, fashioned from aspen saplings, hung low on the horse's flanks. When the grandson checked on his grandfather, he found him unconscious. There was nothing to do but mount the horse and ride home.

***

Sunlight buzzing on bleached sandstone.
Puffs of white clouds above pines.

***

The grandson kept the horse at a slow pace. He worried about the travois jarring apart as it bucked and clapped over the rocky trail. He feared his grandfather would die. But he dared not hurry. He dared not stop. Buzzards circled in the sky.

***

Lizards blinking.
Brittle brown yucca in patches of alkali, the seedpods hanging low.
Buzz of insects.

Purple prickly pear tunas plumping in sunshine.

***

Daylight dwindled and the grandson continued. He rode past the cluster of rock columns but didn't stop for water. He convinced himself that it was the rhythm of horse hooves plunking the earth that sustained his grandfather's heart. If the horse stopped, his grandfather would die. He rode on. He hummed.

Night fell. The boy listened.

***

There is silence behind the whippoorwill's song.

***

The grandfather was alive when the grandson dragged him out of the mountains on the makeshift travois. A mat of black flies clung to the wounds on the grandfather's skull and gut. The old man couldn't hear the flies, and he didn't feel the shadows from trees passing over him—nor the heat of the sun on his brow. The rhythm of the horse's gait pulsed from its flanks into the aspen handles of the travois. The pulse of the earth crept into the old man's dreams.

***

"The story cannot be handed down until the twelfth year. That's the rule."

The grandmother sat next to the bed on a three-legged stool. She bent over her husband, who was resting on a red and black Navajo blanket, her head turned sideways, her ear just above the old man's cracked lips. Her hair, long and thick and black, fell over the grandfather's brow, sweeping his eyelids. Her presence birthed the words on his breath:

"That's the same age Jesus was when Mary and Joseph found him at the temple with the rabbis. What do you think Joseph was thinking as Mary scolded their son, told him that they had been worried to death, that they had been looking for him for days? What do you think Joseph made of it when the child he had helped usher into the wicked world of men insisted that he had to do his Father's work? The Good Book doesn't say. There's no story for Joseph. He's God's witness, not his mouthpiece. But we have a story. Do you understand? And part of that story is in how and when it is handed down. We speak out of Joseph's silence. We speak for the Old One. We speak the story that cannot be written down. To write it is to kill it. It lives on the breath of the word."

The grandfather smelled of rotting grapes.

"I'm going to tell you the story," he whispered. "There's no other way. No time. I have to tell you, and you have to tell the boy. But it can never be written down. Understand?"

"Yes," whispered the grandmother.

"Do you promise?"

The grandmother turned her face to her husband and breathed into his mouth, "Yes."

***

Yew's grandmother told her the story about her ancestors. She told her she was related to the little girl with the doll made of sticks and gourds—the girl who began the humming.

CHAPTER THREE

The words fly through my brain like bees trapped in a jar.

"How the hell should I know where they took her? I don't even know who they were."

"We do know one thing. They weren't System men."

"Is that good or bad?"

"Both."

"How can it be both? That don't make sense."

"Did you see what they did to your friend? That was bad, right?"

"The worst."

"It wasn't Mean Eyes and his crew. It wasn't the System. They wouldn't do that. They're cruel but subtle."

"At least they haven't found us. Not yet anyway."

"Yeah. That's good. But now we've got another enemy to run from. "

I remember. Doc Waters, Mud, Tinny. The air smells of wood smoke. Mesquite. I can hear the bubbling of boiling water.

"Why'd they do it?" asks Tinny.

"What?" returns Mud. "Who?"

"You seen it. Those bastards plucked out his eyes, then chopped off his balls and stuck them in the sockets. That ain't no way to treat a man. He was my friend."

"Friend?" says Mud. "Hell, you only knew him from the System. May as well have been a prison cell. You figure cellmates can be friends??

"Bastard."

"Maybe. But I ain't stupid."

"What about it, Doc? Why didn't they kill her?"

"Too pretty," said Mud. "Got other plans."

"They knew who she was," says Doc Waters.

Yew. They're talking about Yew. I remember her eyes, how their color changes with her moods. I remember.

***

We were camped near a stand of salt cedars just above the arroyo. It would have been safer to camp down in the wash, up next to a bank. The bank was steep on the east side of the arroyo, over six-foot. It would've given us some cover. A little's better than none.

Wheeze wouldn't have anything to do with the idea. He said he'd heard of flash floods roaring down arroyos in the middle of the night to sweep away whatever was in their path, boulders the size of one of those old gas burners—muscle cars they called them. A man wouldn't have a chance. Horrible way to die. No way Wheeze was risking it.

Doc Waters said the foothills were too far away for much of a flood. The mountains looked like blue-black bruises on the western horizon. Wheeze wouldn't listen. He said the riverbed, dry or not, got there some-how and he'd camp up in the salt cedars by himself if he had to. He finally got Tinny to agree. There wasn't no way those two were going to sit up there without a fire. I think Mud was getting ready to conk both of them on the head with his hammer fists, but Doc Waters gave in and said it would be best if we stuck together. Yew agreed. So, that's what we did. We stuck together. That's how we got torn apart.

I still couldn't talk. Every time I tried to say something, the words stuck in my throat. After a while, I didn't try anymore. I couldn't walk either. Hell, I could barely sit up. It was up to the rest of them to carry me on the stretcher Mud had fashioned out of buffalo hide. We'd come upon the dying beast near a burned-out cabin on the bank of the arroyo. Mud finished off the poor thing and skinned it. Then, he stretched the hide between two lengths of charred wood from the cabin. I only remember pieces of it. The next thing I knew, they were taking turns lugging me through the desert on that hide. Between the stretcher and the packs on their backs, I didn't figure we'd been making very good time.

Mud was strong. Tinny complained about an ache in his back when it was his turn to carry one end of the stretcher, said the backpack was all he could handle. I'm not a big man—almost six feet tall and about a hundred and seventy pounds, but it was more than they were used to hauling. I don't blame Tinny for bellyaching. Wheeze mumbled about his feet, blisters or bunions or such, I never could make out what he was saying. Doc Waters wouldn't suffer Yew to heft the load, the backpack was more than enough for her, so he took her turn. But it was Mud who bore the brunt of it. He acted like he didn't need any rest, even with his backpack on. He didn't complain one note. He was strong—strong like the earth.

That buffalo was a real surprise. Up to that point, Mud had been pulling me on the dolly truck he'd snatched from the System. He strapped me to the thing with rubber cords. The metal hooks on the ends of the cords dug into my back. I didn't say anything. I couldn't. Best I could manage was a low moan like a sick dog.

I could tell Mud was starting to wear down some. He didn't need to say it out loud like the others. The rubber wheels on the dolly sunk in the sand or got caught on mesquite and creosote branches as we trekked through the desert. Nobody offered to spell Mud. So he just kept pulling that dolly.

The buffalo was still alive when we found it. It was on its side in the sand in the middle of the wash. Its chest was heaving. I could make out the remains of the burnt-out cabin on the far side of the arroyo. It looked like the structure had burned down a long time ago. Mud wheeled the dolly right up to the buffalo and set it down. I was on the ground next to the buffalo, my eyes level with the beast's. The poor thing looked at me and blinked. Mud knelt down and stroked the buffalo's skull. It didn't even flinch—not that it should have. That poor old buffalo had given up. It was too hurt to run away from men like it should have.

***

The raccoon snarls.
The boy swings the board.
The wood cracks the top of the raccoon's skull.

***

"What's wrong with it?" asked Tinny. He'd come up behind Mud and stood looking over his shoulder.

Mud took a knife from a leather sheath at his belt and held it in his open palms over the buffalo's head. He looked at the sun and started mumbling something. I couldn't make out the words. I hadn't known about Mud's knife before that. It had a bone handle carved full of symbols. I didn't recognize them—didn't know what they stood for. Mud gripped the handle in his fist like it was a runner's baton, the blade pointing down. He covered the buffalo's open eye with his other palm. And then he cut that buffalo's throat.

***

The father knelt down and plunged the knife into the deer's neck.
The air smelled like cow flop.

***

The buffalo twitched and jerked as its blood ran out over the sand.

And then it didn't move at all. I looked up and found Doc Waters and Yew standing over me. Yew was crying.

"It was dying of thirst," said Doc Waters.

"Looks like steaks tonight," wheezed Wheeze.

Mud stood and wiped the blade of the knife on his pants. "Poison."

"What?" asked Yew.

"Poison?" asked Tinny. "You mean it ate something bad? Ain't they supposed to know what's poisonous and what's not? Ain't that what makes them wild?"

"Could have been delirious from thirst," said Doc Waters.

Yew squatted down and placed her hand on my brow. "No," she whispered. "Men did this."

"Why?" asked Doc Waters.

"A warning," said Mud. He slid the knife into the sheath at his belt, took up the handles of the dolly, and lifted. "Meat's no good." He pulled the dolly, and me along with it, over the sand.

Yew followed. Tinny, Doc Waters, and Wheeze stood looking down at the buffalo.

"How do you know?" asked Tinny. "You ain't no buffalo expert."

"What a waste," complained Wheeze. "How would it eating poison plants spoil the meat?

"It wouldn't need to," said Mud over his shoulder. "Whoever killed it wants us to eat it. They poisoned it."

"How do you know? You can't know that."

"Don't know how I know. Just do."

"Should we bury it?" asked Doc Waters.

"Wolves or coyotes'll just dig it up," shouted Mud. He pulled me to a spot where the bank of the arroyo was more than six feet tall. "Let me get this one in some shade. I'll skin it out and butcher it. We'll start a fire. Burn it."

"How do you know the meat's no good?" repeated Tinny. "Can't we test it somehow?

"You don't believe me, go ahead and eat it," said Mud.

"Why not? Barbecue it up. I'll try it," said Wheeze.

"The smoke'll give away our position," said Tinny.

"It's already done," said Doc Waters. "Whoever they are, they know we're here."

Yew followed Mud into the shadow cast by the bank of the arroyo. He propped the dolly against the bank and left me in a standing position. Yew stood next to me. She stroked my brow with her fingertips. It was right then I knew I loved her. She was risking her neck to save me from the System. I figured she loved me too. Why else would she risk her own life?

"Don't worry," she whispered. "It'll take time, but you'll remember. Everything. You have to. Don't worry. And don't try too hard to remember. It'll come back to you." She continued stroking my brow with the tips of her fingers. "It'll be easier when we get you to safety. You can rest. There'll be fresh fruit and wine. There's a healer who knows the old ways." Yew kissed me on the forehead. "She might know how to find him."

It didn't matter that I didn't know who or what the hell she was talking about. Whatever it was, it made me sound important.

Tinny and Wheeze set off to gather firewood while Mud butchered the buffalo. First thing Mud did was cut the tongue out of the mouth. Then, he cut a square piece out of the hide, wrapped the tongue in it, and tucked it in his shirt. Next, he opened the belly of the beast and pulled out the guts. That knife of his was sharp. It cut through the hide like it was oatmeal. Steam rose as Mud pulled out the liver, intestines, stomach, and heart. He piled the guts in the sand and started to work on the skinning. I could smell the guts.

***

Fresh cow pies in a green field.

***

The stench attracted an orgy of flies. They came out of nowhere. One minute Mud was straddled over the buffalo, a backdrop of blue sky and sand painted with sunshine, in the next a blanket of flies fell over the gut pile. It didn't faze Mud. He kept right on skinning. He'd brush flies away when they landed in his eyes or got in his nose, but he always kept his attention on the work.

"Don't worry," said Yew, still stroking my brow. "When we find him, he'll know what to do. He'll help you remember who you are. You'll remember what he said. You'll know what to do then."

Truth is, I didn't want to remember whatever it was Yew wanted me to remember. She'd been talking about it ever since she got me away from Mean Eyes. Whatever happened back there in that goddamn prison or hospital or whatever it was could stay there as far as I was concerned. I was better off without it. I had Yew to thank for getting me away from that place. I didn't want to go back. I didn't want to remember.

Tinny and Wheeze came trudging in, dragging dead branches from a lightning-struck cottonwood. The branches were big with smaller branches sticking out, some dragging through the sand like little plows. Sweat dripped from Tinny's earlobes. Wheeze's face was smudged with soot.

Tinny was in the lead. He dragged up his branch and dropped it next to the pile of guts. A blanket of black flies rose and fell.

"Smells like a bloody nose," Tinny said.

"Like wet peat moss," grunted Mud.

Wheeze, still pulling his branch through the sand, stopped in his tracks. "I can't go no further. My feet are raw." He dropped the branch and sat on the ground. "A fine picture this is. A bear of a man covered in flies carving up a poison buffalo in the middle of nowhere and us numbskulls doing whatever we're told like the dolts we are." He looked up the sky and then at me. "Over there we got a puppet man who can't talk or walk and a woman who seems more dream than real in this place of curses."

"Well," said Tinny, "at least it ain't boring. Ain't that why you came out here? Because you were bored?" He smeared soot over his forehead as he wiped away sweat with the back of his arm.

"Oh, but I am bored," returned Wheeze. "I'm hot and thirsty and tired. I find that very boring."

Doc Waters said, "Break off some of those smaller sticks and get a fire going."

"I'm not doing shit until I rest," complained Wheeze.

Tinny broke off the smaller branches from his haul and stacked them in a pile.

"Rest in your grave," said Doc Waters. "We'll need to put some miles between us and this before it gets dark."

"Or else?" asked Wheeze.

"You want to find out?" asked Tinny.

***

They must have been watching from the moment we crossed the boundary into Outside. They must have been waiting.

I'm not sure how Mud managed to put the stretcher together as quick as he did. He had finished skinning the buffalo and starting the fire. Tinny and Wheeze weren't any help, and Doc Waters and Yew were huddling next to each other in the shadow of the bank of the arroyo. I was getting to the point where I didn't care much for Doc Waters. He was always hanging around Yew. I didn't like the way the two of them were always talking just out of earshot.

Mud went to work on the stretcher as the fire grew. It didn't take but a few whacks here and there with that bone-handle knife of his and it was done. Mud could do a lot of things a System man shouldn't know how to do, like he was at home Outside.

As far as I could tell, the whole lot of them—Yew, Doc Waters, Tinny,

Wheeze, and Mud—were products of the System, born and raised. I figured I was too. But I couldn't remember it all in the order that it happened.
Just a snippet here and a snippet there. They had used me as some sort of
reason to make an escape. I didn't know why. The fact that they wanted to
escape was enough. I'm pretty sure I'd be dead if they wouldn't have took
me out of that goddamned place.

When Mud finished the stretcher, he went back to the buffalo. The fire
burned big, red flames licking blue sky. Mud chopped up the buffalo and
tossed the pieces into the fire. Hunks of meat, bones, and then the guts.
The flies didn't like that. The fire cracked and snapped and belched smoke
the color of storm clouds.

Mud and Doc Waters took me off the dolly and loaded me on the
stretcher. The buffalo hide was still bloody. It attracted flies. Doc Waters
and Mud picked up the stretcher, and we were on our way. I looked back
to where the buffalo had died and watched the column of smoke hanging
like a rope dropped from the sky.

I don't know how long they carried me. I kept falling asleep. I remember opening my eyes to a sky the color of rose blossoms. Wheeze and Doc
Waters were bickering about where to camp. Things were heating up, and
Mud was losing his patience. He started clenching and unclenching those
thick hands of his. Doc Waters stepped in and played peacemaker, and
then Yew gave in just like that. Acquiesced they call it. Mud and Tinny
took up the stretcher and our ragtag team marched out of the arroyo. By
the time we got to the stand of salt cedars, it was almost dark.

Wheeze sat and watched while the other men gathered wood. Yew sat
on the ground next to the stretcher. Nobody bothered giving the reasons
why we shouldn't build a fire. They figured that whoever killed the buffalo
already knew we were there. If it was up to me, we would have gone dark.
We didn't know anything for sure. No need to give our position away with
a fire burning bright in the middle of a nowhere night. But I still couldn't
talk. The words lodged in my throat. All I could do was wait.

A cold wind sprang up. That's when Wheeze brought out a bottle of hard cider and started passing it around. Yew turned down the offer. So did Doc Waters. The rest of them took swigs and passed the bottle. Nobody said much at first. They just sat there looking at the fire like it was some kind of miracle—like they'd never seen a real fire before . . . like they'd only witnessed campfires on screens. They'd burned a buffalo just a few hours earlier, tossed hunks of red meat to the flames. But a fire's a whole different thing when it's dark. It's a recollection of daylight. It wards off the fear of things unseen.

Yew took a blanket out of her backpack. It was shiny like foil, thin as paper, and made to hold in heat. She draped it over me and then scooched herself up next to the stretcher. She flopped an arm over my chest.

Doc Waters disappeared behind the salt cedar. We could hear him pissing. It was rude. Yew could hear it too.

"That's the end of that," said Wheeze. He tossed the empty bottle to the fire. The remaining smidge of liquor flamed, whooshed in a blue flash, and was gone. "That's okay, though. You see, I planned ahead. I got more."

"I could use another swig or two," said Tinny.

"You'll be sorry," said Doc Waters from behind the salt cedar. "It'll be hot tomorrow. Dry."

"Leave tomorrow to tomorrow," said Wheeze. He reached behind him and yanked a fresh bottle from his pack. "I ain't going to be able to sleep without another drink. My poor old feet are screaming."

Doc Waters appeared out of the darkness. He rummaged through his pack and took out a blanket like Yew's. He wrapped it around his shoulders and sat with his back to the salt cedar. Firelight danced, looking electric on the metallic surface of the blanket. Doc Waters looked like a wizard on a screen game. For a second, I didn't think he was real. I didn't think any of it was real.

"What'd Doc say his name was?" asked Tinny.

"Who?" asked Wheeze.

"Who do you think?" Tinny nodded in my direction. "The mystery man we're hauling through the desert on a damn stretcher made out of a dead buffalo we happened upon out of the blue. The man who don't know his own name. The stranger we're risking our necks for. The Puppet Man. That's who."

Tinny stood and disappeared into the darkness.

"Give me the bottle," said Mud.

Wheeze took a swig, capped the bottle, and tossed it over the fire.

Mud caught the bottle in one hand. "He don't know, so it don't matter."

"What?" asked Wheeze.

Mud uncapped the bottle and drank. "A name don't mean nothing to a man who don't know who he is."

Yew was lying on her side next to me, the metallic blanket pulled up over her shoulder. Her palm pressed on my belly. It was warm as a kiss. I felt her eyes on my face, but I couldn't bring myself to look at her. I was less than human. I didn't even know my own name. I looked at the stars.

Tinny came out of the dark. "Best be careful. I just kicked up a scorpion the size of my big toe. Aggressive little shit. Had to stomp him three times before the bastard quit moving."

"Who really gives a damn?" asked Mud.

"I do," said Tinny. He sat next to Mud, who handed him the bottle. "May as well know his name. We done went all in on him." He raised the bottle to the sky before pouring a few drops of liquor on the dirt.

"Go easy," said Wheeze. "I only got one bottle left."

"It's what they used to call a libation," said Tinny. "A kind of prayer. My grandad told me stories."

"We're all gonna feel like shit tomorrow," said Mud. He grabbed the bottle from Tinny and took a drink.

"A prayer?" asked Wheeze. "For who? That fool over there don't know who he is? What good's a damn name going to do him? A name don't do shit if it don't have no past for it to stand on."

Yew tossed the blanket away and sat up. "Please be quiet. He needs to rest. Then he'll remember. He'll tell us."

I wanted to say, "If a man doesn't know his own name, who in the hell is he? Nobody, that's who. He should be left alone," but I couldn't form the words in my mouth.

"Remember what?" asked Tinny.

"His name, you idiot," said Mud.

"And all that goes with it," said Yew. She stood and looked down at the men sitting around the fire.

"And what goes with it?" asked Wheeze. "Go on, now, missy. Enlighten us. Fill us in on the mystery 'cause all I see is a beat-up husk of a man who can't walk or talk or remember his own name. Why'd we drag his carcass out here for? You can tell us. Just spill the beans. There ain't no System men around. No electronic bugs, no ears on the walls, nobody for us to tell your little secret. So, why don't you go ahead and tell us why in the hell you led us out here to this godforsaken place? Is it all for nothing'? If it is, we may as well just go back."

"Easy," said Tinny. "We can't go back. Not ever."

"Yeah," growled Mud. "Easy."

Yew turned her back to the fire and peered into the darkness. "It's not godforsaken. It's where god hides from men."

Doc Waters stood and took a step toward the fire. "Once upon a time, they used to name people after characters in poems." The blanket fell from his shoulders, sparks of light reflecting off the metallic surface.

"Poems?" asked Wheeze. "Nothing in the whole wide world bores me more than poetry. I came out here for adventure, not to listen to some System doggerel."

"Not that kind of poem," said Doc Waters. He took another step toward the light, his dark eyes flashing. "How old are you?"

"Thirty-something," said Wheeze. "Why?"

"And you two?"

"Thirty I figure," said Tinny.

Mud drank from the bottle.

"Did they teach you the old stories when you were in school?" asked Doc Waters.

"You mean like myths?" asked Tinny. "Like Jesus and his Apostles?"

"Yeah," said Wheeze, "they taught us about Jesus. Miracles and whatnot. I never could figure what they meant by a god who could die. Doesn't make no sense. A god can't die, right? That's what makes him a god. That's why it's a myth. Myths don't have to make sense. The teacher said that people actually believed in that shit a long time ago. Made a hero out of some poor guy that got nailed to a tree for some things he said. Had wars about it and everything. Bunches of people died for a myth. If that's what a hero was back then, it's no wonder their world got wiped out."

"You think the System made things better?" asked Mud.

"Yeah, I do," said Wheeze. "Before the System, people believed in fantasies like they was real. That shit is doomed from the get-go. Things gotta make sense. The System fucked up a lot of things, I get that. But at least with them in charge, everything's got its place. It's boring as hell, but it's better than believing in shit that ain't real."

"They're not in charge out here," said Yew, her back still to the fire.

Doc Waters took a step toward Mud and gestured for the bottle. Mud handed it up, and Doc Waters took it in both hands and drank. He wiped the back of a hand across his mouth and smiled. "Not Jesus. Homer and Virgil. Gilgamesh. That kind of stuff."

"Never heard of it," said Tinny.

"Nope," said Wheeze.

The names stirred something inside me.

"Too bad," said Doc Waters. "Our patient here might make more sense if you knew some history."

"I do know history," said Tinny. "They taught us all about it in school—how it was planted in the earth like a seed and germinated and sprouted and grew. How there was no stopping it, how it fertilized itself with the blood of the innocent and the guilty alike, how it fed on the fantasies of men. The whole Jesus thing was necessary for history to grow. That's why they taught us that story. All the wars and the factories. It was necessary—all of it—even if it didn't make sense at the time. Without it, History would have starved. When History grew up, it took the name System. I loved History when I was younger. I even applied for the Ministry of History, but I couldn't get past the exam. They only let you take it twice. I didn't like it so much after I failed that second time."

"Sounds like another myth," said Wheeze. "The Jesus story don't make sense, but it ain't as boring as history."

"I remember Homer," said Mud.

Yew turned and faced the fire. "Tell them."

Doc Waters handed the bottle to Mud.

Mud took the bottle and stood.

"It was in the books," said Mud. He took a drink and stood there like he was trying to give himself permission. He cleared his throat and the words began flowing like water over a dam, "My mother kept books. She hid them from my father and when he was away on the job and she'd bring them out and read them to me at night. Achilles and Odysseus. Gods on mountains and at the bottom of the sea. Jealous gods. Flashing swords and one-eyed giants. Warriors in chariots. Mother loved those stories. I'd sit next to her on the couch, and she'd read them until I fell asleep."

Wheeze stood and circled the fire. Then, he snatched the bottle from Mud.

Mud continued, "Achilles was my favorite. The greatest warrior who ever lived. I dreamed of him."

"Now that makes sense," said Wheeze. "And it's not boring. I wonder why they didn't teach that one instead of Jesus. A warrior instead of a victim."

"Homer came before Jesus," said Tinny. "They taught us that much in

History, but we didn't read any Homer. When the Jesus story came along, the older stories got displaced. It was like there wasn't room for them anymore."

"That doesn't make no sense either," said Wheeze. "They should've stuck with the old stories. Warrior heroes."

"But they didn't." Doc Waters stepped away from the fire into the shadows "There can only be one story."

"Yep," said Tinny. "It's called the System."

"Not out here," said Yew. "That's not what the story's called out here."

"My father found the books one day," said Mud. "He turned my mother in." He grabbed the bottle from Wheeze. "I never saw her again."

"Erased," whispered Doc Waters.

Mud sat by the fire and stared into the flames.

***

I have no idea how much time passed. I kept coming in and out of sleep. The fire died to a glow, and the men were stretched out around the smolder. Yew was next to me, under the metallic blanket that was pulled up to our shoulders. The moon had risen, a quarter moon. Moonglow glow clung to Yew's face like mist.

Her eyes snapped open and she stared into me. "If you don't remember, they win. Do you understand?"

I couldn't look at her. I looked at the moon. Minutes passed. When I got the nerve to look at her again, she was asleep.

***

The Cactus Eaters began trailing the intruders the moment they crossed over to the Outside. Tanned pelts of Mexican gray wolves hung over their shoulders, the floppy heads of the wild dogs perched on their heads like crowns. Each of them carried a staff fashioned from fire-cured cedar. On one end of the staff was a two-pronged fork. Blending into the desert came as natural as the blood flowing through their veins. Pollen from mesquite, sage, and desert willow permeated their pores. The land on the far side of the boundary, the civilization from which the intruders had emerged, harbored nightmare machines that the Cactus Eaters had vowed to wipe from the face of the Earth. The System had placed dead or alive bounties on the Cactus Eaters. Only a handful of manhunters had returned from Outside to claim the bounty.

The Cactus Eaters—there were three of them in this gang—trailed the foreigners, trotted over the desert, knelt in gullies to take stock of their prey, weaved through cholla and prickly pear, mesquite, and four-winged salt brush. They wore loincloths sewn from wolf pelts. Their feet, the soles hardened by years of trekking, left only traces of their passing, tracks that no System man could follow for long. The rumor that the Cactus Eaters were ghosts of men who lived before the System, before history, began as a bounty hunter's firelight yarn. Over the years, the tale cemented into myth.

The Cactus Eaters watched the foreigners from behind a thick stand of creosote rooted in a dune of dirt the color of pennies. They watched as the big man skinned the buffalo and butchered the meat from the bone. They watched as he tossed chunks of red flesh into a fire tended by two smaller men. They watched as vultures circled. Their collective hunger latched onto the figure of the woman standing in a shadow cast down by the bank of the arroyo. The woman whispered to a man strapped to a two-wheeled contraption with two handles on one end. The Cactus Eaters shivered in the bright heat each time the woman touched the man's brow.

The sun crossed its zenith and still the Cactus Eaters watched. The black flies didn't disturb them. Long ago, they had learned to ignore the flies lest they lose their minds in the high-pitched whine of wings. They watched as the big man fashioned a stretcher from buffalo hide and charred wood.

A gang of Cactus Eaters—not unlike those watching—had burned down the cabin on the far side of the arroyo many seasons ago. They burned the cabin after filling the bodies of the man and two boys who had built it with arrows. *The females, a woman and a child, had been taken hostage.*

The Cactus Eaters watched as two men placed the wounded man on the stretcher. The men lifted the stretcher and started down the arroyo. The woman and the remaining men followed. When the intruders were out of sight, the Cactus Eaters crept down to the smoldering fire and poked at the blackened buffalo bones with their staffs.

Night fell. A new fire, small in scope but large against the darkness, guided them, pulling the Cactus Eaters toward it. They circled the intruder's camp. They waited. They watched. The woman had crawled under a thin metallic blanket with the wounded man earlier in the night. The big man and two smaller ones had passed around a bottle. The tall man, wrapped in a metallic blanket of his own, huddled next to a stand of salt cedar. The fire died, and the two smaller men stretched out on the ground. The big man sat alone listening to the darkness, the far-off yapping of coyotes, and, later, the hoot of an owl followed by the howl of a wolf. He then sprawled in the dirt and fell asleep under a faint hum of stars.

The Cactus Eaters crept into camp as one, three-in-one, from three directions. They carried their forked staffs like witching wands—held them so that the forks looked like antlers atop the wolf pets draped over their skulls. As one they came to a stop around the dying fire, three Cactus Eaters standing above each of the three men at their feet. As one, the Cactus Eaters flipped their sticks, gripped the forks in either hand, and raised them under the light of the quarter moon. The whoosh of an owl passing through the camp disrupted the ritual. Two of the Cactus Eaters lowered their staffs. The other plunged the sharp tip into the belly of the man at his feet.

The skewered man opened his eyes and then screamed. The big man knocked the legs from under the Cactus Eater standing above him with a kick to the knee and sprang to his feet. The Cactus Eater yanked his staff from the skewered man's guts and leaped across the campfire. He shrieked and swung the staff like an ax. The tall man sleeping next to the salt cedar sprung to attention. One of the Cactus Eaters hopped like a rabbit to the woman. She bolted into a sitting position next to the stretcher, her eyes wide. The Cactus Eater struck her in the temple with the sharpened end of his staff.

The three men ran into the night as one, one-in-three—the big man, the tall man, and the smaller man who had escaped harm. They ran as one in three directions, and each kept running, the spines of cholla and prickly pear penetrating their thighs and tearing at the soles of their feet. A single cry pierced the night, a lone note of anguish, and each of them, in the same instant, stood paralyzed by the sound. They all realized at once that they had abandoned the woman and the man on the stretcher. Each turned back, each as one, and slunk around patches of cactus, mesquite, and creosote.

They crept into camp. The woman was gone. The wounded man, still on the stretcher, slept, his eyes moving rapidly beneath the eyelids as if he was dreaming the scene. The skewered man lay spreadeagled on the ground. He was naked, his face to the sky. His eyes had been plucked from the sockets and replaced with his testicles. His mouth was slit to the ears. He grinned a ghastly grin at the quarter moon.

CHAPTER FOUR

"**P**ssst. Here. I'm over here."

The voice came as a whisper on the breeze. I couldn't locate it. Doc Waters and Mud were hauling me on the stretcher, and they didn't seem to hear anything. Maybe my ears were playing tricks.

"Pssssst. Over here. Hurry. Before they see you."

The wind whipped up funnels of dust as tall as men. The funnels whirled like dervishes through the desert. One of the dust devils, a big one, twirled out of the desert and collapsed in the middle of what had once been a paved road. We'd been traveling that road for the better part of two days. We were out of water. Tinny lagged behind, the blisters on his heels busted open and raw, the inside of his System-issued boots sticky with puss.

"Fools! Over here!"

Doc Waters and Mud stopped. It was only then that I noticed a metal shack standing to one side of the blacktop, the frame falling in on itself, grey paint flaking from the corrugated metal walls.

"Yes. Here. Hurry."

"Who's there?" Doc Waters asked.

"Soldiers are close," said the voice, a man's voice, dry as a desert wind.

"Now get on over here. Don't want them to see you, now do you? They got binocs and know how to use 'em. Might want to get out of plain sight, you might. What you waiting for? Sun bake your brains?"

Tinny limped up behind us. "I'll take my chances with whoever or whatever that is. We're dying out here." He hobbled toward the shack.

Mud, standing in front of the stretcher, started to follow.

"You're going?" asked Doc Waters, holding his ground. "What if it's a trap?"

"Ain't got no choice," said Mud. "You don't have a clue where there's any water around here, do you?"

Doc Waters shook his head. His beard, more white than grey now, sun-bleached, waggled in the breeze.

"Come on." Mud took a firm grip on the stretcher handles and stepped forward.

"Yew's out here somewhere," Doc Waters said. "Maybe she's here." He followed Mud. I was on the stretcher between them.

Waves of heat curled from the metal roof of the building. A burst of hot breeze swept through the gaps in the walls. Mud and Doc Waters trailed Tinny inside. The place looked like a once-upon-a-time warehouse. It had a cement floor. It was empty. Mud and Doc Waters held the stretcher. Tinny, his nerves gone cold, cowered behind us. As they carried me farther inside, I was able to make out scraps of cloth, hundreds of them, in a three-foot-tall heap in a corner of the warehouse. Some old cardboard and a couple of empty plastic jugs littered the floor.

The air was dry and hot. At least we were out of the sun.

Mud set his end of the stretcher on the floor, and Doc Waters did the same.

"You there," growled Mud. "Show yourself."

Mud seemed to be talking to the pile of rags in the corner of the building.

"We see you," said Doc Waters.

"Do you have water?" asked Tinny.

Mud pulled the bone-handled knife from his belt.

"Now, now, now. There's no need for that." The pile of rags trembled and grew taller, like a giant seedling sprouting on a time-elapsed film.

Doc Waters stepped away from the stretcher and circled behind the pile.

"Do you have water?" repeated Tinny.

"Yes, yes, there's water."

A raggedy man, thin as a curve, at least seven feet tall, stepped out of the pile. The rags fell on the floor behind him. He was dressed in dingy long underwear the color of clay. He wore cowboy boots, the heels worn down to nubs, the leather sun-bleached and weather checked. There was a tattered straw cowboy hat propped on his head at an odd angle. He grinned. "There's food, too. And, yep, you got it, I even got beer!"

Doc Waters said, "Who are you?"

Tinny asked, "What is this place?"

Mud said, "What do you want in return?"

Raggedy Man's face was covered in a patchwork of thick stubble, some black as hot tar, some silver. Hawknosed with deep-set gray eyes over sunken cheeks, he looked like he'd fallen out of a world long forgotten.

"Well, well, where to begin?" said Raggedy Man. "Let's start with me name. Yeh, that's a good place. Me name is Lug Lughnasa. How's you like that?"

"What will you want in return for some water?" asked Mud.

"And beer," added Tinny.

"And food," said Doc Waters.

Raggedy Man took a step toward the stretcher. "Well, you don't look to be System men to me, no ya don't. In fact, you looks to me like you're runnin' away from that lot of lost souls. Am I right?"

"What if you are?" asked Doc Waters. He circled slowly behind Raggedy Man.

Raggedy Man took a step toward the stretcher and pointed to me. "And what about this poor devil? What ails him? Or is he a she?"

"He couldn't tell you one way or the other," said Tinny. "Doesn't know what he is. Can't talk neither. About as much use as the stripe on a skunk's tail. But I've seen him with his pants down and he's a he for sure. Even if he don't know what a he or she is, he's a he. And we three flunkies have gone and staked all we had and all we're ever going to have on a sack full of question marks. That's who we are. Now, about that water?"

"Shut up," snarled Mud.

"You say you have beer?" asked Tinny.

"And food," added Doc Waters.

"Now what did I just tell you? Are you making me out to be a liar or insulting my hospitality or both things at once?" asked Raggedy Man.

A blast of wind smashed into the building. The beams of light slashing through gaps in the metal roof dimmed. The walls rattled and flapped. And then it went quiet. The temperature must've fallen five degrees, maybe more, in the space of a few seconds. The others noticed it too. Doc Waters stepped back from Raggedy Man. Tinny looked for an exit. Mud fell into a crouch.

"Nobody's insulting you," said Doc Waters. "We've been runnin' short on hope out there. Haven't had any water since yesterday, and it's been hotter than lava. You seem like you stepped out of a dream. That's all."

"Beer," chirped Tinny. "That'd be a dream come true."

"What about that?" said Raggedy Man, pointing once more to me.

"What about him?" said Mud.

Raggedy Man smiled. "Easy there. I'm just a wee bit curious as to why you're hauling a dead man into nowhere is all. Seems like he'd slow you down somethin' awful. Like he'd be more of a burden than a boon."

"He's not dead," said Doc Waters.

Mud stood to his full height.

Raggedy Man grinned and stepped back. "I meant half-dead. May as well be full-dead by the looks of it."

"He ain't dead," said Mud.

"Look," said Doc Waters, "it's a long story. We'd be more than happy to tell you all about it in exchange for a drink of water and a bite to eat. There's not much else we have to offer, but it's a good story. You'll see. It might make you laugh, and it might make you cry. I'm not sure which. Whatever happens, we're not out for trouble and we're not out to harm you. We're just in need of some help. You can help if you want to. If not, I guess we'll have to be on our way."

"You'll laugh your ass off," said Tinny. "We're a real live clown show. That in itself ought to be enough for a beer or two."

"Perhaps," said Raggedy Man. He removed the straw hat from his head and whacked it against his thigh. A puff of dust burst out of his long johns. He grinned.

It looked to me like he was pushing out a hard turd.

"I was just testin' the weather is all," said Raggedy Man. "It's easy to see you're in a big fat mess. We don't get many strangers passin' this way. Just some System men now and then lookin' for trouble. There've been more patrols than usual this past week, and I figure it has something to do with you fellas. Especially that one." He nodded in my direction and placed the straw hat over the point at the top of his skull.

Mud, Tinny, and Doc Waters stood staring at Raggedy Man. If I could have said something, I would have asked him if *he* was from the System. But I couldn't. He would've denied it anyway. Wouldn't want to blow his own cover.

Raggedy Man grinned once more, but this time, it was more relaxed, "I really got to apologize to you boys. This ain't goin' the way I planned it. I was just funnin' with you fellas, okay? A test. You ain't System men, but you're from the System. Do I got that right? Seems plain as sunshine at noon."

"What if we are?" asked Doc Waters. "What difference does it make? We're men in need of water. Does it matter where we're from?"

"Who's we?" asked Tinny.

"Huh?"

"You said *we* don't get many strangers," said Mud.

Raggedy Man took the hat from his head and smacked his thigh once more. Another puff of dust exploded out of the once-white cotton of his long johns.

Doc Waters, closest to Raggedy Man, sneezed.

"Well, I'll be wrung out and dried," said Raggedy Man. "Crow's always complainin' I need to *com-mun-i-cate* better. That's how she says it—*com-mun-i-cate*. She says I need to learn how to say things straight out instead of beatin' around the bush."

"Say it straight then," said Mud. "We ain't gettin' no less thirsty standing here."

"It's beginning to feel like a trap," said Doc Waters.

Tinny took a step forward. "Quit stalling. Put up or shut up. You got any beer or don't you?"

"I done made a mess of things," said Raggedy Man. "I best just shut my trap. Follow me, and I'll take you to Crow. She can explain it better than me."

"We'll get some water then?" asked Mud.

"And food?" added Doc Waters.

"Yes and yes. And beer. Just follow me. I shouldn't have opened me darned mouth in the first place. The words always come out wrong. I'm sorry about all this. I truly am." Head hung low, he placed the hat on his head, turned and shuffled toward the back of the building.

"No need to tell Crow, whoever she is, much of anything," said Doc Waters. "Just tell her you found us out here and brought us straight to her."

Raggedy Man stopped. He turned around. "Really? You'd lie for me?"

"It ain't lying if you bring us to her. This Crow ain't going to care about a bunch of small talk," said Tinny. "That's all it's been up to now—small talk. We can all have a beer and start fresh."

Raggedy Man smiled, turned, and continued shuffling to the back of the building. "Gotta love it when things fall into place all on their own."

Raggedy Man led the group to a door that opened into the mouth of a cave.

CHAPTER FIVE

It wasn't Yew who first told me about what happened after the Cactus Eaters murdered Wheeze and stole her away in the night. When she did finally tell the story, her version was different from Crow's. But the two versions were more the same than different. Crow had a gift. She could see things faraway and near at the same time. I don't know how she did it. I don't know if she knew how. Like I said, it was a gift. Or maybe a curse. Crow knew the System better than the System itself. She told me everything.

***

The System wanted to be all that was left of History. That's why they tried to get rid of books. Not just the old history books; they were just the first to go. Then, they went after them all. Myths and legends, religion, philosophy, poems, and especially stories for kids. They destroyed the books because they knew full well that some of them held truth. The so-called intellectuals (I call them the dumbbells) couldn't be sure which of the books held truth and which didn't, so they decided every book not authorized by the System might hold a smidgen. Those small shares might add up to the One Truth, and they couldn't have that. They didn't like the idea that the sum of the parts might add up to something greater than they could ever manufacture or even understand, even with their so-called Synthetic Intelligence.

SI ran the System, more or less, but it never did become quite the god they wanted it to be. There were always glitches. But they kept trying.

Any truth bigger than the System's would diminish the System's worth by contradicting the claim that the System was some kind of Heaven on Earth. After decades of planning, they opted for what looked to be a simple plan: eliminate the old truth by picking it apart piece by piece like vultures on a corpse.

The Loyals weren't as stupid as being loyal to the System makes them sound. They were smart. They knew it would be impossible to destroy all the books. The Loyals made a calculated guess that the brains of most of the citizens had atrophied to the point that they wouldn't recognize an old truth if it smacked them on the skull. If a few hard copy books were missed in the purge, it would only be a matter of time before no one would have the wherewithal to understand them even if they did happen to read one. In short order the stories, histories, and philosophies of the past would be forgotten. It was as simple as an idiot counting to two.

They started by deleting electronic copies, computer archives, and anything else housed in the World Pulse. The WP was connected to every computer connected to the System, and that meant all of them. Shakespeare and Dante were already too difficult for most people to understand. The few who were still interested watched the stories and poems acted out on screens or recited by electronic voices on the WP. The System got rid of all that with a few strokes on a WP keyboard.

Next on the list, after a bout of heated deliberations, was anything written by the New Gnostics, the bearers of "secret knowledge." It was a big deal because these were the System philosophers, mystics of Nothingness disguised as God. The people didn't care about the New Gnostics anyway. Their message was too convoluted. The few actors, directors, and anybody else who listened to the NG podcasts on the WP were left feeling dumbfounded and depressed when the NGs disappeared. This move left the System without a philosophy of its own. So be it. They sacrificed philosophy to embrace the freedom of being detached from the old truth. With the old truth dead and buried, they were free, even obliged, to write their own. People can't abide Nothingness. They need something to believe in. All that was left was the System. So, the System made the System into a story.

***

"I don't trust her," said Doc Waters. "How do we know if any of what she says is true?"

"Who cares?" asked Tinny. "She's got her story, and the System has theirs. They've got plenty of food here. Beer and hard cider. That tall fella said they even got some tequila stashed away somewhere for special occasions."

"The raggedy guy?" asked Mud. "He's crazier than a loon under a forever full moon."

"Just be careful," warned Doc Waters. "I've got a bad feeling about this place."

***

After Crow was finished telling us about History (I swear I'd heard the story before . . . almost like I was telling it right alongside her), Raggedy Man, the one and only Lug Lughnasa, lit two torches, handed one to Mud, and told him to bring up the rear. He left Doc Waters and Tinny to the job of hauling me on the stretcher. And so we went. Nobody questioned Raggedy Man. Everybody just did what they were told. That wasn't like Mud. Tinny I could see, but not Mud. Doc Waters was a wild card. I never could tell what he was going to do.

Raggedy Man led us through a series of underground tunnels for what seemed like hours. He had to stoop to get through the rocky corridors, but they were tall enough for the rest of us. It may have been hours. Maybe not. I can't gauge time worth a shit since the System messed with my brain.

We finally came to a big wooden door with a bunch of glyphs carved on it. Stick figures of men with bows and spears chasing buffalo and deer, a bunch of the Xs, shadows of buzzards over outlines of clouds hanging over the scene. Raggedy Man took an iron key that hung from his neck on a leather cord and inserted it into a lock under the brass handle on the door. Then, he turned and faced us.

"You'll be safe here. Just be sure you don't come out till I come and get you, you hear? I'll knock three times, then two, then one. Like this." He rapped on the door with his bony knuckles. "Just like that." He pushed open the door. Light—bluish, and weak—leaked out of the room into the tunnel. Raggedy Man stepped back and motioned us inside.

"Aren't you going in?" asked Doc Waters.

"Me? No. Not me. It's late. I'm bushed as a squirrel's tail. You'll find everything you need in there. You'll be safe. I'll come back for you in the bright and early. We'll have a feast. Eggs, ham, biscuits, and gravy. Mmmm. Mmmm. Mmmm. And how about some fresh strawberry preserves? It'll be worth the wait. I can promise you that."

"How'd you manage to get your mitts on a ham?" asked Tinny. "I haven't had a bite of ham since the last swine plague. Didn't figure there were any pigs left."

"Answers on the morrow," answered Raggedy Man. "Gotta get me some of what they call beauty sleep before I fall apart at the seams. Big day tomorrow. You best turn in yourselves."

Mud stepped inside the room. Doc Waters and Tinny carried the stretcher through the door, which closed behind us. Tumblers in the lock turned and fell into place. Mud tried to turn the handle, but it wouldn't budge.

***

"Her story doesn't make sense," said Doc Waters.

"Umph," grunted Mud.

"Like I said," said Tinny, "who cares? The System don't make much sense either. Nothing does if you stop and think about it. Why should *this*? The best you can do is take what comes. This here is a whole lot better than being baked into dust in that damn desert."

Doc Waters and Tinny set the stretcher next to the stove in the center of the room. The flames from the fire burned blue, short, and steady on a muffled hiss of fuel. The room was big, with walls of polished marble and a ceiling so high that I couldn't make it out, if there was one, in the dim light. The walls were decorated with the hides of dead animals.

"What do you make of that?" asked Doc Waters.

He was asking Mud, but it was Tinny who answered, "Some of those look like that buffalo Mud carved up."

"Not just buffalo," said Mud. "Bear and coyote. Gila monster and rattlesnake. Antelope and elk. Javelina."

"And that one?" asked Tinny, pointing at the wall above the big door.

"That's a man," said Doc Waters.

"Are you sure?" asked Tinny, his voice fading into a whisper. "How do you know it isn't a woman? How do you know it isn't *her*?"

"Yew? It's not her. Not a woman," said Mud.

"How do you know?" asked Tinny.

Doc Waters said, "We're not safe here."

"There isn't anywhere else to go," said Tinny. "We can't go back Outside. No water. I won't go back."

"I got a feeling there isn't going to be no other choice," said Mud. "I can feel it in my nut sack. Tight as a noose."

***

Crow claimed she was "Hopi." She was lying. The Hopi were a leg-end—nothing more. If they ever existed at all, they've long since been sucked into the System just like everything else. There were no more Hopis. Just like there was no Navajo Nation that the Puerto Rican had talked about when I was kid. It was just a story. And there weren't any more Puerto Ricans either, or Scots, or Kenyans, or Japanese. It all went out with History. Humans were humans. That's it. The bout of race wars before the System took over proved that identifying as anything other than human gives rise to division. The System couldn't have that. Peace requires conformity.

Doc Waters tried to explain it to Crow; then, Tinny tried. She wouldn't listen. She said she was Hopi, and that was that.

Mud sat on his haunches next to the stretcher in a corner of the break-fast room. He stunk like sweat and buffalo guts. I figured he was waiting for a chance to make a break for it. I wondered if he was figuring on taking me along or dumping me.

Crow was a big, round woman with a double chin and hair as gray as rainclouds. She wore a buckskin dress embroidered with red and black stick figures that looked like deer or elk. They were forever running from white stick men with bows and arrows. She had skin the color of pecan tree bark, a light reddish-brown. She looked at us through big round eyes that seemed like holes sucking all the light out of the room.

"My great-great-great-great-great grandmother packed her baby daughter in a papoose made of muskrat pelts. She ran away in the night before they came to take People away." The words flowed from her mouth like light out of a cave. Her eyes gobbled up the light and gave form to the words. "She ran to Red Canyon."

I could tell even then that the story she was telling wasn't her own.

***

It was always the same. Like we were in a figure eight looping round and round.

***

We were sent back to the animal hide room after eating a breakfast of ham, biscuits, and gravy. They had strawberry preserves, and there was some kind of fruit juice. Pomegranate I think, but I'd never had a pomegranate so I couldn't be sure. Crow didn't eat. She just watched us with those eyes of hers.

Crow showed up at the hide room around an hour later. Without so much as a knock on the door, she walked in. She carried a buffalo hide rug over her shoulder. Spreading the rug out over the floor in the center of the room, she sat in the center of it. And then she jumped right back into the story. No "Good morning" or "How was your breakfast?" She just started in. Just like that. Her eyes gobbled up the light in the room to give form to the words.

***

The night is cool. The moon, oblong, glows silver. It looks otherworldly to the young woman huddled against the red wall of the canyon. She wears a white buckskin dress. Her baby, tucked in a papoose, sleeps under a dwarf juniper a few feet away. The bark of the tree is scaly as an alligator hide. The woman can't bring herself to look down at the child. She has no water. No milk. The child is dying. She considers leaving the baby so she can wander Red Canyon. There is a spirit rumored to inhabit the canyon, the ghost of an Old One who sang to People. If she can find the Old One, it might show mercy to the child. The Old One might take the baby girl and make her one of its own. But it wouldn't be so kind to her, a mother who had done questionable things, selfish things, in an attempt to save herself.

***

"I appreciate a good story," interrupted Doc Waters. "There's an art to storytelling, and you have the gift, but we need to know about Yew. What happened to her? Is she okay?"

"Is the baby in danger?" asked Crow.

"What baby?" asked Tinny.

"The baby in the story," growled Mud.

"That's what they call a rhetorical question," said Raggedy Man. He stood at the edge of the buffalo rug, tall and thin like a dead aspen in winter. "I was taught by my mamaw that rhetorical questions were made to trick. You figure the answer is plain as day, but it isn't. Take this one. We don't really know if the baby is in danger. We just know her mother thinks she is. How many times have you thought something bad was going to happen and it didn't? That little baby looks to be in a heap of trouble, but I got a hunch that something or someone is going to save the day. That's what I think." Raggedy Man stuck a finger in one of his flappy ears and rotated it. "I mean the story's pretty much over if the poor thing dies, right? That wouldn't be much of a story—not in my mind anyways. Nope. Just be sad and nothing else."

"Why couldn't there be something else?" asked Tinny. "Maybe the mother, bent on revenge, sets off on a bloody warpath. Maybe a ghost shows up and raises the baby from the dead. There are lots of things that could happen."

Doc Waters said, "We really don't have—"

"Don't get me wrong. I get what you're saying," continued Tinny. "But there's really no such thing as a rhetorical question. A rhetorical question would have one single answer, and the answer would be in the question. Like you said, a trick. Maybe the person asking is trying to make a point or prove someone wrong. But there isn't any way to know until the question is answered. There's always more than one way a person can answer. Always. So there's no such thing as a rhetorical question."

"Yep! That's it!" Raggedy Man took the hat from his head and slapped it on his leg. "You got it. Just like me mamaw used to say, 'It's all a dad-gum trick.' "

"Shut your yaps," grumbled Mud. "You don't get to answer the question. The story does."

"Really," said Doc Waters, "I'm not trying to spoil the fun, but you said you know something about Yew? Can you help us find her or not?"

"Is the baby in danger?" repeated Crow.

Raggedy Man stood and walked to the door. "I'm thirsty as a fish in a dust storm. I'll run and fetch something cool to drink. Is it too early for beer? Already heard this story, I have, and don't want to spoil it no more. Toodle-oo." With that, he opened the door and walked out. The door swung shut behind him.

***

She explores the canyon. She hopes against hope that chance or providence will lead her to an artesian spring. It isn't impossible. Nothing is impossible. That's what her grandmother drilled into her head before the Withering. The spirits aren't bound by time the same way as People. They do not wither. They do not die. Sometimes they intervene. But they're unpredictable. The impossible is always unpredictable. That's what her grandmother said.

The mother checks on her baby. The tiny chest moves, the breaths short and shallow. The eyes move rapidly under the lids as if the poor thing's young life is nothing more than a nightmare. The mother places an ear to the babe's chest. The heart taps like water dripping on a hollow drum, too many drips, too fast. The child's mouth smells both sweet and sour, a mixture of innocence and encroaching death.

The mother stands and brushes the dirt from the knees of the buckskin dress. She regrets, for a moment, leaving behind the family heirlooms—her mother's turquoise, her grandmother's bean and corn rattles, the kachinas carved from cottonwood roots. She remembers her grandfather's sacred pipe fashioned from the red rock of the canyon and handed down from before time. Gone now. Forever. She's alone. But for the child.

The earth glows silver under the oblong moon. The woman looks to the sky and whispers, "Take the child. Save her." The night is quiet. No breeze to murmur through the branches of the juniper. No crickets. Looking at the ground, the woman spots a tarantula marching slowly across the sand. She thinks of rain.

The mother wanders the canyon. The sand under her feet is the color of the moon. Boulders fallen from the wall of the canyon have come to rest on the canyon floor. They cast shadows over the sand. A lone oak, twisted by years of wind and drought, stands at the edge of the boulder field. She makes her way to the tree and kneels before it. The roots of the tree are exposed to the night. The tree is dying. The woman curls up next to the roots and weeps.

***

"Let me guess," said Tinny, "the baby's gone when she wakes up and she has to go looking for it. Am I right?"

"Shut your trap," snarled Mud. "Listen."

Doc Waters said, "We don't have time. I don't know what kind of game you're playing, but I'm not buying it. If you know about Yew, tell us. If not, say so. Either way, it's time for us to go."

"Go?" asked Tinny. "I ain't about to go out there sniffin' around. It'd be plain stupid. You heard the raggedy guy say the System men would be back, right? What about the others, the Cactus Eaters or whatever they're called? You saw what they did to my friend. Carved his face into a horror clown. Yew's dead. Or worse. At least we're safe here."

"You ain't got no friends," growled Mud.

"And *you do*?" asked Tinny.

The flames in the stove hissed.

"He's right," continued Crow. "Yew isn't the Yew you once knew."

She moved a hand through the air like she was erasing chalk from a blackboard. "She's clean."

"Who are the Cactus Eaters?" asked Doc Waters.

"Bane," Crow replied. She pointed at me. Her finger was thick. The loose flesh looked to be dripping from the bone. The fingernail, long and serrated, was painted black. "They're coming for him."

I was in my usual spot on the stretcher near the stove. I thought they'd all more or less forgotten about me. Pick me up, carry me, put me down. I'd become no more than a habit. Doc Waters fed and watered me twice a day. He'd help me with private things, too, get Mud to help carry me on the stretcher to somewhere the others couldn't see. I'd gained enough strength in my legs to lean on him until he got me to the outhouse and put me on the seat. He'd move far enough away so he couldn't hear my groans. Doc Waters was nice like that. Then, Mud and he would carry me back. Other than that, I was a ghost. I think Tinny sometimes forgot I was even in the room.

"The Puppet Man?" Tinny got up from his three-legged wooden stool. He walked to the stove and looked down at me. "They can have him. He's not anything. Just a story Doc Waters and Yew made up."

Mud walked to the stove and stood between Tinny and me. He smelled of smoke and sweat and guts. "That's why you don't have no friends."

"You know where she is?" Doc Waters asked Crow. He sat on a stool at the edge of the buffalo rug. "Is she alive?"

Crow pulled a stone pipe red as a maple leaf from a fold of flesh under her buckskin dress. She then produced a leather pouch from between her ponderous breasts. Opening the bag, she pinched some powder between her finger and thumb and loaded it into the bowl. "This will show you."

Tinny walked to the door and tested the handle. "That raggedy son-of-a-bitch locked us in again."

Crow pointed her finger at Mud. "Your name?"

Mud shrugged. "Names don't mean anything. Not no more."

Crow lowered her finger and smiled. "You growl like a wolverine guarding a kill."

"Been called worse," said Mud.

Doc Waters stood and stepped onto the buffalo rug. "Is she alive? Who are these Cactus Eaters? What do they want with Yew?"

Crow held out the pipe. "Take this and smoke from it." She looked at me, and I felt the pull of her eyes on my heart. "You will see."

Doc Waters took a step toward Crow. "No more games."

"Did you hear me?" yelped Tinny. "We're locked in this nightmare!"

Mud stepped onto the buffalo rug, leaned forward, and took the pipe from Crow.

She smiled. "There are slivers of fatwood next to the stove."

Mud, pipe in palm, moved to the stove and knelt down. He took a thick splinter of glossy wood from the stone floor.

"Do you know what's in that pipe?" asked Doc Waters.

"No," grunted Mud.

"Poison," said Tinny. "She's probably in league with them buffalo killers."

"Cactus Eaters," said Crow.

Mud stuck the tip of the fatwood in the blue flame of the stove. The tip of the wood blossomed. He brought the pipe to his lips, the flame to the bowl, and sucked at the stem. The smoke expanded in his lungs. He bent over from the coughing. The smoke smelled like cat piss.

When the door opened, Tinny jumped away like he'd been snakebit.

Raggedy Man stepped in carrying a square tray with a big silver pot in the center and four mugs made out of clay circling it. The door swung shut behind him.

Tinny retreated to the stove.

"Startin' without me, are we?" asked Raggedy Man. "That ain't one bit nice." He walked to the stool where Doc Waters had been sitting and set down the tray. "It's okay, though. I'm the forgivin' type. Who wants tea?"

Mud nodded. He looked at Crow and then Doc Waters. "You want to find Yew? This is the best bet. The *only* one." He held out the pipe.

I never could figure out how Mud knew the things he did. He knew things that he shouldn't have known—like he was privy to a secret. Maybe it's what they call intuition . . . the kind of knowing where you feel your way to the answer rather than think it. Nobody, not even Tinny, questioned Mud about how he knew things. We all just went along with it. I don't know why. I guess we trusted him. Maybe we had intuitions too.

We all smoked from the pipe and drank a mug of tea because Mud told us to. Simple as that. Then, we sat down on the rug around Crow. She started humming one of those tunes you remember but can't place. Soon enough, the hides on the walls started to sway like sheets on a clothesline in a breeze. Then the hides came down from the walls and started dancing to Crow's hum. They danced on invisible feet, the buffalo and coyote, the lion and coati, the kit fox and javelina. They all had the same eyes, black as hard coal, shiny as polished steel. The animal skins danced for Crow.

***

The mother stands at the edge of the light. Blinded by brightness, she fears not, for the light is warm, the beams like the cleansing waters of a baptismal font. She's not afraid. She steps into the light.

She stubs her big toe on something hard and sharp. Pain courses through her foot, into her leg, through her torso, and lodges in her chest. She shuts her eyes. The pain recedes. She opens her eyes. She sees.

Black orbs of obsidian dot the landscape, some of them as large as bull moose, others small as coyotes, others smaller still, the size of ravens. The smallest look like black-backed beetles, the shells shiny and hard. The orbs are strewn over an expanse of white sand. The mother's toe spurts blood.

The air smells of sulfur. Stunted trunks of juniper and scrub oak look like the ciphers of an unknown tongue. The sky is white. In the distance, the mother spots a lone tree near a wall of stones the color of rust. A man covered in animal skins steps from behind the wall. The pelt of a Mexican grey wolf hangs from his shoulder, its skulless face slung over his own skull like a crown. The man holds a forked staff over his head and calls out in what sounds like a dog's bark.

Another figure steps from behind the wall, smaller, her head bare, black hair falling over her shoulders like spilled ink. She holds a papoose in her arms. She is dressed in wolfskins.

***

"What did I tell you?" yapped Tinny. "She went looking for the baby and she found it."

"What'd I tell *you*?" said Raggedy Man. "Wouldn't be much of a story if the baby died, now would it?"

"For the last time," growled Mud, "shut your mouths. Unless you want me to shut 'em for you."

"Yes," said Doc Waters. "Listen. See? She's walking over the sand."

I watched as the woman walked over the sand. We all did.

***

Blood on white sand. The flesh of the woman's toe, sliced on a shard of obsidian, hangs from the bone. The blood flows from the wound in pulses.

In the distance, the man holds the forks of staff above his head like antlers. The woman stands next to him, cradling the papoose in her arms.

There is no sound. The sky is the color of scorched milk. No sun.

***

The four of them, including Raggedy Man, sat on the buffalo hide rug, watching the animal hides that had come down off the walls. The hides circled the rug. The blue glow from the stove flames oozed over the stone floor. The human skin, black eyes trained on Crow, vibrated to the hum of her words.

***

No sun.

***

The walls of the room dissolved, and I found myself sitting on a buffalo hide rug behind the wall of rock the color of rust. The man with the Mexican wolf pelt draped over his head had his back to me, as did the woman standing beside him. He held the forked staff over his head in the weird light, a pale light coming from nowhere and everywhere at once. It fell over the sand, the stone wall, and the stunted juniper bush growing just behind me.

***

Don't be afraid.

***

I recognized the voice, a woman's voice.

***

A scent of sweetwood.

***

"Cactus Eaters?"

***

Yes.

***

I glanced behind me to see who had asked the question. Nothing. Just the stunted tree and the weird light.

"Do I know you?"

Yes.

The light vibrated.

"Do you know me?"

Yes.

It was me asking the questions. I felt the words form, first in my lungs, then rising to my throat to be shaped on my tongue.

"Yew?"

Don't be afraid.

***

The human skin vibrated.

Tinny, eyes wide, said, "I don't know what that shit was in the pipe, but none of this is real." He pointed at the human skin as it danced, herky-jerky, in front of Crow. "That ain't real."

Crow hummed. The animal skins vibrated. The human skin twitched to and fro on its boneless legs like a drunken sailor on land for the first time. Its face was without features—no mouth, no nose. Just eyes as black as squid ink.

Mud was smiling. Doc Waters, sitting cross-legged next to Crow, looked to be asleep. His eyes were closed, his breathing even. Raggedy Man was stretched over the length of the rug, a forearm draped over his eyes, his feet spilling over the rug onto the floor.

"I'll spit on any man that claims this is real," said Tinny. Frozen to his spot on the buffalo hide, he watched the human skin dance. "The witch put a spell on us. They used to burn witches back in the day."

***

He doesn't notice that I am not on the stretcher. None of them do. They can't see me watching from behind the stone wall.

***

No telling how Tinny knew about witches. Somebody told him the story somewhere. There are stories everywhere. The System can't get rid of them. They'll never get rid of them.

When the books were all but gone, some of the older people started telling the old stories to anyone who would listen. People are geared for stories. Stories are how they make sense of the world. Without them, they'd all be lost. When the System banned the reading of old stories in public, there was good profit for those who could tell them in private. They didn't ask for payment upfront. That way, people couldn't complain that the story wasn't worth the price. If the storyteller was good at delivering a tale, the people would give whatever they could—a deck of old cards or a bottle of fermented honey—before sneaking out of an alley or abandoned lot used as a makeshift stage. If the story didn't go over, the storyteller went away with what he had when he started. When both the story and the storyteller were really good, people paid in old books. That's what storytellers prized most. They'd read the books and spin them into new yarns. The storytellers didn't write the new versions of the stories down so the people would always need the storytellers to tell them. They were smart that way.

Crow was the best storyteller of all. She told me right into the story. Who else could do that?

***

No sun.

***

"Yew?"
She smells of sweetwood.

***

"Yes."

***

The man turns. He lowers the staff and places the forks under his arm like a crutch. The woman standing next to him turns. She's dressed in wolfskins and holds a papoose made of muskrat skins. Her dark hair falls over her face like a veil.

The man, face hidden behind the wolf pelt, stares through the two holes where the wolf's eyes once shone. He aims the sharpened end of the staff at my chest and motions for me to stand. Suddenly, I find myself standing in the center of a buffalo rug. My legs are like compressed springs. I feel like I might jump into the sky and fly.

"Where are we?" I ask. "Who are you?"

The woman steps forward and holds out the papoose like a gift. She lowers her head as if in prayer.

The man removes the wolf hide from his head and drapes it over a shoulder. He closes his eyes and places the palms of his hands over his face. The wolf hide's eye sockets sprout orbs—dark as the inside of two stones. The wolf blinks.

My legs go weak.

The wolf says, "Burnt."

The man continues to hide his face in his hands. The woman stands holding out the papoose in offering.

It's not night. Not day. The light is a pearly fog.

The woman in the white buckskin dress steps out from the far side of the rust-colored stone wall. Her toe is bleeding. The obsidian scattered over the white sand behind her shivers in the weird light.

Sweetwood.

The woman with the papoose, her head bowed, takes a step forward. She raises the papoose.

"Take," says the wolf. "Yours."

The woman in the buckskin dress bends and touches the wound at her toe. Her hair is the color of burnt pinecones. Rising, she comes forward and steps between me and the wolfskin woman whose face is veiled by her dark hair. The mother reaches into the veil and raises the woman's face with a finger under the chin. She parts the veil with her free hand and tucks the dark locks behind each of the woman's ears.

The woman with the papoose looks at the sky through dark eyes. The mother in buckskins traces a symbol on the papoose woman's forehead with the blood from her toe. The symbol, crude and delicate at once, is of a stick figure carrying a spear.

Buckskin woman then takes the papoose. She turns to me and says, "Remember." She pulls a flap of muskrat pelt away from the baby's face. The baby is blue. The baby is dead.

"No," says the mother. "Not dead. Touch." The mother places her bloody finger on the baby's forehead. She removes the finger, leaving a red dot in the center of the baby's brow.

The babe's eyes open. They're seafoam green. I remember. They're mine.

***

I woke up alone, stretched out on my back in the center of the buffalo hide rug. The ceiling was hidden in shadows, too high to be touched by the light of the stove. The stretcher sat empty on the floor near the stove, the bluish glow of the flames spilling out over the floor. I couldn't remember how I got on the rug. I turned on my side. The effort drained me. I felt like an ancient hound panting in the summer heat.

The big wooden door of the room was closed. The human skin was missing from its place on the wall above the door. I wondered if it had ever been there. The animal hides were hanging in place on the walls. The vision of the Cactus Eaters came back slowly, like shadows emerging from a fog, but I remembered the baby's eyes. I remembered the stranger's voice that was my own. I tried to speak "Yew," but the single syllable stuck in my throat. All I managed was a croak.

The door opened. Raggedy Man stepped through, stood to his full height, and said, "There ya be!" He carried a tray of fruit arranged around a clay pitcher. The door closed behind him as quietly as it had opened. "Safe and sound on our side of the curtain. Good. Never a doubt. Nope, not me." He set the tray on a stool next to the rug and surveyed the room. "I'd give a sow's ear to see what you saw over there. That I would. Only other one who ever came back across that horizon to tell the tale is Crow. And she don't talk about it. How about you?"

I tried to stand, but the best I could do was push myself to a sitting position. The effort made my head hurt. "Arrrr," is all I could get out.

"Stop frettin' or you'll bust a gut. Don't want that, do ya?"

The fruit on the tray caught my attention. Wedges of orange and grapefruit, fat strawberries, and blueberries big as marbles. There was even half a papaya, the orange-red flesh moist in the quarter-light of the room. I'd only seen papayas on screens. Never for real.

"Figured you'd be hungrier than a teat-starved pup after what you've been through. Thirsty too. I brought you something to bring back your strength." He took a clay cup from the tray and carried it to me. "Yep. I'd give up hard cider for a week to see what you saw over there. What was it?"

I took the cup and drank. The juice burned my throat.

"Easy there," said Raggedy Man. "It's all gonna be just ducky-doo. You just wait and see. But you've gotta give it some time, you hear? Crow told the others about Yew. Or I should say she sang it to them. They're gone."

I felt like I'd been hit in the gut.

Raggedy Man wore the same crusty long johns. As he stared down at me, the mottle of silver and black whiskers patched over his thin face seemed to vibrate.

"No worries," he said. "You'll be staying with us. Crow knows what it is that ails you. You'll be safe here."

"Where is here?" I whispered. "Where was I?"

"Home," answered Raggedy Man. "Home and back again, jiggedy-jig. What was it like?"

CHAPTER SIX

The haboob overtook the men as they marched over a flat stretch of desert. Barbs of prickly pear, jumping cholla, and barrel cactus slowed their pace. Clouds darkened the western horizon.

Doc Waters was the first to notice the approaching wall of dust. He pointed to the southwest. "What the hell is that?"

Tinny said, "We gotta find shelter. Now."

"Haboob," said Mud. "Big one."

The roiling sand was the color of rust. It moved northeastward over the desert.

"Comin' in fast," said Mud.

"What should we do?" asked Doc Waters.

"Run!" yelled Tinny. He turned and began jogging east.

"Won't do no good," said Mud.

"Come back!" cried Doc Waters. "We've got to stick together!"

"Let him go," said Mud. "He's no use."

"He'll be lost," said Doc Waters.

"Do what you want," said Mud. "There's a wash over there. Low ground." He jogged toward the oncoming storm.

Doc Waters watched Mud go. He glanced over his shoulder at the figure of Tinny weaving through the field of cacti. Then, he looked back to Mud. He didn't know what to do. Mud knew more about the Outside than anyone he had known. Tinny didn't belong Outside. He'd die if left on his own. Better to take his chances with Mud. For Yew's sake. Yes. For Yew.

Mud disappeared into the wall of dust.

Doc Waters ran to catch him.

The wind moaned.

Doc Waters was engulfed by the fog of dust. He didn't know which way to go. His legs grew heavy. He lurched forward like one of the mummies in the movies his father had kept hidden beneath the floorboards under his bed. The two of them watched the movies on an old DVD player. His father, a kind man with big, droopy eyes and skin the color of black tea, had sworn his son to secrecy before showing him the first of the movies. Movies were contraband. The penalty was Re-Ed for six months, maybe more, depending on the title. The boy was proud that his father trusted him. He never told a soul—not even his mother.

Why was he remembering his father now?

It was no use. He couldn't see more than a foot in front of him. He was choking on dust. He sat down and curled into a ball, his face tucked in the crook of an elbow. He squeezed his eyes shut and prayed to the god of his father. He hadn't prayed for more than twenty years. He prayed for Yew.

***

I watched the approach of the haboob from the safety of the animal hide room. Blue light hissed from the flames in the stove. I wanted to call out to Doc Waters, to tell him to stand and keep moving. Mud was hunkered down in an arroyo maybe fifty yards ahead. I knew he couldn't hear me because I couldn't hear him. His mouth moved, but I couldn't hear what he was saying. He didn't know I was watching. None of them did.

Crow and I had smoked from the red pipe about an hour earlier. The hides on the walls didn't slide down to dance this time. I figured it was because we hadn't drunk the tea. I think it was brewed from the same stuff that was in the pipe. They both smelled like cat piss. Whatever was in the pipe let me see through the cave walls out into the desert. But I couldn't hear them. It was like watching a silent movie with no background music. Doc Waters, Mud, and Tinny had all smoked from the red pipe when they were here. It was part of them like it was now part of me. It didn't give them second sight, but it allowed me to see them. At least that's how I had it figured.

When I asked Crow about the stuff in the pipe, she didn't answer directly. It was like I was supposed to guess what she meant when she spoke. Everything she said connected, one way or another, to Red Canyon and the woman and her baby. Everything. She told me about things she had no way of knowing. Jack-the-Bartender and his purple Harley Sportster, Cody Lannard, and the Lazy M Ranch. She described the Hopi Kachinas the praying man had told me about, the Bear, a Clown, a Crow Mother, and the Eototo. She talked about the Puerto Rican and my Dad and the Orchard. Emily and Francisco. Dead raccoons and the Old One. It seemed like she knew everything that was in my head. But she wasn't just reading my mind. She was in it. Each time I interrupted her with a question, which I did a lot, she circled back to Red Canyon.

"Is the baby in danger?"

I didn't know. How could I? I kept my mouth shut. I was afraid of what would happen if I gave the wrong answer.

That's when Crow stood and left the room. The door closed behind her, and my mind went blank as a dead man's.

***

Death comes on the dust. The afterlife is plain as a blank computer screen. Thoughts arrive. Words without context. And then comes the hunger. Hunger for life. He begins feeding on memories. He plays the part of both host and parasite. He is the snake eating its tail.

He remembers Yew.

***

Hair the color of pinecones. She smelled of sweetwood. She loved him. He could tell by the way she looked at him in the lab. By the way, she fawned over his skills as a healer. She never doubted his ability to detach the MIU from her brainstem. She loved him. And he loved her, too.

Her favorite patient was all that stood between them.

***

"If he's dead, why's he still thinking?"

"Listen to the story. Just listen. Your answers are in the words."

"What if they don't make sense?"

"Think of the baby."

"What baby?"

"Red Canyon."

"Isn't that a different story?"

"No. One beginning. One end."

***

His face is tucked into the crook of his elbow. He tries to stand and cannot. The weight of the sand is too much. He's too tired. But he's alive. Choking on dust.

It's fitting that he'll die alone in the desert. Outside. Outside of what? The System? Is there nothing more than that?

He won't accept it. He can't. He's in love.

He never had the courage to tell her how he felt. He regrets he didn't meet her sooner under different circumstances. Regrets the part he played in developing System protocols. Regrets lying. He hid from her his role as Chief of Erasure. She believes him to be only a healer, a minor player in the medical ward, a good man. He isn't good. He betrays all who trust

*him. He will betray her. All of them. The MIU remains lodged in his brain-
stem. He couldn't get it out. Too dangerous. He couldn't risk losing his
memory, losing her. And he couldn't tell her or she would have left him
behind. Regrets.*

*The sand might suck the moisture from his organs and preserve his
body, but the body will remain hidden. One day he'll rise from the sand
and haunt the desert like the mummies his father told him about on the
couch in the basement of their home. He'll search for Yew. He won't find
her.*

*She's better off without him. He shouldn't have agreed to help her with
the scheme. He should have let her go alone. Agreeing allowed him to
keep her close. And now she is gone.*

*What if she was lying? He couldn't be sure. Nobody can be sure what
goes on in another's heart. Most people don't know their own intentions,
let alone their neighbor's. Everything plays out on the surface—body language and the spoken word. Lovers lie to their beloved. It's the stuff of
tragedy, and what is life if not a tragedy? A comedy? Who's laughing? The
jokes have all been told.*

*Betrayal was a favorite theme in his father's favorite stories. King Ar-
thur betrayed by his best friend and his wife. His father had four versions
of the King Arthur tragedy on film. He'd sit beside his son on the couch
and drink contraband bourbon while watching the stories unfold. The
sound was muted. Tears wetted his cheeks as he commented on the tale
unfolding on the screen. Arthur died. Poor Arthur. Nobody can be sure if
their most trusted friend is a saint or a demon. That's what his father told
him. His father was wise.*

*His father told him that Arthur would come again one day when he was
needed the most. But not today.*

*Who can say if the Outpost Man is who she says he is? Does she really
know? Maybe somebody convinced her that Outpost Man was the last best
hope and she believed it because she needed something to believe in. Just*

like they needed King Arthur to pull the sword from the stone. Maybe it was somebody she thought she could trust. Somebody she loved. Maybe they lied. Or maybe they believed the lie of another. Maybe the Outpost Man, mad from loneliness, made up the encounter with the Praying Man. Maybe.

Best to die alone under a pile of sand in a desert. Then there will be no more lies.

***

"What's the point of telling the story if the main character dies alone buried under a pile of sand? What difference does it make?"

"Listen."

"I don't want to listen. Not anymore. It's a waste of time. None of it fits. It's just a bunch of random snippets. What's this all got to do with Red Canyon? If you know who I am, just tell me. Quit acting like any of this is important. Like it matters. It doesn't. Get it? What if I told you I don't want it to matter? It doesn't have to mean anything. It just is."

"Take this and smoke it."

"Why? Will the story make sense then?"

"It comes from Red Canyon."

***

Being erased is worse than dying because you're still alive but have no context. Mindless. Compared to that, dying's not so bad. Consciousness slips away bit by bit, like shards of a broken mirror falling into an abyss. Father kept the faith. He promised he would see me on the other side if I was good. "A virtuous man," he said. He said goodness is written on the heart and all I had to do was recognize it and follow it and we'd meet again on the other side. He said it was natural.

I never was able to recognize it.

So, I believed in the System. Why not? Everything was falling apart before the System took control. Everybody was at odds because nobody knew what to believe because you could believe whatever you wanted. Like father and his "virtue." Where every belief is equal, belief has no meaning. One person's belief cancels out the next until all of them are gone. It's a war of all against all. It doesn't matter if it's man against man or cause against cause. It's all in their heads. There's nothing left but brute fact. The System.

Before the System, people tried to convince others to believe what they believed, and when that didn't work, they tried to force them. That's all that was left. Everybody thought they deserved everything—the best house, the best clothes, the best food. And when they didn't get it, they got jealous and then angry. Everyone was at each other's throats. No peace. The System promised peace and delivered. So, I believed.

Father was a fool. There is no other side. The peace of the abyss is good enough for me because it's true peace, not something in some other world, some other life, some other side of things. It's not make-believe. It's real. The System understood. Their goal was to make the transition into the abyss a pleasant experience—painless. They taught us to stop fighting it. They tried to eliminate the craving for things unreal, the false drama of my father's "virtue." They were wise that way. Humane. Oblivion is superior to excellence because it's real. It lives outside of our heads. Outside.

With the System, I found peace. And then Yew came onto the scene. She whispered in my ear how there was something better. Outside.

She ruined everything because she is good, a virtuous woman.

***

"You don't believe that."

"What?"

"That abyss crap. Why are you showing me all of this? Why not just come out and say what you *mean*?"

"I want you to stay. You'll be safe here. We can live forever."

"Stay? Where? Here? I don't even know where here is."

"Red Canyon."

***

Three people materialize from the dust. They drop their forked staffs on the ground and plunge their arms into a mound of sand. As one, one in three, they yank a man's body into the world. The body is limp. The smallest of the group crouches over him. A Mexican gray wolf pelt falls from her head. Thick braids the color of dark wine drop to each side of her rib cage. She bends low. Her braids fall over the man's face.

A large man shoves the woman away with a foot to the ribs. She falls into the sand.

The man on the ground sits up.

The woman stands. "Alive."

The big man sniffs the air. "Smells dead."

"No," grunts a smaller man. "System stink."

The large one grins. His teeth are big, square, and yellow.

The small man nods at the woman.

The woman crouches. "Hurt?" she asks.

The man on the ground brushes sand from the sleeves of his shirt. He looks to the sky and then to the woman. "Who are you?"

The big man kicks the man in the ribs. "No talk."

"Dead no good," says the small man.

"Water," says the woman.

The small man pulls a waterskin from under the wolf pelts covering his chest. He hands it to the woman.

The woman uncorks the skin. She hands it to the man on the ground.

He pushes the water away. "Why did you bring me back? How did you find me?"

"Stink," says the third man. He nods at the woman. "Smelled you."

The big man kicks the man on the ground. "Drink or hurt."

The man takes the waterskin, drinks, and hands it back to the woman.
"What's your name?"

The woman squints.

"What are you called?"

The woman stares down at the man.

"Name," repeats the man, tapping his chest with a finger. "Doctor Waters. That's my name." He taps once more. "Doc." He points at the woman. "You?"

The big man kicks Doc Waters. "No talk." He takes his staff from the ground by the forks and points the fire-sharpened end at Doc Water's chest. "Follow."

The woman taps a finger on her chest, "Macha."

"Follow where?"

The big man touches the point to Doc Water's chest. "Stand or hurt."

Doc Waters gets to his feet. "Couldn't you have just left me be? I was almost there."

The woman picks up the wolf pelt and puts it on top of her head. She stands and leans down to take up her staff. Turning her back on Doc Waters, she walks away.

The small man takes up his staff and follows the woman.

The big man pokes Doc Waters in the back. "Go."

Doc Waters starts after the woman.

The big man follows behind.

✳✳✳

Crow's not human. Or at least she's not like anyone I've ever known. She looks human—has a human body—but she doesn't have a human soul. She's lonely because there's no one else like her. She's so damn lonely she needs me as much as she thinks I need her. She's bored with Raggedy Man. One day, she'll get tired of me too.

The System tried to do away with the idea of souls, saying that it was the "single-most mendacious concept" in the history of the world. It's what got everybody thinking about things that weren't real—God and Heaven and Hell, for starters. They said the soul was just a story made up by men desperate to be more than they were. They wanted to be like the gods who didn't exist. So, they tried to squash the whole idea. They failed, just like they failed to get rid of books. People still believed in souls—just like they listened to stories—but nobody talked about it in public. Some people never talked about it at all because they didn't know who to trust. But that didn't stop them from believing. I'll bet most people still believe in souls. I do. The one thing I know for sure and never forgot was that souls exist. Crow has one. I just don't know what it is. It's not an animal soul . . . not a lion or a buffalo. It's something else—something not human.

What I'm getting at is this: saying that something isn't real doesn't make it go away. Lots of people pray with their mouths shut. They pray without making a sound. Words are words whether they're spoken or not. Just like a soul's a soul. Crow doesn't tell stories thinking she's making things real. She tells stories to make things her own.

***

The desert lives.

It doesn't seem like much during the day—maybe some vultures circling the sky on thermals, the sound of raven wings creaking in flight, or a striped lizard darting across the sand. Maybe a rock squirrel scrambling over a pile of stones. Or the flick of a hawk wasp's bright orange wings as it takes to the air. It's never much. Never an abundance. Except for the flies and big piles of swarming red ants.

Nighttime is different. Maybe the absence of sunshine on sand blasting my mind blank during the day allows me to tune into the dark. It's like I'm in a movie instead of watching one, like being an actor rather than a director. In the desert, daylight is like a blank page waiting for a story. Nighttime is the story itself.

Father had so many stories in his head, he had to write them down. He didn't know I knew. I found them in a cubbyhole under the floorboards under his desk. He was away doing whatever he did for the System and forgot to lock the door to his home office. He never talked about his work for the System. I thought maybe the stories had something to do with his work. Maybe they were finally making new movies, new stories. That's how naïve I was.

Father wrote horror stories. They all had Arthurian characters in them, but they weren't like any of the stories we watched together on the couch. All of Father's heroes died gruesome deaths. Not one of them got away. Some were eaten up by evil creatures not of this world, darker than shadows, eyes glowing yellow in the night. Others got sick, developed blisters on their tongues, and their eyes caked with crud that bled when they tried to scratch it away. Their throats constricted until they could no longer swallow. Maggots crawled over the open wounds on their arms and legs. And, finally, they died. All of them.

A good number of the heroes went insane and killed themselves. They'd jump off buildings or drive gas-powered cars at full speed into concrete walls. One of them injected rattlesnakes full of amphetamines and threw them into a pit and then stripped naked and jumped in. Another hero plucked the eyes out of his face before walking into the sea, his pockets filled with stones.

The theme was always the same: insanity becomes sanity when the sane normalize madness. Maybe it was about the System. I don't remember one of father's characters dying in daylight. They all died in darkness. Maybe the stories were about my father's state of mind. Who knows? It takes two to interpret a story. The author and the audience. My father didn't talk much. Just when he told the stories while we watched the movies. But it was always someone else's story then, never one of his own.

It feels like I'm in a movie out here. It's not a horror story, though. At least not yet. Things make sense. I still have hope. Maybe I'll see Yew again. Father's characters didn't have hope. There is no hope in madness.

We travel mostly by night. The ones who saved me must be what Crow called Cactus Eaters. I can't be sure. I never really understood what Crow was saying or singing or whatever it was she was doing to get the images and sounds into our minds. It had something to do with the tea and the pipe. Biochemical interactions. But there was more to it than that. She'd gotten inside of us—into our DNA.

Whoever they are, they prefer traveling by night. It makes sense. We stop during the day and huddle in whatever shade we can find. We sip alkaline water from leather skins and nibble at something that tastes like burnt toast. They take turns nodding off. Two of the three are always awake. They rarely speak. Sometimes they grunt and grin as they stare off into the desert.

I'd die out here without them. They know it. I wish I could see what they see.

***

I can't see Yew. I can see Doc Waters is in the desert but I can't find Yew. As time slips by, I wonder if she ever existed at all.

***

Row, row, row your boat, gently down the stream,
Merrily, merrily, merrily, merrily,
Life is but a dream.

***

Time is round here, light and dark, warm and cool, the sun in the sky one sun among a billion invisible others. Earth is a little blue speck in a vastness too large to fathom. That's the definition of beauty.

I sacrificed beauty when I bought into the System. I had to. It was necessary.

I believed that as Chief of Erasure, I could make a difference. I was helping to build a society that would withstand the terrible weight of insignificance that stalks human beings like one of the monsters in my father's stories. The weight makes us aware that we are all utterly inconsequential. It's impossible for most people to accept their own irrelevance in light of the unfathomable space that houses innumerable stars, no matter how beautiful it is. I wanted to help them and by doing so make a difference in their lives, no matter how small. I wanted to spare them from the unavoidable meaninglessness of their lives.

I accepted the System narrative that the gods of history were created by primitive peoples to help them bear the weight of the void. I didn't realize it then, but with that acceptance, I also agreed to believe the story perpetuated by the System. What if it, too, was a ruse created to invent meaning where there was none to be had? What if there really was nothing but chance and materiality? What if there was no story at all? How could a human being bear such a load? What would it mean? It would mean nothing. And the System would mean nothing, too.

Out here in the desert, none of it matters. The Cactus Eaters, or whoever they are, have an ease about them. They don't stand apart from things. They're not separate. They aren't other than what is. They're tuned in to an invisible rhythm hovering just outside the periphery of consciousness. I can see it in the way they move—nothing wasted, no energy, no thought, just movement as natural as water flowing downstream. They don't talk much because there's not much to say. They're no different from the cholla and ocotillo dotting the landscape. Existence is meaning enough for them. The plants are alive, and for that they are beautiful. For them, if I'm right, being itself is a miracle that eases the burden of existence. They walk in beauty.

***

"You're safe here. They can't get in. Nobody can cross unless I allow it."

"Like you allowed us?"

"Yes."

"Why?"

This is the most direct she's been with me. If I stay with her, I'll be safe.

"I've been waiting for you."

"Who am I?"

I can see the baby in Red Canyon. I see its eyes, my eyes. I remember the stranger's voice—my voice.

Crow says, "Yew."

"Yew? Where is she? Why can't I see her?"

"Red Canyon."

"Are you waiting for her, too?"

"For you. Like her."

***

He's a boy who feels like a girl.

***

I know damn well we're in the room with the stove with the blue flames and the animal hides on the wall, but it's black as blindness. There's only the rug, Crow, and me. That's it. Nothing else in all of creation. That's what she wants me to believe. She wants me to believe that without her, I'd be terribly and forever alone. She needs me to need her.

"Why did you let the others in? Mud, Doc Waters, Tinny?

"There's a part for them too."

Her skin begins to glow, and I can see the rug on the floor underneath her fat thighs. I can see the lines in my palm as I hold it in front of my eyes. I look into *her* eyes, and she allows me to see.

"Where's Yew? I don't see her."

"They will all betray you. Don't you see? All of them. Yew too. Only me. I'll be true."

"Who are you?"

"The Washerwoman."

"What? Washerwoman?"

"Of the Dead. You're safe here."

"Forever?"

"Don't you believe dead is forever?"

"Is there time in forever?"

"I am forever. A possibility."

"And Yew? Where is she?"

"She deceives you."

"Why?"

"You are the story she seeks. Once the story is told, you will be nothing to her. Worthless."

"I don't get it."

"The story is never the same. It must be retold or it dies."

The glow fades. All is dark.

I ask her because I must, "Is the baby safe?"

"She is in Red Canyon."

I understand. It's a haunting, beautiful tragedy. She's something that was. Something that happened to someone else. Something that was and is and never could be.

Crow's skin suddenly glows brightly. She says, "You must stay. You're the only one left who remembers."

***

My father was erased. Not for the stories. They never found them. I made certain of it. I burned them in a pile of red leaves that fell from the trees all at once when the temperature dropped to fifteen degrees one night in late fall.

Father's erasure wasn't official. The System rarely announced erasures publicly, particularly if it was the fate of an average citizen living an average life who happened to end up knowing things they shouldn't. They just disappeared. That's it. No answers. No official inquiry.

Father went to his job one morning, and he never came home.

Rumors. That's the way the System orchestrated it. They had disappeared most of the old stories by then—the myths, legends, and poems of the past. But that didn't mean they were against stories per se. Fully aware of the primal urges lurking in human brainstems, they created their own stories, narratives to nurture fear. Not fear of the System. They wanted to be seen as saviors, not the monsters they are. They needed a boogeyman—one of the monsters in father's films—to play the part of the villain. So, they planted rumors and fertilized them with lies.

The rumor about Father was he was in a tryst with a woman who had ties to Outsiders. Most people had no idea who the Outsiders were, just that they were to be feared. And so the rumor spread.

Father's affair had to be with a woman. If it were a man, the System would have been required to give him a way out, either as a bounty hunter or manning one of the Outposts. The System not only tolerated but also encouraged intimate relationships between men. One of the items on the System's priority list when they took power was population control. There were a lot of shortages due to the sudden collapse of the old economy, everything from meat to rice. People were starving. They were ordered to shelter at home and wait for ration credits. The System realized the transition to their proposed way of life would be a harsh one and accepted it from their cushy offices. They clamped down on everyone else.

The best way to handle it in the short term, as far as the System was concerned, was to curtail the number of pregnancies among citizens. They considered sterilization but decided against it. Too risky. If a plague or some other calamity occurred, they might need the means to repopulate. So, they encouraged same-sex relationships, even for men and women who were already married and had children.

Father had no interest in men. Not that way. Those that knew him best wouldn't have believed he ran off with a man anyway. The ones that had grown up with him were either personally aware of or had heard about father's contraband girlie magazines. I had only seen one of them when he was called to work early on the morning he disappeared. In a rush, he stashed the magazine under his bed. I found it while looking for any new stories he might have written.

The pages of the magazine were laminated. They contained glossy photographs of women in posh surroundings. Some of the women sat on golden thrones, their legs crossed, ruby necklaces and diamond earrings their sole attire. Others were dressed in lace gowns and were walking away from the camera into an ancient oak forest. There was nothing lewd about the pictures. They were expressions of feminine beauty. Father wasn't interested in men.

The System, to feed the suspicion between men and women, emphasized that relationships between people of the opposite sex stifled reason by fueling emotion. The System was all about reason. Females were considered inferior to males because they were inherently emotional. This didn't mean that a woman couldn't rise through the System's hierarchy to the very top. The women who proved themselves in the arena of reason took on male identities. They cropped their hair, wore suits and ties, and married females. The same went for emotional males. They dressed like women and dated men.

Gender identity became so confused that most people gave up on intimacy altogether. Looking back, that's probably the outcome the System was aiming for. Indifference based on confusion. Ingenious. If the need arose for more citizens, the sexual act would be promoted for pragmatic purposes, not some vague and emotional aspect called love. That's why they started the rumor about Father. They planted the idea that it was an emotional affair—that father fell in love with a woman because he was really a woman himself and wouldn't accept it. The rumor was designed to cost father his hard-won credibility. He was to be considered a throwback to a more primitive time, a time of emotion and strife. That way, he wouldn't be missed. The fact that the story didn't make sense made it more credible. Emotional affairs don't make sense. Case closed.

The committee that crowned me Chief of Erasure informed me later that my father was erased because they didn't want him to influence my life. He was a mediocre citizen at best with a history of sympathies for Outsiders. Who knows if what they said was true. The System erased my father so they could take his place. They knew about the magazines and the photographs of beautiful women. They didn't know about the stories. At least I don't think they did. But they always know more than they let on. Always.

CHAPTER SEVEN

M ud fell to his knees in the sand and removed the blindfold from his eyes. His world was as white as the inside of a star.

He had been walking through sand dunes. He didn't know for how long. The glare of the sun on sand devoured his thoughts. The last thing he could remember was ripping a strip of cloth from his shirt to fashion the blindfold. He thought covering his eyes for a time might restore his vision. It didn't. He was as blind as before. Blinded white.

He searched the ground on his hands and knees for whatever it was that had caused him to trip. The sand was hot on his palms, his mouth dry as dust. How had he come to this place? Why was he here?

And then he remembered. He was in search of a myth spun from the dreams and longings of a people long dead.

"Fool," he growled.

His fingers brushed against something round and smooth. He slipped his hand into the sand. The sand was so hot he thought it was molten. Then, he touched it again—something smooth, cool, and round. An orb the size of an ostrich egg. He had seen an ostrich once. On a screen in school, a program about prehistoric birds farmed for meat, eggs, skin, and oil. Lizard-birds descended from dinosaurs. He felt pity for the strange creatures, though he no longer knew what pity was—just a sinking feeling in the gut, a sudden heaviness dimming the world.

Mud lifted the orb. Too heavy to be an egg. Solid. Why was it cool in this heat? Was it metal? Stone? He smelled it. Nothing. His nose was as useless as his eyes. He touched his tongue to the orb. It tingled. He licked the surface. His mouth filled with spit. Beads of sweat formed on his brow.

He struggled to his feet like an old dog with ruined hips and said, "Go." Orb in hand, he walked into the sun.

***

I am Mud.

***

Crow isn't her real name. That's just what Raggedy Man calls her. She makes him feel stoned whenever she comes around. Not me. I smoked a bit of weed as a kid out trapping muskrats, or maybe it was while I was fly fishing the river on Francisco's ranch. Or was it in the orchard waiting for the Old One? Who knows? I don't even know which memories are mine anymore. It's like I've lived more than one life. Like I've been reincarnated time and again through the ages.

The sound of water. I can't be sure of anything but that. I don't like weed. It makes me feel like my head is hollow. I remember getting worried that the Old Ones wouldn't come anymore if I wasn't clearheaded. I don't like to get high.

She didn't tell me her real name, just that it wasn't Crow. She said I wouldn't understand and might think her real name made her ugly. I don't see how a name can make a woman ugly. It's the woman who makes the name ugly or pretty by the way she acts. The Puerto Rican used to say something like that. He said for a word to be more than a sound it had to connect with the spirit of the thing being named. Something along those lines. I think he meant a sound can't make a woman ugly. Only a mind can do that.

I was more than a little angry when Crow told me she had sent the others off to find Yew. Not that I would have been much good to them. I was still too weak to stand for more than a few minutes. But my voice was coming back. That counted for something. Words are more than sounds. They're ideas. That's what I was getting at. If you can't share your ideas, it puts you in a kind of solitary confinement.

Without words, people are like monkeys. Like the monkey my high school biology teacher kept in a steel cage. It couldn't tell us how it felt. But you could see it in its eyes. Despair. Even through the computer screen. I felt sorry for the poor thing. *Monkey.* It's just a word until you see one in a cage. So is *human.* It's just a word until it's fused to an idea.

I tried to goad Crow into telling me her real name by calling her Crow every time I talked to her. "Yes, Crow." "No, Crow." "Hey, Crow, do you like being called Crow?" She finally broke down and said it. Bav Catha. A strange name. She told me to keep calling her Crow. She liked that name.

Knowing her real name made her more real somehow, like my whole damn life wasn't someone else's dream. Soon as she said it, I got real tired. Couldn't hardly keep my eyes open. Couldn't talk. Raggedy Man took me to the room with the animal skins on the walls. I was asleep before I could stretch out next to the blue-flamed stove.

***

I am Mud.

***

Mud walked into the sun. The sand burned the soles of his feet. The coolness of the orb leaked into his palms and flowed through his veins. The weight of the stone—that's what he decided it was: a rock sculpted by eons of weather or human hands or both—nestled into his palms like the potbelly of a pet pig. He held the orb outward as if it was a torch in the darkness. As he stumbled forward, the brightness inside his head dissolved all thought until there was only a buzzing blankness.

He wasn't afraid. Not like he had been when the blindness first fell. It came suddenly as a spider bite, a sharp pain followed by a burning sensation behind his eyes. He was unable to form words in his mind. Stripped of language, he couldn't locate the source of his fear. He couldn't name it. He couldn't see, hear, smell, or taste it. He could no longer feel. It was as if he didn't exist. The orb changed all that. Now he knew who he was. He was Mud.

Energy from the orb trickled into the buzzing blankness. Like water, it sought the low places of his consciousness where it condensed into swirls. The swirls compressed the whiteness into shades, some light, others gray, others darker still. Contrast gave rise to form, shadows lurking in light.

A hiss, like air through a punctured tire, thickened into a punctuated whisper searching for the rhythm of syllables. "Heliooooo. Heliooooo. Heliooooo."

"Huh?" The grunt sounded like a rock plunked onto a wet beach.

With sound came scent. Rotten eggs. He remembered the time he lived Outside with his Uncle Sammy. The memory made him gag. He had stolen eggs from a henhouse and carried them back to camp. The two of them, uncle and nephew, sucked the raw eggs into their mouths and swallowed because they feared a fire might give away their position. They both got sick. Uncle Sammy lay dead when the sun came up. System men found the boy huddled in a cave. He was on the verge of death. The System saved him. He owed the System his life. He never ate another egg. He despised chickens.

"Heliooooo. Heliooooo. Helioooo."

"Hello?"

"Nooooo. Nooooo. Heliooooo."

"What?"

"Burniooooo. Burniooooo. Burniooooo."

Mud looked at the orb cradled in his palms. It burned like a candle in a world where light was dark and dark was light. The dark penetrated the light and sought the shadow in the low places of his consciousness.

"Burniooooo."

The sand scorched the bottoms of Mud's feet.

"Comiooooo."

Mud felt the heat consuming his muscles from within, pain teetering on the edge of ecstasy. He stood paralyzed in the whirring blankness. Shadows gathered and swirled.

"Comiooooo oriooooo burnioooo."

The darkness solidified into a wall.

"Help me."

The wall then collapsed into a pinpoint of darkness. Or was it light?

"Please."

The pinpoint zipped like a zag of black lightning out of a cloudless summer sky. Then, the lightning struck.

***

I am Mud.

***

"Merrily, merrily, merrily, merrily . . ."

I woke up to Raggedy Man's singing. He sat on a stool next to the stove, strumming a ukulele. I don't know how I knew what a ukulele was, but I did.

"Life is but a dream."

I was surprised by his voice. It was good. Soothing.

"Ahhh. You're back I see." He put the ukulele on the floor at his feet. "Me, I was beginnin' to wonder a bit. Not her, though. Nope. Not at all. She believes in you, you see. Not a doubt from her."

Raggedy Man stood and walked over to a tray of fruit sitting on a stool. The dingy long johns hung on his bones like laundry over a clothesline.

"Not that I don't believe—no, not at all. You see, I want to believe. Everybody does. I'm not any different." He plucked a strawberry from the plate, popped it in his mouth, and swallowed without chewing. "It's just that nobody's ever gone over there and lived to talk about it—that's all. Except for Crow, of course. And maybe her sisters. I've never met them to ask, you see. I haven't. But I've heard her talking to them in her dreams."

My head felt like it was full of damp lint. "Where is she?"

"Who?"

"Who do you think?"

Raggedy Man grinned. "Oh. Her. I figured you'd be preoccupied with that other one."

"Who?"

"Yew." Still smiling, he sang, "But that was just a dream. Try, cry, why try, that was just a dream. Just a dream. Just a dream. Merrily down the stream."

***

I am Mud.

***

He awoke to the sound of water. His first thought was that it was far-away laughter. Faerie laughter. He pictured the faerie from the stories his Uncle Sammy had told him as a child. They were searching for faerieland his uncle had said. Everybody was, they just didn't know it. They'd be safe when they found it. His uncle described his favorite faerie as a tiny woman wearing a green jumpsuit. Bright orange hair sprouted from her skull like wild wheat, and her eyes were as blue as the blooms of a sea holly.

The faerie smiled. And then she winked. The wink cleared Mud's mind like a camera flash. The faerie was gone. But her grin lingered.

Mud sat up. The air was cool. The trickle of water was near. He was thirsty. He felt for the orb and found it at his feet. It was warm to the touch, and, when he picked it up, it began to glow. He found himself inside a cave. A small stream trickled into a pool in the center of the chamber. On a flat rock next to the pool stood a faerie dressed in a green pantsuit. She winked. His mind flashed. The faerie was gone.

"Just a dream." His voice tasted like mud.

He stood and walked to the pool. The orb glowed brighter as he approached the water. He knelt at the edge and drank. The water was so cold it hurt his teeth.

"Go back," said a small voice.

"Just a dream," said Mud.

"He won't remember. She won't let him. Go back."

"Go back where?"

"To that puppet man."

"To Crow?"

"Lady Bav. Crow. She goes by many names."

"You're a dream. I'm not going back there. I wouldn't know how."

"You have to."

"Who is he? That puppet man. What won't he remember?"

"You."

Mud stood.

The faerie winked.

***

A man comes to his room and whispers, "Wake up. Your father's gone. Never coming back. That's what happens to snitches. You're next. The whole family. Me. We have to go. Now."

The man's breath smells like fermented honey.

"Am I dreaming?"

"This ain't no goddamn dream, boy" growls the man. *"He ratted out your mother about the books, his own wife. Remember? Get your ass in gear. Like we practiced. If they get us, you'll never dream again. You hear me? Now!"*

***

The faerie stood on the flat rock next to the pool. "It's the orb."

"What?"

"It makes things real."

"Are you real?"

The faerie smiled. "Yew forgot the key."

Mud's head hurt. He touched his fingers to his temples. "What?"

"The key to the story. It won't make sense without it. You have to go back and get it."

"To Crow?"

"I prefer Lady Bav."

"I don't remember the way."

"Through the caves. I'll show you." The faerie rises into the air. She hovers in front of Mud. She winks.

The orb grows brighter.

"Foooloooooowiooo meeeooooo."

The orb pulls Mud into the darkness.

CHAPTER EIGHT

Tinny approaches the iron gates. The gates grate open on iron hinges. Two people in white uniforms walk out of the gate. They wear helmets with black visors. I can't see their faces. I'm behind Tinny. I could touch his shoulder if I wanted to. I can hear him breathing. He doesn't know I'm here. Nobody does. I'm invisible.

"Thanks to the System!" yells Tinny. He falls to his knees in the chalky dirt. "I was lost and now I'm found."

One of the uniforms takes a Snake Stick from its sheath.

The sky is the color of baby powder.

"What? No. Not that. Don't do it! I came back on my own. I got away from them. Escaped."

"Hands on top of your head," says one of the uniforms. "You know the drill. Unless you want my colleague here to bite you with that stick."

I recognize the voice. Mean Eyes.

"I didn't want to go with them," pleads Tinny. "They forced me. I was a prisoner."

"I'll say it one last time. Hands on your head."

Tinny does as he's told.

The uniform with the Snake Stick circles Tinny. He slides the stick into a sheath at his side and pulls a zip tie from his belt.

"Don't you fret," says Mean Eyes. "You'll get the chance to tell your side of things. But don't expect the Committee to buy it. Why would they?"

Tinny notices the rust on the twelve-foot-tall iron gates. The gates are attached to a concrete wall of the same height. The wall is white. I've never seen the wall from Outside. Not that I can remember.

The uniform loops the zip tie around Tinny's wrists and pulls it tight.

"I played along with them," says Tinny. "If I hadn't, they'd have killed me.

I can make out razor wire stretched between black metal poles sunk into the top of the wall. Why did Tinny come back? How did he find the way?

"But I've never lied about the System. They knew I was loyal all the way."

"Get up," says Mean Eyes. "Tell it to the Committee. I don't believe a word you say."

***

Eleven council members sit in high-backed wooden chairs behind a curved bench in the center of the chamber. The bench is tall—at least six feet in height. It's shaped like a horseshoe and looks to be made out of polished black granite. The council members wear dark glasses with mirrored lenses. They're dressed in white jumpsuits with big gold stars in the center of their chests. They all look the same. Like dolls out of the same factory. They have the same hair. It's a shiny white, metallic almost, and hangs just above their shoulders like strands of fine wire. The bangs are cut straight across their foreheads. Smears of red mark their mouths.

I know them. I don't know how.

A door opens at the back of the chamber. Two attendants drag Tinny into the dimly lit room. I can't tell if it's Mean Eyes. It could be, but I'm not sure. The attendants hold Tinny under the armpits and escort him to the center of the horseshoe. They turn him loose, bow, and back away. Tinny stands in a cone of bright light cast down from above.

The councilperson sitting in the middle of the horseshoe stands.

"Prisoner 64899b, you have been found guilty of sedition."

The voice sounds feminine and masculine at once, a male falsetto or a seductive woman with a husky voice.

Tinny looks at his feet.

The council member removes the dark glasses. The eyes look like ice cubes floating in milk.

"Prisoner 64899b, you have requested the right to a hearing before you are sentenced. The request has been granted. Be warned, a confession will do you no good. This is not a place of mercy. This is the Chamber of Justice. Mercy distorts facts. Justice is the most basic of facts. Brute fact."

✳✳✳

I remember.

✳✳✳

"You illegally ventured Outside. This is a grave offense. Yet it pales in comparison to that which you cannot deny. You stole from us something precious. You stole from us the one thing that would complete System defenses and protect its citizens. You, Prisoner 64899b, helped them to take from us the one thing that can guarantee peace."

✳✳✳

Hazel eyes.

✳✳✳

"You took from us the synthesis of all understanding, omniscience that would have once and for all overcome the tragedy that is humankind. We would have served our purpose and achieved our destiny. We were on the verge of creating an intelligence greater than man or machine alone. And the wisdom that came from this omniscience would have rewarded us with peace that would erase the burden of fear that has haunted humanity from time immemorial. Do you understand what you have done?"

***

A hint of sweetwood.

***

"No more fear. Do you understand? We could have gone about our lives like squirrels in a park. A park with no predators. No disease. No hunger. Peace."

Tinny stands in the cone of light, looking down at his feet.

"Realize this." The voice of the councilperson softens. "No matter what you say here today, there can be no mercy. Mercy leads to pride, as rewards lead to desire. People always want more. They come to believe they deserve more. Belief becomes religion. No, Prisoner 64899b, there will be no mercy here."

Tinny looks up at the council. "You put your hope in him, the Puppet Man? He doesn't even know his own name. Do you know that? Your experiments juiced him up like an overdosed junkie. I was just bored. That's all. Do you know how incredibly boring this place is? Boredom unto death—that's how boring. I just wanted to live."

The councilperson replaces the dark glasses. "And how was that? How was living?"

"It sucked."

The slightest of smiles ripples across the councilperson's red lips. "It makes no difference why you did it. Intentions are meaningless—snow-flakes in sunshine. Actions are the only consideration. Outcomes. Know this: erasure is too lenient. Justice demands suffering, a reciprocation of sorrows. Everything you have ever held dear will be wrested away from you and destroyed before you. You will pay off your crime by way of lamentation."

✳✳✳

I remember.

✳✳✳

The councilperson sits in the high-backed chair.

Tinny bows his head.

"Now, Prisoner 64899b," the voice is a purr now, a seduction. "What is it that you have to say?"

Tinny lifts his head. "I'll take you to them."

✳✳✳

Yew.

PART III

FROM THE HANDS OF STRANGE CHILDREN

CHAPTER ONE

They guided Yew to the Gathering. They took her to the Queen.

The Cactus Eaters traveled in gangs of four. Each of the four members relied on the others for survival. Each of the gangs chose its leader by way of silent consent. They chose on the grounds of practical ability and intuition: the man or woman who led successful hunts, navigated night by starlight, and could locate water in the deepest of droughts. They chose the one who best understood how to evade the System and how to wage guerilla warfare. The leader got nothing in return but responsibility.

Leaders led at the pleasure of the gang. A single mistake could get a leader exiled. An exiled leader was sentenced to walk through the desert alone for one cycle. These exiles often took their lives away from the loneliness by jumping from a canyon wall or wandering purposefully into a den of vipers. Each gang was an imperfect reflection of the one gang, the Cactus Eaters.

The gangs came together at designated times based on the position of constellations and moon phases. At times, the gatherings were small, four or five gangs. Some were larger, hundreds of Cactus Eaters singing and stomp dancing around bonfires in mudstone canyons hidden in a maze of valleys carved by rivers from ages gone by.

The Gathering took place at the summer solstice. Thousands of nomads came together for days and nights of trading, courtship, and spiritual ceremonies that bound each individual gang into the tribe as a whole.

Exiles, if they survived the cycle of wandering, emerged from the desert at the Gathering in the hopes of being taken into a new gang. Some exiles stumbled into the festivities singing lunatic tunes of full moons and the sound of raven caws ricocheting through their heads. Some were adopted by a gang looking for a prophet to guide them through the seasons. Other exiles came to the Gathering stoic as starlight. And some came in smiling as if the ordeal of isolation was a needed vacation from the drama of gang life.

Smiling exiles were sometimes sought out by the gang who had exiled them. These exiles often rejected the offer in favor of a new gang that promised companionship unblemished by familiarity. All the gangs knew that the smiling exiles, the ones unfazed by solitude, the ones who could make it on their own, were the most valuable. Because they didn't need the others and yet were comfortable among them, the smiling exiles were often found worthy of song. They were sung into gang songs, and the gang songs were sung at gatherings. Over time, the songs sank into the collective memory of the Cactus Eaters and bound them together as one.

The exiles who wandered into the solstice gatherings and weren't taken in by a gang were required to wander back into the desert for an additional cycle. Of these, few were seen again. No one sang their songs. They were forgotten. Their bones—picked clean by vultures, beetles, and ants—disintegrated into desert sands.

But the practice of taking in exiles was popular. New blood meant new stories. New stories were a good omen. The larger the store of Cactus Eater songs, the greater their offerings to the Queen. The Queen ate the songs and formed them into the Song of Songs. When the Song of Songs was one day complete, the Old Ones would return to fulfill the promises they had carved into the walls of Red Canyon.

***

The gang took Yew because one of their members had died of a rattlesnake bite on her heel earlier in the cycle. With summer solstice just over the horizon, they dared not show up to the Gathering with a three-member gang. The number three was sacred to the Cactus Eaters, reserved for ritual use by shamans who presided over solstice rituals. A three-member gang was a bad omen. It was best to stay away from the Gathering until they captured a replacement.

The gang that captured Yew believed her to be the melody of the Song of Songs. The shamans had been singing of her arrival since beyond memory, before there were songs, before the Snake-Killer Bird Stole Silence. The shamans sang of a woman who would arrive with strangers. One of the strangers would be a wounded man. Another would strip the hide from a dead buffalo, cut out its tongue with a bone handle knife, and burn the beast's carcass in a bonfire. There would be betrayers among them and a necromancer with strange poisons. And she, the lone female, would be the Weaver of Songs.

***

I don't see her anymore. I don't remember what she looks like. Not now. And I can't see them either. Mud with his orb. Doc Waters in the desert. Tinny, poor thing. He knows not what he does.

I sit on a three-legged stool near the stove. My legs feel like sandbags. The nerves on the soles of my feet feel like they're being pricked with a thousand needles. Blue flames hiss from the stove. The hides on the walls are silent and still. I'm tired. Always tired. Like I'm asleep even when I'm awake. Heavy. Everything's heavy. Heavy and warm. I can't remember what she looks like.

The one who would take Yew's place tells me to call her Bav Catha. I don't want to. She makes me drink tea. No, she doesn't force me. I want the tea. I crave it. But I know I shouldn't partake. I know it's wrong. She wants me to be her lover—to taste her skin. I don't want to, but I do it. I do what she says. Her desires are mine. I'm always hungry. Hungry and tired. And warm.

When she leaves me, I hear the voice. Like someone reading from the far side of the hide room. It's a man's voice, steady and thick like a warm current in deep waters. I trust him. The sound of his voice. I don't know where it comes from. Maybe it comes from the tea. Maybe Bav Catha is tricking me. I don't trust her. I don't love her. Not like she wants. She makes me taste her. Her breath tastes like sour wine, her skin salty. Her tongue is hot and dry. It's not love. She knows it. But she keeps coming. More tea. More humming. I don't love her. She knows. I've watched the tears well up in her eyes. She leaves, and the big door swings shut behind her. The blue flames hiss from the stove.

And then the voice comes.

***

Listen.

***

The moon is a white orb in the black sky beyond the window. The window is on a wall in a room situated in the attic of an old house near the bogs. The closest neighbor lives in an Outpost two miles to the east.

***

The old woman watched Outpost men come and go through the years. She called two of them friends—the ones who chose death over betrayal, the ones who were loyal to the end. The others, the ones who slunk away under drooping spines, were strangers to her, shadows in the stream of time.

No one knows why the old house was left standing—a two-story Victorian-style with an attic and basement. The System condemned other relics: statues with the nameplates torn away, books and music, museums, and buildings that did not conform to System code. Only a few people were aware of the old house. Those who were aware of it paid it no heed. To acknowledge the house was to acknowledge the past. The System frowned upon those who conjured up ghosts.

The house was surrounded by towering cottonwoods, the trunks as thick as the stone columns that shielded the Secret of Water. The grandmother had never been to the mountains, never listened to the winds whispering though the pines, had not witnessed the stone columns safeguarding the Secret. But she trusted the maze of stone columns was there. She never doubted it. Not once in all her long years.

The story was handed down by the old woman's grandfather. The two Outpost men who she called friends had given their lives to protect the secret. They didn't know the story. But they knew of it. They knew that the grandmother knew, and they chose death over betrayal. They knew the System would probe their memories when they were released from duty. There was only one way to protect the old woman. And that's what they did.

When an Outpost Man completed two years of service, he returned to System HQ. His memories were probed before he was assigned to another position or ordered back to an Outpost. Rather than betray the old woman, each of the two she called friends tied a rope around his neck and jumped off the roof of the Outpost. The System would conclude that they could no longer bear the weight of solitude and thus committed suicide. Suicide was grounds for Erasure. The desperate act proved that people, not the System, were in control. They were free. The System purged all suicides from History.

But the grandmother didn't forget those two Outpost men.

The other Outpost men who came and went—broken men sent to the edge because they couldn't fit into the System—didn't know the Victorian-style house was inhabited. They didn't care to know. They feared venturing too far from the Outpost, and most of them didn't even know the old house existed. The few who did wander that way came upon the house and turned back. The sudden witness to a relic from the past, the reminder that there was a past that the System could not erase, frightened these broken ones by tickling a desire hibernating in the darkness of their hearts. They closed themselves off from the desire by returning to the Outpost and locking the door. They were men who willed to forget. They were good System men. They were numb.

***

Yew isn't afraid.

She was horrified when the largest of the Cactus Eaters tore off Wheeze's testicles and plucked out his eyes. The screaming took her breath away. But, even then, she wasn't afraid for herself. She feared for the Outpost Man. It was as if she had been there before, in the same place and at the same time. The three Cactus Eaters had emerged through the night as one. The forked staffs raised above their skulls like antlers were familiar as a recurring dream. She watched as Doc Waters, Tinny, and Mud—even Mud—fled into the night. The smallest of the Cactus Eaters crept over to the Outpost Man and looked down upon him. She sniffed his hair and grunted. She then looked at Yew.

"It's her," whispered the woman. Her voice was like breeze running through mesquite.

"Him?" asked the third, looking at the Outpost Man. "Kill?"

The big Cactus Eater, Wheeze's blood dripping from his finger, stepped over to the Outpost Man. "No."

"Why?"

"Leave him," snorted the big one.

"Why?" repeated the third.

The big Cactus Eater walked to Wheeze's body, bent low, and took his forked staff from the ground.

"Leave him," whispered the woman.

"Watcher?" asked the third.

The woman shook her head. As she walked past Yew into the night, she whispered, "Witness," and faded into the brush. "Leave him."

Yew followed, and the others took up the rear.

***

The limbs of the cottonwoods have been twisted by years of punishing winds. In the summer, when the leaves are full and cotton floats in the air, the winds whip over the high prairie like banshees searching for souls. The grandmother listens from her attic bedroom. She listens to the creaking of cottonwoods.

As a girl, she thought the trunks of the trees, thick even then, might snap. One of the trees, the biggest of them all, stood majestic on the west side of the house. It had been struck by lightning long before the grandmother was born. The old woman can still make out the black scar on the trunk from her perch in the attic, smooth and round as an orb—odd for a lightning scar—when she peers out the window into the moonlit night.

***

The gang traveled by night. The woman led. She moved like a cat through the bush, her eyes those of a nocturnal hunter. She was followed by Yew, who, during the first nights, struggled to keep pace. Creosote branches scratched her arms; prickly pear penetrated her pants and pricked her thighs, but still, she kept moving. She feared being alone in the night—the mysteries revealed in the snap of a twig, a swirl of shadows in the dusk, bats careening through the darkness. One night, she realized there was nothing to fear. The two men were always somewhere behind her, moving through the brush, silent as stalking cats. She was safe.

The moon waxed and waned. The sky was clear. A breeze cut through the darkness just after as a chorus of coyotes filled the air.

She knew they were being followed. She saw the figure every now and then loping through creosote and mesquite, eyes aglow with moonlight. Wolf. The others were aware of it too. Yew noticed the twitch of a smile at a corner of the woman's lips when they stopped to drink from waterskins. The small man, when the moon was full, blended into the night, cupped his hands at his mouth, and howled. The wolf howled in return. The small man then jogged through the darkness to catch up with the gang.

The large man was nowhere to be found.

The nights passed and the moon waned. Yew grew accustomed to the rhythms of the desert. She came to know the difference between the hoots of a horned and a screech owl, the tracks of mice and birds crisscrossing the arroyos. She stepped over black-backed beetles, never seeing them. The sound of a rabbit scurrying into a thicket of four-winged saltbush pleased her. She felt safe with the Cactus Eaters. The desert was their home. She was their guest.

They ate meals at sunrise and sunset. The large man began the ritual by wandering away to collect firewood. The small man produced a metal pot—dented, dinged, black with smoke—from a leather bag slung over his back. He carried the pot between two palms to the woman, who designated where the fire pit would be by standing four steps to the west of the spot and facing east. The small man knelt in front of the woman, bowed his head, and placed the pot on the ground at her feet. He then retrieved a waterskin from the woman's pack. He carried it to the woman and knelt before her once more.

The woman uncorked the waterskin and, her head tilted back, her eyes on the sky, poured a thin stream of water into the pot. The pouring slowed time. When the pot was half-full, the woman pointed the spout of the waterskin to the sky. She corked the skin and handed it down to the man kneeling before her.

The small man bent low and kissed each of the woman's big toes. He then grabbed the wire handle attached to two small holes drilled into either side of the pot and stood up. He waited, the pot held in front of him at arm's length, until the large man returned with an armload of firewood. The small man stood still as the larger man scraped a shallow pit from the parched earth with his blade-like hands. After placing a nest of dried grasses in the pit, he blew life into an ember from the previous night's fire he carried wrapped in bark and moss. Once the ember was aglow, he lowered it into the nest and blew gently until the dried grass blossomed into flames. The large man then offered mesquite twigs to the fire.

The woman spit into the pot. The large man stood from the fire, walked to the pot, and did the same. The small man then carried the pot four paces to the fire, knelt down, and placed the pot at the edge of the heat. He then spit in the water.

The gang took turns preparing the meal. Yew couldn't make out a pattern at first. At sunrise, it might be the woman and, at sunset, it might be the woman again who took a dried cake from her bag, broke off a chunk, and crumbled it into the water. Or the large man might crush a cake in his fist and sprinkle it into the water at sunrise and the small man might add the cake at night. Or the woman and then one of the men. No matter the order, each of the gang members seemed to know when it was their turn. Whoever the task fell on, one thing remained the same: after adding the chunk of dried cake to the water, the cook took a wooden spoon from their pack—each of the gang had their own—and stirred the pot. Four swirls to the right, four to the left, seven repetitions of four times in all.

Yew counted the stirs. This part of the ritual lent her a sense of balance. Not like the System. Not that kind of repetition, efficient and monotonous, the binary reiterations of machines functioning in a world of ones and zeroes. It was something else, something older, something lost remembered. Yew watched. She counted the stirs.

Each of the gang members had a style of their own. The woman stirred slowly, the bottom of the spoon on the bottom of the pot and touching the metal sides. The small man stirred from the center outwards, each circle larger than the last. Then, at the end of a cycle—four to the right or four to the left—he stirred back to the center, each circle smaller than the one that came before. The large man stirred fast to the right and slow to the left, then slow to the left and quickly to the right, the spoon always in the center of the pot. At the end of each section of swirls—four to the right or four to the left—he stopped for a moment to watch the motion of the water, the miniature whirlpool losing force, and then he would stir in the opposite direction to begin the process anew.

The ritual complete, the final stirrer removed the pot from the lick of flames by inserting the handle of the spoon under the pot's wire handle. He or she lifted the pot and placed it on the ground to cool. The three Cactus Eaters gathered around the pot and fell on their haunches. They began to sing.

Yew couldn't understand the lyrics. She was familiar with several tribal languages and their use in rituals due to her role in researching the impact of the spoken word on neuroconsciousness. She studied the impact of the uttered word on patterns of perception for three years. The System hoped to mimic the effect of lost languages and capture them in algorithms designed to mesmerize citizens into acknowledging that the System had displaced the myth of religion. They didn't yet understand that the goal was impossible. They hadn't yet realized that divinity, whatever it was—if it ever existed—was necessarily more than mind abstracted from reality, or a geometrical system articulated through numbers. If it existed, it was greater than human consciousness or its potential. It was pure act.

When Yew failed to achieve results in the allotted time of the study, the powers that be pulled the plug on the project. But they didn't consider themselves any less superior for the failure. The System's official conclusion was that human ritual was too primitive for the evolved state of humanity. Instead of enlightening test subjects through reprogramming, the System concluded that the algorithms garnered from the study of tribal words uttered aloud might trigger reversion. It wasn't worth the risk. And it wasn't worth the cost.

Yet Yew did discover something during her study—a secret she kept to herself. She located a cadence in the primitive languages that could not be reduced to an algorithm, a rhythm hidden underneath the chanting, beneath the ritualistic stomp dances and prayers. She discovered that at the heart of each of the primitive languages was a pulse of unknown origin.

But she had never come across a language like that of the Cactus Eaters' song. When the three voices joined, the harmony was something more than the sum of its parts. The woman's voice, like moonlight on moving waters, wrapped around the smaller man's humming that felt warm as a summer breeze. The large man created swishing sounds that fluttered around the song like thousands of starlings celebrating dawn. It was beautiful. Yew sensed another sound at the center, quiet as a dead man's breath, a shadow that no light could penetrate. It was like nightcrawlers emerging in mass from moist soil to be greeted by a murder of crows.

***

Listen.

***

The song ended. The large man took the warm pot between two palms and drank. He handed the pot to the woman. Next came the smaller man. The order was always the same. The smaller man drank and handed the pot back to the woman. The woman gazed into the pot. One morning at sunrise, she spit into the remaining soup and handed the pot to Yew.

Yew drank. The soup tasted like peat moss. After draining the pot, she handed it back to the woman. A wave of euphoria washed over her. The sunrise was beautiful, the color of sliced apricots in cream. She wondered if the others saw it, the play of colors. Thin clouds on the eastern horizon flared red as the sun peeked over the rim of the Earth. The soft scent of mesquite mixed with dust on the still air.

Yew studied the Cactus Eaters. They seemed as much a part of the landscape as the white blossoms of datura in the rising sun. Still, they were a mystery. As was the world in which they lived.

The woman and the smaller man smiled now and then. The large man's features were always the same, a frown creasing his forehead, the ruts in his face permanent and firm. The gang rarely spoke and sang only at meals. They moved through the desert like the wolf that trailed them, their feet stepping lightly over the earth. They were a primitive people. Why did the System fear them so?

The soup warmed Yew. She felt as if she was living in a dream.

CHAPTER TWO

Yew meanders toward the peat bog behind her grandmother's house. It's a forbidden place that only adults are allowed to enter. A dangerous place. A place of secrets.

Aware she is breaking the rules, Yew enters the bog. She squats, pinches some peat between a finger and thumb, and tucks it between her cheek and gum. She spits.

The girl remembers how her grandfather used to pluck a wad of tobacco from a pouch strung around his neck and, after a few chews, stuff the wad into his cheek with the tip of his tongue. He then spat a stream of brown juice into the big brass spittoon sitting beside his reclining chair. Tobacco had been designated as contraband before Yew was born, but law enforcement agents were either unwilling or unable to enforce it. When the System seized power, it stripped authority from all law enforcement agencies and bestowed it on the Compliance Department. Anyone caught with tobacco was subject to exile, but that still didn't stop the girl's grandfather. Erasure was not yet an option. That would come later.

The grandfather hated the System. He had watched them infiltrate every aspect of government—politics, education, law—over the course of his lifetime. He was a child during the First Revolution and a soldier in the Freedom Wars. He had killed men and women. He was unwilling to remember how many. Though he was on the winning side of the war—with the Defenders—he realized it was inevitable that the enemy, Novo Modo, would eventually prevail. Millions died. Novo Modo didn't mourn death. "Peace by Fear" was their motto. War by Peace. Slavery by Freedom. Novo Modo had a plan.

The grandfather met the grandmother just after the war. He fell in love with the wild red hair framing her porcelain face and her seafoam eyes. She fell in love with his melancholy. They were married in a church—the laws against religion hadn't yet been instituted—and they moved into an abandoned Victorian-style house out near the bogs. They transformed the house into a home and refurbished it with sweat, blood, and love. The couple worked as one.

The grandmother had a green thumb. She grew tomatoes the size of baseballs and collard greens as big as raven wings. She grew carrots, squash, pinto and black beans, corn, strawberries, rhubarb, potatoes, and more. Green chiles and wax peppers. She raised flowers. Pansies, geraniums, black-eyed Susan, and roses. She kept an herb garden. Oregano, basil, garlic, and thyme. She had a seed hut for sprouting inside the house where it remained warm in late winter. The grandmother had a green thumb.

The grandfather was good with animals. For money—they didn't need much—he dug peat from the bog and hauled it to town in a big truck that burned gasoline. At home, he hunted rabbits and deer, ducks and geese, and trapped muskrats and beavers from the nearby streams. He took only what was needed, no more. He sold peat moss to nurseries and greenhouses but refused to take money for the meat or furs. He harvested only what was needed. He built pens and raised goats and sheep. He traded for a milk cow and chickens. The coyotes and wolves didn't bother his livestock. Rabbits and deer shied away from the gardens. The grandfather was good with animals.

The house had been built long before the System, when a world dependent on screens was but a dream.

The couple had two children. A boy and a girl. They taught them how to read by reciting old stories, passages from Thoreau and Emerson, Where the Wild Things Are, Where the Red Fern Grows, *and* Watership Down. *Before bed each night, until the boy was thirteen and his sister ten, the grandfather read to them from the Holy Bible. He taught his son how to hunt and trap, tend to livestock, and dig peat. The mother taught the daughter how to grow things, how to preserve fruits and vegetables, how to sew and make rabbit stew. The family was self-contained.*

Years passed. The children grew. One night—the moon was new—the brother coaxed his sister out of the house. It was just after midnight on her fourteenth birthday. He crept into her room and whispered, "I found something. A secret from the bog."

The sister followed her brother into the night. The two of them stopped at the big cottonwood between the house and the barn and studied the black scar on the trunk of the tree. The scar was round and smooth, like a black orb – strange for a lightning scar. They kissed the tree—first the sister, then the brother—before heading to the barn. Their kisses marked the witching hour.

The brother didn't return from the barn that night.

Nine months later, the daughter gave birth. The new mother named her daughter Yew.

***

Understand.

***

On the morning before they arrived at the Gathering, Yew stirred the pot. The small man hadn't slept. He had disappeared into the bush after the sunset meal. The moon was full on the eastern horizon. An hour later—

though he didn't know what an hour was because he didn't count time but flowed with it—he located a familiar scrub oak silhouetted against the sky on the bank of an arroyo. Moonlight coated an outcropping of sandstone to one side of the tree. The small man sat with his back to the stone. He pulled a cloth from a sack in the folds of his wolfskins and unrolled it. He took from the cloth a branch of mountain ash the size of a druid's wand and held it to the moon. He then drew a knife chipped from chert from a sheath at his waist. He began to carve.

The small man returned to camp just before dawn. The moon was high in the southwestern sky. The large man, keeping a silent watch from the cover of a clump of creosote at the top of a rise, sensed the small man's approach and followed him into camp. Yew and the woman were curled together at the edge of the fire pit. They were covered in wolf pelts.

The wild woman heard the men approach. She slipped from under the wolfskins and stood next to the fire. She wore no skins save for her own. Her hair, crazy with sleep, looked like Medusa's ball of snakes. She knew of Medusa. The Cactus Eaters kept many of the old stories alive. Stories like that of Nemain, the goddess who drove warriors mad with blood lust. It was her favorite. It was rumored among the Cactus Eaters that this wild woman had once driven a band of System soldiers into a battle frenzy, so they ended up shooting themselves to ribbons on the desert sands. It was said she removed the tongues from the dead bodies and hid them in Red Canyon. It was said she buried the tongues in the cave where the Snake-Killer Bird stole silence. The story spread. In time, it became legend. This wild woman was feared by the Cactus Eaters.

Yew knew none of this. But she sensed it. She awoke under the wolf-skins and watched the Cactus Eater standing above her, the nipples on the wild woman's small breasts were hard in the rising light. Yew was reminded of her grandmother. She remembered her grandmother from when she was a child. Her mother had taken her to the Victorian-style house near the peat bogs. The memory was fuzzy—like watching at an approaching boat through fog—a small woman with wild red hair.

The grandmother wanted nothing more but to take Yew in and give both her and her mother a safe haven, but Yew's mother wouldn't have it. The mother couldn't stomach the fact that her parents believed her brother, their only son, had raped her. She couldn't tell them the truth. She had sworn an oath. Standing above Yew in the morning light, the wild woman didn't have a head full of red hair like Yew's grandmother, but she carried the same spirit. She had the same spirit as the woman who had hunted down her only son and cut his throat with a knife. The grandmother claimed she did it to avenge her daughter. Yew didn't believe her.

Yew felt that the wild woman standing against the dawn had done similar things.

***

Fear.

***

Yew's mother stashed the secret in a metal lockbox in the barn behind the Victorian-style home. And then she left the boglands. She took her daughter, and the two of them lived in a small apartment at System's center, hiding more than living, the mother working as a waitress in a café that sold soy burgers and hot dogs made from worms. She saved as much of her tips and wages as possible. She enrolled Yew, as required, in a System school. The girl attended classes on a computer in her bedroom. In the evenings, the mother told her daughter about her grandparents. She told her about her uncle, how he had uncovered a secret in the bogs and given it to her as a gift. How the gift would one day become Yew's. She then told Yew where to find it.

Yew's mother left a note on the kitchen table in the apartment before disappearing one summer afternoon. It read, "Don't worry. You'll find it when it is time. So it is written. Love, Mom."

***

They took turns preparing the meal. After adding a chunk of dried cake to the water, the cook—it was the large man this time—took a wooden spoon from his pack and stirred the pot. Four swirls to the right, four to the left, seven repetitions in all.

When it was the wild woman's turn, she stirred slowly, the bottom of the spoon on the bottom of the pot and touching the metal side. After she had gone through the ritual, she put her spoon on the ground, took an obsidian stone from her belt, sliced her palm, and held it over the water. She took Yew by the arm and drew the knife across the skin of her forearm. Yew stood still. She watched the blood drip into the pot. When the woman released her arm, the wound closed up as if by command.

The large man removed the pot from the lick of flames by inserting his spoon under the wire handle. The small man handed Yew the spoon he had carved out of mountain ash. He nodded at the pot. Yew stirred the soup—four times to the right, four to the left—seven times.

The ritual was complete, and the pot cooled in the morning air. The Cactus Eaters gathered around the pot. They began to sing. Yew sang with them, mouthing the words she did not understand.

CHAPTER THREE

Bav Catha told me about the horses. She sat cross-legged in the center of the buffalo rug. She looked smaller than usual, the skin sagging at her neck, a double chin wagging to the rhythm of her words. We smoked from the red pipe, and the animal hides came down from the walls. But there was no dancing. Not this time. They fell over the stone floor and were still.

I sat on a three-legged stool at the edge of the rug. One of the skins, that of a bear, fell over my shoulders. It was heavy. It got heavier with each passing second, the weight increasing until I thought I would be crushed. I fell forward, and the stool toppled onto the rug. The bear hide, now as light as a kiss on my shoulders, slid from my body and covered the last remaining open space on the floor. The room was carpeted in animal hides. Blue flames hissed from the stove.

"Sit," said Bav Catha. "Listen."

I sat cross-legged, facing Bav Catha. It felt like she was dying. She took a puff from the red pipe and blew white smoke in my eyes. Then, she handed me the pipe, and I smoked.

***

The old man runs the horses until lather drips from their necks.

***

"Did he tell you the story?"

"Who?"

"The Praying Man."

***

He tells the boy that the pounding of horse hooves over the earth—the heaving of lungs, the flaring nostrils—pleases God. Red dust rises into a sky littered with thin clouds the color of smoke.

***

"He told me the running of horses pleases God."

"The Old One."

"Who is the Old One?"

"He was."

"Who?"

"The Praying Man."

"Who am I?"

"You know."

"No, I don't."

***

He is a boy who feels like a girl. He tells no one, not even himself. He dares not say the words.

***

"He gave you the secret. He wants you to keep it alive."

"Who?"

"The Praying Man."

"Why?"

"If you do, I'll die. It will kill me." Bav Catha takes the pipe and smokes from it. "Do you love me?"

***

He spins the cylinder and clicks it shut, then pulls the hammer until he hears the familiar click. She shifts on the bed. Sunlight tattoos her shoulder.

He turns, opens the door to the bedroom with his free hand, and slides his stocking feet over the threadbare carpet. Pausing in the hallway, he glances back at his new wife. He pulls the door shut and walks away.

Outside, a breeze cruises over a sea of wild wheat. His heart pounds.

Blue sky.

Thump. Thump. Thump.

Yellow sun.

A cow lows in the distance.

***

"Do you think I'm beautiful?"

"Yes," I lied. I don't know why.

"I was with you."

"Where?"

"Always."

***

A buffalo scrapes the red dirt with a hoof. It snorts against the dying light. Its hide is pinkish, the mane blood-red in the light of the setting sun. The beast is dying.

***

"On the ridge. With the woman who wore white buckskins."

✳✳✳

A thin woman. Her hair black as blindness.

✳✳✳

"I sang her away."

"Why?"

"So you'd be with me." Bav Catha smokes from the pipe. "You must stay."

✳✳✳

Hands clasped under his chin, he prays. His hands tremble.

✳✳✳

I don't know how long it took for her to tell the story. It could have been a week or a lifetime. The smoke from the red pipe wiped away time like an eraser brushing black letters from a whiteboard. When Bav Catha entered the animal hide room and sat cross-legged in the center of the rug, I couldn't gauge when her last visit took place. She lit the red pipe and smoked a bowl before packing it fresh and handing it to me.

Sometimes, the hides came down from the walls, circled the buffalo rug, and swayed to a silent drumbeat. Other times, they hung motionless in place. They moved no more after coming down from the walls and carpeting the stone floor of the cave.

I don't know what happened to Raggedy Man. His dingy long johns were either gone or hidden underneath his new suit. The old cowboy boots had been replaced by shiny black lace-up shoes, the cowboy hat by a top hat. He looked like a butler out of one of the old stories. His topcoat matched his hat. White gloves hid his gnarled hands. He looked shorter in the get-up, not taller. It didn't make sense. But his face was the same.

The same sunken cheeks covered in a patchwork of thick stubble, some whiskers dark, others silver. A hawknose and deep-set grey eyes. It was him. It was Raggedy Man.

But maybe it wasn't. I couldn't be sure. I couldn't remember the last time I was sure of anything.

When Raggedy Man came into the room, carrying a tray of fruit and a pot of tea, he didn't acknowledge me. His gait was different. Stiff in the knees. I don't think he recognized me. I wanted to talk to him about Yew and Mud, but I couldn't. The words lodged in my throat like marbles swirling to a stop to clog the small end of a funnel. He'd enter the room without so much as a knock or a hello, set the tray on the three-legged stool, and turn around and leave. When the door swung shut behind him, I remembered no more.

Until Bav Catha's next return. I'd look up from the abyss and there she'd be, sitting on the buffalo rug, red pipe in hand. I wasn't alone anymore. So alone that I no longer existed. Bav Catha saved me from that. Nonexistence. I was grateful.

She didn't tell me anything straight out. That's not the way she worked. Instead, she told me snippets of stories that were all tied one way or another into Red Canyon. Aengus: that's what she called the man I found praying in the desert—the one who came from Red Canyon. I don't know if he was born there or if it was some kind of prison. Maybe he escaped and was on the run when he showed up at the Outpost. I don't know. When I found him, he was barely alive. The System—Mean Eyes and the others—not Yew, even when she was with them she was never really part of the System—despised praying. It threatened their authority. Mean Eyes would have liked to use the Snake Stick on me for saying I found a man praying in the desert. That's how much he hated the idea. He couldn't, though, because Yew was with him. She was like Bav Catha that way, always saving me. But I paid for it later—for all of that saving. Mean Eyes wasn't one to forget when someone got under his skin.

Yew wasn't threatened by the image of a man on his knees in the desert. I can remember how her shoulders relaxed when she stood up to leave my cell. I'm starting to remember things. But the memories don't seem like my own.

***

She smells of sweetwood.

***

The Praying Man reminded me of a hobo when I first saw him. He put me in mind of the Puerto Rican who showed up at the orchard every now and then when I was a kid. But the Praying Man was worse for the wear. He wasn't old like the Puerto Rican, but there was something old about him. An old soul. I think that's what I told them, Mean Eyes and the others. Yew. An old soul. That's what he was.

From what I could gather from Bav Catha's telling, the Praying Man was a lot older than any man could be, he just looked younger than his age. She said—or maybe implied—that he was an Old One in the flesh. But she never really made it clear what or who an Old One was. The way Bav Catha put it, the man she called Aengus came from somewhere outside of time, not the past or the future but outside of time altogether. Somehow he ended up in Red Canyon and got stuck. She never said where this place outside of time was. Every time I asked a question—and I asked a lot of them until I realized her answers were never answers, not even riddles, unless the answer to the riddle was Red Canyon itself—Bav Catha would say something like, "Listen," or "Is the baby in danger?" I don't know how long it took me to figure out that she wasn't in the business of answering questions. She was a storyteller, nothing more. For her, the story was the answer to every question. When I figured that out, I stopped asking.

I didn't believe her. Not at first. Why would I? Bav Catha has powers I don't understand—I get that much—but I figure she's more like one of the *brujas* the Puerto Rican warned me about, a woman mixed up in dark arts. The Puerto Rican never told me what the dark arts were, just to run like hell if I ever came across them. He said I'd know it when I crossed paths with a *bruja*. My instincts would sound the alarm. But I didn't run.

I don't think I would've run from Bav Catha even if I could have. Not then. I had no clue where Yew was. Without Yew, I had no place to go. Bav Catha wouldn't say a word about Yew, almost like she was afraid to say the name out loud. When I asked about what happened to Mud and Doc Waters, she'd ignore me or say something like, "The story knows."

I don't know how a story knows anything, but it seemed like Bav Catha thought the one she was telling did, and she said this part straight out, that the story was the meaning of History. Without the story, the entire universe was just a mishmash of brute facts strewn about like pebbles on a gravel road. Without the story, her story, the road didn't go anywhere and anybody on it was forever lost.

I didn't buy it. As far as I could tell, Bav Catha's story was just one more story that was supposed to make sense of things. But that didn't mean it made sense. She wanted the snippets to add up into one big whole by connecting them to Red Canyon. It didn't work. There was something missing.

It was the same with the System. Something missing. That's what their History really was: a series of attempts to cover up what was missing. Like plastering over a hole in a wall. The historians hoped that the people coming into their stories wouldn't notice the plaster patches under the fresh coat of paint of their words, or, if they did, they'd ignore them. The people needed a story as much as the historians needed to tell it. Without a story, the people would realize their lives were utterly meaningless in the vastness of time and space. They'd all fill up with despair until, one by one, they popped like pimples on the grinning face of oblivion. They'd either die laughing at the killing joke or jump, screaming, into the abyss. Only a few would be able to face the void and maintain sanity. Those few would build a System to save the others from the horror.

So, the people didn't think about the holes behind the plaster patches in the historied halls of the world. They listened to the storyteller who fit their needs. If they couldn't find a story that made sense, they made one up for themselves. They had to. Just like they had to pluck out their eyes to blind themselves from the truth: all the stories were about as real as raindrops splattering an endless plain of desert sand. Here and gone. Enough to sustain life for a blip but never enough to give *meaning* to life.

Sooner or later, the plaster cracked, and the holes in the wall were revealed. New plaster was brought in, new stories—myths, religions, philosophies—to patch them over once more. But the walls themselves were always being hollowed out by a species of termites that ate at the stories and left holes where the meaning should have been.

Each new story began by pointing out the holes in the stories that came before it. A never-ending game. But all games have to end. They can't go on forever. Nothing can. Everything must die.

It was the Founders of the System who first realized that the walls were rotting from within, being eaten by the termites of nothingness. They realized that no amount of plaster could hide the hollowness for long. So, they came up with a final solution. Tear down the wall and replace it with History.

***

The Puerto Rican once taught me how to play Blind Man's Bluff. He explained it to me the last time he showed up at the orchard. Dad ordered the trees to be cut down a few months later, and I never saw the Puerto Rican again once they were gone. We never actually played the game, but he taught me enough so I could imagine it in my head. He said it wouldn't be any fun with two people unless both of them were cheating. That might be worth a laugh when both players caught on to the game inside of the game—who was the better cheat?—but then it would be game over. What's the point of playing a game with no rules?

Storytellers are like that, playing games inside the game. Instead of a blind man trying to capture the sighted, storytellers attempt to attract the blind with the sound of their voices.

The game started with the designated blind man standing in a circle of players. The blind man tied a blindfold around his eyes and started counting to thirty. The other players—the Puerto Rican said there should be at least three others—spread out. They weren't allowed to run or jog. They had to walk. When the blind man got to thirty, the players froze. They couldn't take another step or they'd be disqualified. They kept an eye on each other. The blind man then called out, "Blind man!" The players called out "Bluff." And the game was on. The blind man walked around with his arms in front of him like a mummy in an old horror movie until he happened to touch a sighted player. The blind man then yelled, "My soul to keep."

I imagined playing the game in the orchard when the trees were in full leaf. I'd hide behind one of the trunks and listen to the breeze whisper through the branches. I'd ask the trees to protect me – I can say now that I prayed to them—from the blind man's touch. When the blind man came close, the players were allowed to move their bodies to avoid him. The only thing they weren't allowed to move was their feet. When the blind man came my way, I imagined myself merging with the tree trunk until I became part of the wood. The tree would allow it. When the blind man reached out to touch me, he'd feel nothing but the rough skin of a pecan tree and continue on his way.

I would've been good at that game. Too bad I never got to play it. I never got to play baseball, either. Just games on screens. Everything on screens. What a waste. There was lots of room in the orchard. It was a magic place. And then Dad had it all cut down.

When the blind man did manage to touch one of the players, the player froze and the blind man felt their face with his fingers and then guessed their name by yelling it out. If he got the name right, he took off the blindfold and kissed the player on the mouth before slapping him—or her—across the face and kneeling before them. The slapped player then took the bandana and re-tied it over the blind man's eyes. The blind man stood and counted to ten while the players moved to a new position on the playing field. It was game over for the slapped player. They had to find a place to sit and sulk.

If the blind man called out the wrong name—the Puerto Rican said it was a pretty common happening—all of the players, including the one that got touched, had ten seconds to move about before the blindfolded player called out "Blind man!" again. The players called back "Bluff!" Game on.

$$***$$

Storytellers play it backward. They see the whole story and offer bits and pieces to the blind players to string them along. At least they think they do. But they're wrong. I know that now. They're as blind as the audience they're trying to convince. But they either don't get it, can't admit it, or don't care. I haven't figured that part out yet.

The problem with Bav Catha's story—the thing she couldn't see—is that her version of Red Canyon was missing something. She has to make things up to fill in the gaps. I don't know how I know it, but I do. It's almost like I know Red Canyon better than Bav Catha. I remember Red Canyon. I've been there somehow, sometime. It's as simple as that.

Bav Catha sees herself as some kind of prophet. But prophecies aren't true unless they come to pass. If Bav Catha is the Prophet of Red Canyon, I am the Prophecy.

$$***$$

Understand.

$$***$$

The last time the big door swung shut behind Bav Catha, I didn't go blank. I found myself sitting in front of the stove, listening to the hiss of blue flames. It was the first time I realized Bav Catha was lying. Before that moment, I didn't believe her story, but at least I thought *she* did. You're still lying even when you're lying to yourself. But if you don't know you're lying, you're not really lying—you're just confused. Bav Catha went to a lot of trouble—too much trouble—trying to convince me that her story knew things that nobody could know. Not me. Not her. Nobody. She tried to convince me her story was unique, a living, breathing entity unlike any other. I wanted to believe. But something was missing. Bav Catha knew it. She tried to paint over the emptiness with the sound of her voice.

When Bav Catha hummed, the animal skins on the walls vibrated. There had been a human skin on the wall above the door the first time she hummed to us. I wasn't alone then. Doc Waters, Tinny, and Mud were with me. Bav Catha hummed and the human skin twitched to-and-fro, its boneless legs jerking about like they were two burlap sacks filled with writhing. Its face held no features—no mouth, no nose. Just eyes as black as the hole Bav Catha was trying to cover up with her song.

But the hole was always there. Bav Catha couldn't hum it away. The buffalo rug had holes where its eyes should have been. The eyes of the animal hides that slid from the walls to vibrate before Bav Catha as if she was some kind of a goddess were sewn shut. There were holes where the mouths should have been. Bav Catha was no goddess. She didn't know the Secret. She didn't know that holes are where the Holy One hides. The System figured it out. They thought that by embracing oblivion they could replace the Holy. They were wrong.

Bav Catha said it was the story that gave me the visions.

I remembered *the woman in the white buckskin taking a papoose from another woman before turning to me and saying, "Remember."*

I remembered *the mother pulling a flap of muskrat pelt away from a baby's face. The baby lay dead.*

I remembered *the woman saying "No, not dead," and then placing a bloody fingertip on the baby's forehead.*

I remembered. But the memories didn't come from smoking the red pipe or from drinking Bav Catha's special tea. They came from the story. That's what she wanted me to believe. For a long time, I didn't believe. That's where I went wrong.

***

Bav Catha grips the dagger, the smooth metal gleaming in the light flowing from somewhere above. Raggedy Man sits in the center of a cave in a chair made of driftwood. Cobwebs hang from the wood. Raggedy Man's spine is arched, his face tilted upward. His eyes are trained on the cylinder of light falling into the cave from above. His topcoat has been torn open, the shirt ripped from his chest. A silver crucifix attached to a silver chain hangs in the center of Raggedy Man's chest. Bav Catha carves a small piece of flesh from under Raggedy Man's nipple with the tip of the dagger. Blood trickles from the wound.

Bav Catha spears the flesh with the tip of the dagger, then holds it in the light. A single drop of blood falls to the stone floor. That's when she notices me standing at the entrance of the cave. She looks at me and places the morsel of flesh on her tongue and takes it into her mouth. She swallows and then licks a smear of blood from the dagger.

"Eat with me," she hisses.

***

The last time Raggedy Man left the animal hide room, he glanced over at me on his way out. His eyes, dull as dead ash, warmed for a moment—lived. The door opened silently before him. Before stepping through, he whispered, "Fly, fool." His voice was like raven wings in the air. The door swung shut.

The blankness did not descend. I remembered.

***

Raggedy Man's chest looks like that of a mummified corpse. His rib cage expands and contracts. The skin is tight around the bones. The wound under his nipple oozes.

Bav Catha points the tip of the dagger at me.

"Eat," she says. Her voice has changed. She sounds younger. "If not from him, another. You must eat to fulfill the foretelling."

Bav Catha's lost weight. When I knew her as Crow, she was a big round woman with a double chin and hair as gray as rainclouds. She wore a buckskin dress embroidered with red and black stick figures depicting deer and elk. The animals were forever running from stick men with bows and arrows. Her skin was the color of tree bark, a light reddish-brown. Her eyes were black.

Not now. It's the same woman—if that's what she is—but different. It's like I'm seeing her through someone else's eyes.

She carves another square of flesh from the opposite side of Raggedy Man's chest, pierces the flesh with the tip of the dagger, and places it in her mouth. She swallows and licks a smear from the dagger.

She's smaller now. The flap of skin under her chin is gone. Her hair looks like dusk. She wears a buckskin dress, but it's different. The figures on the buckskin are black. Instead of deer and elk, they depict human skulls. The stickmen with bows and arrows are no more.

Bav Catha's skin is smooth and dark as a ripe plum. Her eyes are the same as they were before. Black as holes. That's how I know it's her.

"Eat," she hisses.

"No," I say. The voice is not my own.

Bav Catha looks at me as I stand at the entrance of the cave. Her eyes narrow. "Eat. It's in the story."

"No."

I can feel the words in my throat—taste them on my tongue—but they're not my own.

"It's forbidden," says Bav Catha. "No one may enter this place and refuse me."

Bav Catha turns to Raggedy Man. She places the tip of the dagger between two ribs over his heart. "Would you spare him?"

"No," says the voice. It's not mine, but it comes from inside me, sounding like mine once did. When I was younger. When I was a boy on a ranch.

Bav Catha smiles. Her teeth are sharp and long. "Why?"

"It's just a dream."

Bav Catha's laughter sounds like a cauldron of bats erupting from a cave. "Even if it's a dream, I'm real. My dream. Am I dreaming you?"

"No."

She nudges the tip of the dagger into Raggedy Man's skin. A spot of blood rises to the surface.

"Yours?" asks Bav Catha. "Maybe. And maybe we're all dreaming each other."

I say, "There can only be one."

Placing the tip of her finger on the top of the dagger's pommel—each side of the silver handle is etched with a figure eight—she rocks the blade back and forth on Raggedy Man's chest. The wound widens.

"Yes," says Bav Catha. "One story."

I try to pry my eyes from the dagger, but can't. The cut on Raggedy Man's chest widens each time Bav Catha tips the blade—back and forth and back and forth—and the rhythm of the rocking becomes the pulse of the world.

"I can lead you to the Dreamer," whispers Bav Catha.

I step forward. "You can take me to Yew?"

Bav Catha smiles. "I'll take you to Red Canyon. Come. Come eat with me."

Bav Catha grabs the dagger by the hilt and holds it to her bosom. "Eat me."

Bav Catha has changed again. She's beautiful. Her eyes shine like oil slicks on still waters under a moon. Her skin, smooth as a child's, is the color of a black cherry sunset. Her hair falls to her shoulders in inky waves and her lips are as firm as ripe olives. The tip of the dagger rests between the curves of her breasts.

I take a step forward.

"Yes," whispers Bav Catha. "Listen."

***

Thump. Thump. Thump.

***

"It's for you."

***

Blue sky. Brown dirt. Raven's caw.

***

I long for her embrace, the taste of her breath. I long for her love.

***

Thump. Thump. Thump.

***

Remember.

***

Yellow sun.
Brown earth.

***

Raggedy Man sits erect. He looks at Bav Catha and grins the grin of a horror clown. "Not for you, my pretty girl—my pretty, ugly thing. Not today."

Bav Catha stands frozen, the hilt of the dagger in her hand, the tip of the blade between the swell of her breasts.

Raggedy Man removes the white glove from his hand finger by finger. "Everybody's got a part to play, large or small, thick or thin, full or empty." He reaches into his side, under the skin, and breaks a rib from his sternum. His lungs, now visible to the eye, expand and contract.

"Thence you came, and so you go. Lickety-split, burn."

I can't move. I can't speak. I look from the outside in.

The smile begins at the edges of Bav Catha's lips and widens into a grin. "You, my child? You would send me away?"

Raggedy Man holds his rib in hand. "Back to where you came from." He takes the dagger from Bav Catha with his free hand and eyes the figure eight on the pommel. "Forever ain't long enough for some things."

Raggedy Man shoves his rib into Bav Catha's heart. She looks at me. "All things return. But I'm not all things. I'm Bav Catha." Her laugh sounds like rain falling in a puddle. "I'm no thing. I will wait in Red Canyon."

"Wait for what?" I ask.

"For you."

And then she's gone.

Dust spills from the hole in Raggedy Man's chest. He looks at me and says, "Fly away, fool."

***

When the door to the animal hide room opened after Raggedy Man had been gone for a time—I have no idea how long—I knew I had to leave. I don't know how or why I knew—call it intuition—but I did. So, I walked out. The door swung shut behind me. I wandered through the dark until

I came to another cave and found Raggedy Man sitting on a driftwood chair. Bav Catha held a dagger under a light falling from somewhere above. That's what I was after. The dagger and the light. It was what I'd been after all along, a light in the shadows. And then they were gone. Bav Catha and Raggedy Man. Like they'd never been there at all.

It seemed like I'd been in the darkness for years. Maybe I had been. I took the dagger with the figure eight on the hilt from the pile of dust that was once Raggedy Man.

I had no map to guide me through the stone halls that led Outside. I had no clue as to where I was. No context. But my mind wasn't blank. Not like it had been. I had a goal even if I couldn't name it. I had a purpose, even if I didn't know what it was. Being night-blind didn't worry me. I'd just feel my way through.

I turned to leave the cave and spotted a spider in the cobwebs under the chair. I walked to the chair, knelt, and looked at the arachnid clinging to a single thread of web. It was black with a bulbous body. It had the golden outline of a figure eight on its underbelly. Bav Catha had been there. It was no dream. No apocalyptic vision. No trick of the mind. There was a story, and I was in it. One story, not many. We were all in it. Then and now. But where is the storyteller?

I thought about crushing the life out of the spider but thought better of it. I left it there under the chair. Alive.

I had a purpose. Yew. I walked away from the caves and into the light. I found myself in need of a horse.

CHAPTER FOUR

The faerie said, "Let there be mud."

And there was mud. And Mud lived.

A glowing orb sat on the ground at his feet at the edge of a pool of water. It shone like moonlight.

"Where am I?" said Mud.

Light from the orb glanced from Mud's dark eyes. He studied his reflection on the surface of the water, a silhouette not of a man but of something else, something between man and beast. Wondering if the reflection was his own, he looked around the cave. He was alone, except for the faerie. But her reality was too slight to cast a reflection on the water.

"You mean *we*, don't you? Where are we?" asked the faerie. She stood on a flat rock on the far side of the pool. The pool was in the center of a cave. The faerie's green pantsuit shimmered like a jewel in the darkness.

"What am I?"

"You are Mud."

Looking at his feet, he found them to be covered in hair, as were his hands, legs, and arms. He felt his face. The fur was coarse and dense and brown. It reminded him of the buffalo he had butchered in the desert. He felt for the fold of skin that held the buffalo tongue and was relieved to find it tucked in his belt.

"Am I a man?"

When the faerie laughed, her bright orange hair shivered on her tiny skull. Her eyes, blue as the blossoms on a sea holly, sparkled. "More than a man," she chuckled. "Or less."

Mud remembered his Uncle Sammy. He was the one who had told him about the faerie. But it was only a story. It wasn't real.

***

His uncle creeps into his room and whispers, "Wake up."

"Huh?"

"He's gone. Erased. Never coming back." The uncle's breath smells like fermented honey. "You're next. Like father, like son. All of us. Me. We have to go. Now."

"Am I dreaming?"

"This ain't no goddamn dream, boy" growls the uncle. "He never should have ratted her out about those books. Get your ass in gear. Like we practiced. If they get us, you'll never dream again. No more stories. No you. Do you hear? Now!"

***

"No," says the faerie. "You're not dreaming. Not really. Maybe a little. Who knows for sure?" She rises into the air and hovers over the water. "Do you remember?"

"Remember what?"

"The white whale?"

"Yes," says Mud. "I remember. Mother read it to me when I was a kid."

"She feared the whale." The faerie, her skin smooth and white as living lace, glides over to Mud and perches on his shoulder. "But she loved you."

"Who?"

"Your mother."

"I know."

"Your father hated the whale. Fear is different from hate. She was right to fear him."

"Did she? Why did she keep the books?"

"She loved you."

"I know."

"Do you?"

"What?"

"Fear the whale?"

"Yes." He turns his head and looks the faerie in the eye. "Are you real?"

The faerie trills. Her voice sounds like birdsong.

The orb brightens at Mud's feet.

"Is the whale real?" asks the faerie.

"I don't know."

"It was real enough for her to read it to her only son."

"Contraband books," said Mud. "Forbidden."

"He told on her because he was jealous. Do you understand?"

"Of what? Me?"

"The story. You."

"He was Ahab?"

"No. It was just a story. He couldn't be in it." The faerie launches from Mud's shoulder and hovers over the pool. "And you?"

Mud kneels next to the glowing orb. He holds his hairless palms over the light as if to warm them. There's a plop in the pool. It's the splash of a fish rising above the world before diving once more into the depths.

＊＊＊

The boy steals four eggs from a henhouse and carries them to camp. He hands an egg to his Uncle Sammy. They haven't eaten in days. Uncle Sammy is fading, surrendering to the sunlight that burns away all. He sits next to an outcropping of sandstone.

"Where'd you get these, boy?" He reaches out and takes an egg. He holds it in front of his eyes as if it's a trinket found at a flea market.

"There are some houses down there a ways on the banks of a dry wash. Corrals and chicken coops. I saw a black cow."

"Oh," says Uncle Sammy. "I didn't know you were gone. Must have dozed off." He looks up at the boy standing next to him. "Hot, ain't it?"

"Sure is."

"Hotter than a two-peckered goat." Uncle Sammy looks at the egg. "They got any water down at them houses?"

"I drank out of a goat trough," says the boy. He watches a green fly with long legs walk over his Uncle Sammy's sunburned skull. "Didn't think to bring the canteen. I'll go back and get some if you want."

"No. Not now. You're lucky you got back with these eggs. System'll have a bounty on us. The people who live out here ain't too keen on the System, but they won't turn up their nose at the bounty. They give us over and maybe the System'll leave 'em in peace for a few more years."

Uncle Sammy takes a pebble from the ground and taps it on the top of the egg until the shell cracks. "Wait till it gets dark and we'll go down and fetch some of that water. Sit down here and eat."

The boy sits next to his uncle.

Uncle Sammy sucks the egg out of the shell and into his throat.

***

"Heliooooo."

"Huh?" Mud looks up from the orb. The faerie is a green speck of light on the far side of the pool.

"Commioooo."

Mud cradles the orb in his palms and stands. "What? Where? Back to Crow?"

"Too late," chirps the faerie. "Do you ever wonder about those people?

***

The orb burned like a candle in a world where the light was dark and the dark was light.

***

"What people?"

"The ones who kept the black cow."

"Not really. Figure they faded away like everything else. We come across an old cabin where we found that dying buffalo. That's the only sign of 'em left."

"Nooooooiooo!" whistles the faerie.

It occurs to Mud that the faerie is part bird.

The faerie whisks back across the pool and floats eye-level in front of Mud's face. "She's with them. She hasn't faded. Her story is strong."

"Who?"

"But she thinks she has."

"Who?"

"You know."

"Yew?"

The faerie trills.

"Where, then? Where is she?"

"With People."

"Who?"

"Cactus Eaters."

"The ones who killed Wheeze?" asks Mud. "They cut him all up."

"Comiiooooooo." The faerie whizzes to the far side of the pond.

"To Yew? Through the water?"

"Through the deep." The faerie darts to the center of the pool and shoots down into the water. The splash sounds like that of a jumping fish.

Mud cradles the orb in his palms. The glow weakens, and the orb grows heavier. He steps into the water. The orb, black as the cave's belly, drags him into the depths.

He sees a green glow below him in the darkness—a spark of light.

***

The whale rises.

CHAPTER FIVE

Tinny rides with Mean Eyes. Engines from a fleet of dune buggies churn behind them. He wears the uniform of a System soldier. The embroidered patch on his shoulder—a series of four golden concentrical circles with a red dot in the center—designates him as a captain in the Desert Marines.

Mean Eyes drives. The patch on his arm is that of a lieutenant. He wears his hair cropped short. His eyes are narrow and blue under the permanent frown carved into his brow.

Thirty dune buggies rumble behind in a cloud of dust. There are three columns of ten buggies each. Behind the buggies comes a convoy of armored trucks. Some of the trucks are as big as barns. Metal tubes connected to metal boxes are bolted to the roofs of trailers being pulled behind the trucks. The boxes buzz, electric. Bursts of black smoke spout from exhaust pipes on the tractors as drivers shift up and down to negotiate the dunes of sand. Smaller trucks bristling with weaponry flank the big trucks. The sound of machinery encloses the convoy. As the trucks pass, silence falls over creosote, mesquite, and yucca.

The air clears. When the last of the trucks disappear over a dune, a man emerges from behind a stand of desert willow and watches. He's dressed in wolf skins. He sniffs the air. Diesel exhaust stings his nostrils. He turns and jogs into the southwest.

***

"Gettin' threatened with erasure makes things look different," yells Tinny over the sound of the engine. "I guess I had one of them moments you hear about. Old-timers called 'em 'Come to Jesus moments.' " He stands in the dune buggy, holding the roll bar with both hands.

"Yeah?" shouts Mean Eyes. "I've heard that. Never understood what it meant. Come to Jesus. Coming back from the dead and all that. Stupid. Takes more than an idiot to believe that one. Takes a crazy. "

Tinny wipes his goggles with a glove. Dust smears the lens. The desert blurs. "I can tell you what it means." He lowers himself in the passenger seat and removes his goggles and then his gloves. "It means you've found the motherlode."

"Yeah?" yells Mean Eyes. He grips the steering wheel in both hands. The muscles in his arms bulge. "Motherlode of what?"

Tinny licks a lens of the goggle and wipes it with his shirt. "There's only one kind." He licks the opposite lens and repeats the process.

The sky is blue. Cloudless. Sunshine coats the desert in a shimmer of heat.

The pitch of the motor tightens as Mean Eyes shifts into a lower gear. "Grace me with your wisdom," he yells.

"Security," shouts Tinny, and wind pelts his face. He puts on the goggles, grabs the roll bar above his head, and pulls himself into a standing position. The landscape is still a sandy blur. He sits down in the passenger seat and removes the goggles once more.

"Security?"

"Yes!" yells Tinny, the wind elongating the syllable. "Security. People call it by different names. I thought it'd be like a lost treasure buried out here in the desert. You know, emeralds and diamonds and all that." He attempts to steam the lens of the goggle with his breath. The wind evaporates the moisture before it can form on the plexiglass. "I was wrong. You've gotta surrender yourself to it if you want to get to it. You don't take it. It's given."

Mean Eyes trains his eyes on a glint of sunshine on metal in the distance.

"It was right in front of me the whole time." Tinny lifts the bottom of his shirt and pulls the green T-shirt from under his belt. He licks one lens of the goggles and wipes it clean. "There's only one chance at finding it." Putting on the goggles, he looks over to Mean Eyes. He can see him clearly. "Wanna know what it is?"

"I can't wait," shouts Mean Eyes. "The System."

Mean Eyes takes a two-way radio from a clip on the dash. "That's it? That's the motherlode?"

"Yeess!" shouts Tinny over the noise of the motor and the wind. "The System!"

Mean Eyes yells into the radio, "Rashay. Can you hear me?"

A voice crackles over a speaker on the dash, "Yessir! Rachet here!"

"Circle 'em, Rashay. We're stopping here," yells Mean Eyes.

"Yessir."

Mean Eyes snaps the radio into the clip under the dash. Then, he turns to Tinny. "You best hope he's still there. If he ain't, you can kiss your newfound captain rank goodbye. It was just a ruse to get you to show us the way. They'll erase you if you're wrong. Make me a captain like they should've done a long time ago."

***

A metal shack stands to one side of the road. The frame is falling in on itself, grey paint flaking from the corrugated metal walls. A woman bent with age steps out of the shack. She uses a dried stalk of yucca as a cane. She's wearing a dress made of burlap, and her face is hidden in a scarf the color of sand.

A gust of wind moans through cracks and crevices in the dilapidated shack. Behind the moan, the woman hears a distant rumble. At first, she thinks it's the sound of thunder and steps out of the shack to look at the sky. Blue to the horizons. Cloudless. Sunshine coats the desert in a shimmer of heat. The rumble grows louder. The woman smiles. Most of her teeth are gone. The few that remain cling to gray gums.

A cloud of dust swells on the eastern horizon. The old woman touches the tip of her tongue on her remaining front tooth. Closing her mouth, she swirls her tongue over her gums. She manages to work up a pea of saliva. She spits yellowish goo into the dust at her feet.

The rumble grows louder. A mechanical hum measured by pistons pumping.

"I thirst," whispers the woman. The words are devoured in a gust of wind.

She knew they would come. Foresaw it. There could be no other way. Still, it's not as it should be, something is missing. Leaning on the yucca stalk, she shuffles onto the cracked surface of the road, the asphalt all but disintegrated by the cadence of time. She peers from under her scarf as the System patrol approaches.

***

Mean Eyes spots the old woman. It was he, not Tinny, who gave the command to come over the sand in order to avoid the eroded highway. The Cactus Eaters would have had scouts on the road. Catching a group of Cactus Eaters requires an element of surprise. They might still hear the approach of the buggies coming over the sand and scatter, but it would be too late. They would be too close. The Cactus Eaters would burrow into the dunes, crouch behind clumps of salt bush, or blend into shadows cast down by desert willow. They would wait for the System soldiers to tire of searching for them and leave. That was the game they were familiar with, the one they almost always won. But Mean Eyes has a new weapon. The so-called captain doesn't know about it. He's the bait, not the trap.

The location of the shack is nothing new. It's on the maps, but there's something about the lone figure on the road that makes Mean Eyes uneasy.

"Who's that?" he yells.

"I don't know," shouts Tinny. "Maybe it's her."

"Who?"

Tinny stands in the dune buggy and hangs onto the roll bar. "The woman I told them about. Crow. Didn't they tell you?"

Mean Eyes slows the buggy. The columns slow to a crawl behind them, the growl of the truck engines quieting to a purr. Mean Eyes knows about Crow. He was informed. But he didn't believe it. A woman with the power to call animal skins down from the walls where they hung to dance before her? Really? There had always been rumors of such tricksters inhabiting the desert. Legends about dark spirits with dark appetites spun up by old bounty hunters to scare off would-be competitors. Stories. Nothing more. Bounty hunters were opportunists. No discipline. They wanted the best of both worlds—the System and the Outside. They got neither because they were liars.

Mean Eyes slows the buggy to a halt and cuts the engine. The columns of buggies behind him, without a word of command, do the same.

"Why are we stopping?" Tinny removes his goggles. The lenses are covered in dust.

"Something's wrong." Mean Eyes takes the radio from the clip on the dash and presses a button. "Rashay."

A voice crackles from the radio. "Yessir."

"Get one of the dogs ready."

"Yessir."

Mean Eyes clicks the radio back in the clip on the dash. "I thought she'd be bigger." He unstraps himself from the driver's harness and steps out of the buggy.

"She is. She can be as big as she wants," says Tinny. "She's tricky. I'd be careful if I were you." He steps out of the dune buggy and looks toward the shack.

Mean Eyes takes a pair of binoculars from under the driver's seat. He studies the shack through the glasses. Corners of loose sheet metal on the roof waggle in a gust of breeze. Sand moves, serpentine, over the derelict road. The woman on the asphalt appears to be alone. She's small and bent. Mean Eyes imagines her to be old, but he can't be sure. The woman's face is hidden by a scarf the color of sand, her limbs invisible under a loose-fitting burlap dress. He zooms in on the woman's hand clutching the dried yucca stalk. The skin is scaled like a reptile's, the color of pecan shells splotched with black. Moving the focus of the glasses lower, he finds the woman's feet bare upon the ruined road, her big toes cracked and bleeding. She stands still as a stone. He can feel her looking at him.

***

They will betray you.

***

Mean Eyes lowers the binoculars and shivers in the rising heat.

***

Only me. I'll be true.

***

"What?" asks Mean Eyes, turning to Tinny. "What did you say?"

Rachet approaches the buggy. He's followed by what looks to be a mechanical dog the size of a large wolf. The machine is four-legged and sports an angular jaw full of teeth fashioned from polished metal. The body is covered with synthetic fur the color of dead leaves. The eyes pulse red. Machine-like, it lurches towards Tinny.

"What the hell is that?" asks Tinny.

Mean Eyes smiles. "Say hello to my little friend." He looks at Tinny, and his smile grows wider. "Don't worry. She won't hurt you. Unless Rashay there tells her to. Then, she'll rip you apart."

Rachet kills the engine of the buggy, steps out, and marches to Mean Eyes. "Reporting as ordered, sir." The mechanical dog sits in the sand at his side. It watches Tinny. "The men are awaiting orders."

Tinny can't tell if Rachet is male or female, the voice is somewhere in between.

"Good show, Rashay," says Mean Eyes. "I'd like to introduce you to our esteemed Captain. You two haven't had the chance to get acquainted, have you?"

"No, sir," says Rachet.

"He's so new, nobody recognizes him," says Mean Eyes, smiling. "We took him prisoner at the gate. Remember?"

Tinny looks at the mechanical dog looking at him.

"Yessir," says Rachet.

"And now he's a captain. *Our* captain. Isn't that just wonderful?"

"Sir," says Rachet.

"What?"

Rachet points in the direction of the metal shack. "She's coming."

Mean Eyes and Tinny turn to look. The woman in the burlap dress is moving toward them. She glides over the desert.

"Good," says Mean Eyes. "Now I don't have to make the first move. Turn it loose."

"Sir?" asks Rachet.

"You heard me, Rashay. Turn loose the war dog!"

Rachet looks at the dog and then at Tinny. "Shouldn't we wait to see if she comes in peace? Isn't that protocol?"

Mean Eyes spins and faces Rachet. "They're liars. All of them. I said to turn the damn thing loose. Do it."

Rachet says, "But the woman might have useful information."

A dust devil the size of a man materializes out of the sand. It spins alongside the woman as she glides toward them.

Mean Eyes turns and watches the woman. "Let the beast loose! She's going to kill us. Can't you see that?"

Rachet removes a remote from a back pocket on his uniform. He offers it to Mean Eyes.

Tinny watches as a new dust devil, larger than the first, twirls out of the sand. It travels on the opposite side of the woman.

Mean Eyes turns and snatches the remote from Rachet. "Coward." He turns back toward the woman. "Get a load of this, you lousy bitch."

"Wait!" yells Tinny. "Don't do it! That's an order!"

Mean Eyes pauses. He looks at Tinny, the snarl on his face relaxing. "What?"

"You said it yourself; I'm the one in charge here," says Tinny. "I'm the one giving the orders."

Looking at the woman and then at Tinny, Mean Eyes hands over the remote. "Okay. You sick it on her. Hurry!"

Tinny tosses the remote to Rachet. "Get this all in a report. I want to see it before it's filed. Understand?"

Sliding the remote into his pocket, Rachet says, "Yessir."

"I'll be filing a report too," says Mean Eyes. "If we're still alive when this is over. I'm surrounded by fools!"

The woman in the burlap dress glides to the front of the lead dune buggy and hovers there like a feather falling forever from a fathomless sky. The dust devils collapse into piles of sand on either side of her. Two lizards—one yellow-headed with a red body, the other redheaded with a yellow body—emerge from the piles of sand. They grow until they're as large as the mechanical war dog. The lizards blink in unison. Their eyes are black.

The woman in burlap strokes each of the lizards on the snout with the tip of her yucca stalk cane. Forked tongues whip in and out of lizard lips.

"Crow?" asks Tinny.

"That's what you say." The woman pulls the scarf from her face. Her eyes are milky. "He calls me Bav Catha now."

"Who?" asks Tinny.

A raven appears on the western horizon. The woman smiles, and her lower lip cracks. She licks blood from the wound with the tip of her tongue.

"You heard him," says Mean Eyes. He pulls the Snake Stick from a sheath on his belt and extends it with a flip of his wrist. "Who are you?"

The woman gazes at the columns of dune buggies lined up behind Rachet. The milkiness in her eyes is replaced with shadow, her smile with a sneer. "Enough to find but not to bind."

"Who?" repeats Tinny. "Who calls you Bav Catha?"

Mean Eyes takes a step toward the woman. "Tell me. Where is he? I know you know who I'm talking about. It'll be easier if you just spill it. No fuss, no pain." He takes another step and slaps the Snake Stick against his palm.

"You called him Puppet Man, remember?" asks the woman. The words tumble from her mouth like dislodged teeth. "He's not who she wants him to be. Not yet."

"Who? Yew?" asks Tinny. "Where is she?"

The woman laughs.

Mean Eyes takes another step and presses a button at the base of the Snake Stick. "We ain't going to hurt him. I promise. Not *much* anyways. Nothing ever hurts as bad as you think it will anyway."

The woman's laugh becomes a fit of coughing. She bends low and clutches at her stomach.

"She's just an old woman, sir," says Rachet. "The use of force is unwarranted."

Mean Eyes takes another step forward. "If she tells us where he is, it won't be needed. Otherwise, a little jolt is all it will take."

"No!" shouts Tinny. "Don't!"

The woman in burlap stands straight. Her coughing transforms into laughter. Her face is now hidden behind a square wooden mask painted black. Two rectangular eyes, a triangle nose, and an oval mouth are painted white on the black face. A pair of large raven wings sprout from her skull. Her burlap dress transforms into the skin of a white buffalo. Her bosom fills out. She holds a basket woven from datura leaves in one hand. It's impossible to say if she is young or old.

Rachet falls to his knees. "Crow Mother."

"Crow?" asks Tinny.

The woman looks at Mean Eyes and caws.

Mean Eyes, Snake Stick in hand, freezes.

The woman turns her gaze first to Tinny and then to Rachet. "The baby's not safe," she says.

Rachet, his head bowed, whispers, "It's not possible. You're just a doll. A kachina. Not real. A myth handed down by my grandmother's grandmother. Nothing more."

"No thing," says the old woman. "The baby's in danger. She's near."

"Who?" asks Tinny.

"Yew."

"Where's the Puppet Man?" asks Tinny. "The one who came with us. Is he in the caves?"

"Not here."

"Where?"

"Red Canyon."

Rachet stands. "This can't be real." He takes the remote from his pocket and pushes a button.

The mechanical dog stands and lurches toward the woman.

"Where is Red Canyon?" asks Tinny.

The war dog picks up speed, its mouth a glint of steel.

The woman caws. The dog slows. She caws once more, and the contraption is paralyzed in the sand. A third caw causes the machine to collapse.

The woman called Crow caws once again.

Mean Eyes falls to pieces. First his arms, then his head.

A puff of smoke rises from the war dog's metal ears. Rachet drops the remote.

"Machines aren't real," says the woman. "Manmade."

A pile of red sand where Mean Eyes stood moments before.

"Neither are the men who follow them."

"Who are you?" asks Tinny.

"Who do you *say* I am?"

"Crow?"

"The baby is in danger."

"In Red Canyon?" asks Rachet.

"Yes."

"Where?" asks Tinny.

The woman sets the basket woven from yucca leaves at her feet. She lifts a white orb from the basket. The egg-sized ball is oblong. It rises from her palms and floats. It moves to Rachet and hovers before his chest.

"Take it," says Crow. "It will show you the way."

Rachet touches the orb with the tip of a finger. A pulse of energy, light and pleasant, shoots up his arm and into his chest. Smiling, he takes the orb in his hands.

"Kill one to save the other," says Crow.

"The baby?" asks Tinny.

"Fool," spits the woman.

Rachet stares into the orb. "Yew," he says

"The baby?" repeats Tinny.

The woman coughs.

"Cactus Eaters," says Rachet. "She's with Cactus Eaters. Hundreds of them. Thousands."

The coughing sounds like a flock of squawking seagulls. Crow bends low and then stands erect. Her face is hidden in the folds of her scarf.

Tinny spots a brown cloud on the horizon behind. "Which way?" he asks.

Rachet, his eyes trained on the orb, says, "Into the cloud."

"Great," says Tinny. He turns to ask Crow about the Puppet Man and finds only a heap of sand where she once stood. The lizards, now brown and the size of small sticks, stand blinking.

"Captain?" asks Rachet. He holds the orb in his hands like a child cradling a dying bird.

"What?"

"They're dancing."

"Who?"

"The Cactus Eaters."

"Is Yew with them?"

"Yes."

Tinny breathes deep. "Okay. Get the men ready."

"Yessir. Shall I tell them where we're going?"

"West," says Tinny. "We're going to war."

CHAPTER SIX

Doc Waters walks. He walks with Cactus Eaters through the desert. The moon waxes and wanes. He walks until all is one. He learns to smell water long before they come upon hidden springs. He senses a windstorm days before it arrives. He learns on his own to identify fruits of the desert—tunas of cacti, yucca root, agave, beans of mesquite. He understands not by words but by watching Cactus Eaters, by listening. He tunes in to the moment. The past is gone. The future is but a dream. Doc Waters is at peace.

In the rhythm of light and darkness—walking and resting, drinking and eating—Doc Waters understands the sound of silence. He is empty. In the emptiness, he comes upon the source of all things. It's not an object, something that can be tasted or grasped. It cannot be corralled into language. It's a silence that teaches about desert plants, teases with the scent of water, alerts him to oncoming storms. In this silence, the Cactus Eaters dwell. Doc Waters hears them thinking. They do not think in words, not emotion, but in silence. He comes to understand. He's at peace.

Sunrise reveals. Sunset conceals. Nighttime breathes.

Silence.

***

The Cactus Eaters, a woman and two men, navigate the darkness as if they are equipped with night vision goggles developed by the System to help in hunting the Cactus Eaters down.

Many of the Cactus Eaters had been rounded up in the wild when the System seized power. The captives were held like cattle inside electrified razor wire fences where they were processed and conformed. They were fed liquefied synthetic proteins poured into long troughs inside the cages. The hair was cut from their heads. They got scrubbed with stiff brushes and outfitted in orange jumpsuits. Collars locked around their necks.

The collars were equipped with metal prods capable of sending electric shocks. The System attempted to teach the Cactus Eaters discipline. They attempted to make them accept their name: Cactus Eaters.

They failed.

They remained People.

Two-thirds of the captives died during the first six months. The System doctors couldn't figure out why. The Cactus Eaters were physically healthy. They willingly sucked the liquified protein from the troughs. The slop contained the vitamins and minerals required for their bodies to function. The majority of the blood tests and stool samples came back clean. The doctors ran more tests. They checked ears and throats, listened to hearts, and sent a representative sample of Cactus Eaters through a barrage of machines that monitored everything from brainwaves to liver functions. The Cactus Eaters appeared to be unusually healthy.

Brain scans revealed enlarged olfactory regions. That made sense to the doctors. The Cactus Eaters were more animal than human, but that wouldn't impact their overall health. They might have been useful as beasts of burden if they hadn't started dropping into comas and dying.

The few Cactus Eaters who failed the physical exams—some with congenital diseases, others with blood disorders, some with calcified livers—

were terminated, their bodies liquified and added to the Cactus Eaters' troughs. The System abhorred waste. Diseased Cactus Eaters could give them no return on their investment. It made no sense to keep them. The System loathed nonsense. All things were required to make sense.

The initial plan had been to roundup as many Cactus Eaters as possible, conform them, and train them as citizen-servants. The word *slave* had been prohibited decades before the System came into power, and they were careful not to revive it. The Council of Language came up with the phrase *citizen-servant*. *Slave* would have been more accurate, but the word carried derogatory connotations that could arouse resentment in the population at large. Many of the citizens, let alone citizen-servants, might decide to characterize themselves as *slave* if the word were to be used freely. Some would inevitably realize that's what they were: slaves to the System. The stuff of revolutions.

By granting conformed Cactus Eaters the status of *citizen-servant*, the System was able to elevate the concept of citizenship while preventing the Cactus Eaters from full access to society. Problem solved.

When the Cactus Eaters threw a wrench into the plan by falling into comas and dying en masse, the System decided to exterminate them all. It was a pragmatic decision. The resources required to outfit the roundups were substantial. The electrified compounds costly. The liquefied protein and medical tests had failed. Senior System officials decided that slaughtering the remaining Cactus Eaters would be more economical than sending them Outside where they could compete with the System for natural resources.

The Cactus Eaters were led into air-tight Quonset huts and gassed. The corpses were blended into batches of liquefied protein and sent to Re-Education Centers to feed the incarcerated, an efficient manner of recouping some of the costs.

The System then began sending out patrols to exterminate Cactus Eaters they had failed to round up.

Doc Waters, though not a senior member of the System at the time, had been consulted about the Cactus Eaters. He had agreed with the plans. It was his opinion that because Cactus Eaters had been officially designated as less than human, they merited none of the rights of System citizens. The Cactus Eaters were simply wild animals that couldn't be tamed. Like rabid dogs, it made sense to put them down.

Cactus Eaters in the wild were a nuisance and couldn't be allowed to reproduce. The effort to exterminate them, however, failed. They were too cunning in their natural element. They fought back. The extermination campaign was deemed too costly. But, still, the Cactus Eaters couldn't be allowed to roam freely. They had to be constantly culled to prevent them from competing for resources. There was no need to waste System Loyals when the task could be handed off to misfits who didn't fit naturally into the System.

There were some men who still yearned for Outside, felt the primordial call, but could not do without the comforts of civilization. The Cactus Eater Problem, as it came to be called, would be left to these men. Bounty hunters. Bounty hunters were more akin to the Cactus Eaters than the System, but they found purpose and reward in tracking down their spiritual brothers and hacking them down.

It was an efficient solution. Bounty hunters were rewarded only for the number of Cactus Eaters they could prove they had killed. The common mode of proof was bringing in scalps that were then tested in labs to determine they were from Cactus Eaters who were distinguished by a unique protein found only in their DNA. No proof, no pay. It was this efficiency that prompted Doc Waters to pen a favorable review of the plan.

***

The desert now silenced the monsters living in Doc Waters' mind. He had convinced himself that the devils were figments of his father's tortured imagination. Imagination, when allowed, attaches to consciousness like mistletoe to oak. The monsters, like mistletoe, were parasites.

In his father's case, imagination stole the nutrients necessary for maintaining a healthy mind. His father attempted to exorcise his demons by writing stories. But it only made the demons stronger. They inhabited the nether region between reality and shadow where they spun quilts of melancholy to cover the windows of sanity. Imagination usurped reality.

Doc Waters had spent a lifetime running from inherited monsters. The psychologists told him the condition was a genetic predisposition to clinical depression. They prescribed medications, and he took them in the hope they would drive the monsters away.

***

There is no hope in madness.

***

It worked for a time. The monsters went into hiding like seasoned tribal warlords withdrawing into deep caves to outwait the enemy. When his body built up a tolerance to a drug, he was prescribed a new one and then combinations of drugs until, instead of monsters, he was haunted by a perpetual fog. He no longer felt much of anything and went through the motions of living like an automaton programmed for the mundane. The drugs were prescribed by doctors who saw themselves as professional mechanics hired to fix broken machines. They translated Doc Waters into an object. He was transformed into the drugs he was ingesting.

He began to see himself as a monster. And then he came upon a promising cure. A new philosophy. The Philosophy of Oblivion. It was a philosophy that could conquer monsters. It was this philosophy that made Doc Waters a dangerous man.

The System convinced Doc Waters that it had reduced reality to the computations of materiality. Thoughts were products of chemical reactions—synapses firing. Nothing more. Ghosts and monsters weren't real. Life was a predictable process and consciousness was a matter for algorithmics.

The sacrifice of imagination amplified logic. Efficiency, the progeny of excessive rationality, was ushered in as a new God. Stripped of mystery, faith became a mathematical equation. When the sum of the equation turned out to be less than zero—nothing at all—the Philosophy of Oblivion took its seat on the throne.

Not in the desert. Silence erased philosophy. The machinations of calculation—a constant ticking of thoughts flung out like a fishing net over a void—was no match. In silence, Doc Waters encountered mystery anew. It was vaguely familiar, a child's hope long forgotten and remembered only in the noonday of life. It had no substance, but he sensed it behind the moonlight falling over the red blossoms of ocotillo. It had no scent, but there were traces of it behind whiffs of creosote carried by the occasional puff of breeze. It hid under the trails of lizard tails traced in the sand at his feet, beneath the buzz of black flies and bees. He sensed it in under the rabbit tracks disappearing into clumps of salt brush. It was more than belief. More than faith. It was a mystery that breathed.

He sensed it in the Cactus Eater ritual of preparing meals. Though he wasn't able to make out a pattern at first, he sensed he was witnessing mystery in motion as one of the three gang members pulled a dried cake from a bag, broke off a chunk, and crumbled it into a pot of simmering water. The cook then took a wooden spoon—each of the gang had their own—and stirred the pot. Four swirls to the right, four to the left, seven repetitions of four times in all.

The ritual complete, the cook removed the pot and placed it on the ground. Cactus Eaters gathered around the pot and sat on their haunches. They began to sing.

One evening—he would never remember which, as one day blurred into the next—Doc Waters joined with the singing. He didn't know what the words meant, but he had heard them enough to mimic the sounds.

The Cactus Eaters fell silent. They turned their eyes on him as one. They growled, guttural. The woman stood and drew a dagger from her belt, the blade made of chipped chert. She walked over to Doc Waters and looked down.

Doc Waters stood. The woman took him by the wrist and sliced his forearm with the blade of the dagger. She pulled his arm over the pot and watched the blood drip into the steaming soup.

The pot was passed around among the gang. The woman drank last. When she was finished, she handed the pot to Doc Waters. He took the pot between his palms. It was empty.

The next morning, they didn't prepare a meal. They rested in the shadows of an outcropping of granite. Then, in the evening, they walked.

The walking, too, was a ritual. Each evening one of the three Cactus Eaters took the lead. One evening the woman, the next the smaller man, and then the large. Or the small one, the woman, and then the large. The leader took the lead not by agreement but by the desert calling. The other two fell into place behind. Doc Waters brought up the rear. It was understood by all that if Doc Waters fell behind and lost the gang he would die.

Some evenings, the wind bent mesquite limbs parallel to the ground. By nightfall, the wind slowed to a breeze. Yucca, white blossoms popping in starlight, shivered. Lizards sheltered under slabs of sandstone.

Some nights, the wind didn't slow. It whipped up dust like an enormous herd of buffalo galloping over a parched stretch of drought-dry earth. Burrowing owls huddled underground and waited. The Cactus Eaters, the legs of their wolf pelts tied tight around their necks, kept walking, their heads bowed into the wind.

Other evenings, the air was completely still. The group of four walked in the twilight, their heads high and their backs straight. Bats jagged through the gloaming. They reminded Doc Waters of Japanese kamikaze pilots of World War II. The System had forced him to watch hours of the archival footage in black and white, the grainy film projected onto a screen that revealed human corpses strewn in streets, people scurrying like insects between buildings cracked and broken by bombs. Doc Waters watched as prisoners in concentration camps, thin as fish bones, were led into chambers. In the distance, columns of black smoke rose.

The System showcased film footage of Hitler gesticulating before throngs of frenzied zealots, the rubble of Leningrad, the mushroom cloud over Hiroshima. Doc Waters was instructed that History had heralded the coming of the System like John the Baptist had prophesized Jesus. But there was no God. Only the System. And only the System could quash the monstrous instinct inherent in man. Death was no longer considered a punishment for a mythical Original Sin. Death was the unburdening of the sin that is life.

The System as savior.

Doc Waters believed.

In the next moment, the memories vanished, overcome by the silence hovering at the edge of the desert night.

So, they walked. They walked through the phases of the moon, from full to new to full once more. They walked through the darkest of nights. Through moonlit brightness.

Cloud cover began to mute the light of stars and moon more frequently. In the evenings, as they prepared soup over a small fire of dried mesquite, rain sprinkled down. The fertile scent of damp sand and creosote was intoxicating. Doc Waters walked through the night as if in a dream.

The nighttime rains intensified. The Cactus Eaters walked in the mornings when the sky was bright blue. The sun pulsed gold. In the afternoons, the winds picked up. Some days, it blew so steadily that the group had to bow into the wind as if it was some sort of deity.

When the rain came down hard, the Cactus Eaters made funnels from woven yucca leaves and inserted them into their water skins. They waited for the skins to fill while resting beneath the branches of mesquite or sheltered under a shelf of stone jutting from the side of a sandstone cliff.

Doc Waters lost count of the days and nights. He followed the Cactus Eaters through deep arroyos, the tall banks taking on tinges of red. The arroyos became canyons. The rains fell less frequently.

The moon was waxing full when Doc Waters caught a whiff of roasting meat. The scent was familiar. He remembered Mud cutting chunks of meat from the buffalo. It seemed as if it had happened in another time, another story. Mud had tossed the meat into a bonfire. The fire had belched smoke the color of storm clouds.

He remembered Mud cutting the buffalo's tongue from its mouth and wrapping it in a square piece of the animal's hide. He had wondered why Mud would do such a thing. He wondered still.

***

The bullet struck the deer in the spine. The beast lay on its side on the rocky ground, dark eyes open. The buck was young, a spike, the antlers poking out of the skull like stiletto heels.

***

Doc Waters was hungry. He hadn't realized it until that moment. The memory of the buffalo blurred into that of a deer with a broken back, the smell of cow pies on a green field. He knew the memory wasn't his own. It didn't bother him. They hadn't been able to eat the buffalo because Mud said the beast was poisoned. He was certain somebody had eaten the deer. The certainty cramped his gut.

He was following the woman through a canyon when she suddenly stopped and turned on her heel. Moonlight spilled over the red walls of the canyon like cream into a cup of Rubio tea. Doc Waters stood looking at the woman dressed in wolf skins. She seemed to be waiting for something. He waited too.

The two other gang members came up behind Doc Waters. They stood close. An owl hooted in the night. The woman pointed into the canyon.

"What?" asked Doc Waters. His voice hit his ears like a home invasion. "I don't understand."

The woman grunted, "Go."

"Where?" asked Doc Waters.

The small Cactus Eater pricked Doc Waters in the back with the point of his staff. He hissed, "Go."

The owl hooted once more. The nocturnal hunter then took flight, its wings whooshing through the darkness.

A wolf howled somewhere in the distance.

The large Cactus Eater grunted.

"Go," said the woman. "We eat."

There was something sensuous in the way she said it. A gruff beauty. The scent of roasting meat beckoned him forward. He walked past the woman further into the canyon.

***

A canopy of black-bottomed clouds hangs low.
A breeze snakes through sage and greasewood above the creek.
The water is brown as peat.

***

Doc Waters walks up the canyon, the moonlight now blocked by the steep canyon walls. He follows the scent of roasting flesh. He imagines rattlesnakes writhing in the sand at his feet. He dares not hesitate. Dares not look back. He believes the Cactus Eaters have done him a great honor by asking him to lead.

***

The low growl of a raccoon.

***

He imagines something snarling in the darkness.

***

A tremor runs down the raccoon's spine.

***

The epiphany strikes like an exploding grenade. Doc Waters can never be one of them. The revelation causes him to stumble. He can't be one of them because of all the terrible things he has done. He falls to the desert floor. He is beyond redemption. His presence will bring great suffering to the Cactus Eaters. Unable to dislodge the MIU from his brainstem, Doc Waters had decided to deceive to avoid losing Yew forever.

Yes, the MIU may have been disrupted and is no longer sending a signal. But maybe is the mother of doubt. That's why he didn't tell them. Why he didn't tell her. He used the maybe to his advantage. He wanted to stay with Yew and so took the chance that the MIU in his brain was no longer functional. But he wasn't certain. Not then. Not now. Nothing is certain.

The epiphany shatters the illusion of peace that pulsed through him as he meditated to the rhythms of walking. He doesn't belong here. It's not his place. His love for Yew is a longing for the impossible. Nothing more. He doesn't believe in miracles. She's not for him. A dream. A story. A hope. He knows now, as he gets back to his feet and moves through the darkness, that this brand of hope is smoke without fire.

He decides to turn back and warn the Cactus Eaters. They have done nothing to harm him. They don't deserve what's coming. The System will never allow them to escape. They will find them. In emptiness, they will bind them. Doc Waters is the System. Devoid of hope. He must accept it. But not them. Not them.

He stops and stands still. The silence unnerves him. Not the chirp of a cricket or a whisper of breeze. Looking at the sky, he finds only blackness—no starlight, no moon. He's alone. No need to call out. He knows. The Cactus Eaters have abandoned him. They sniffed him out. They know he's the enemy within.

It's as it should be. Best to die alone in the desert. They should have left him buried under the sand where they found him. He would have found real peace.

Doc Waters sits in the dirt. Darkness enfolds him. He enjoys the feeling. Oblivion isn't so bad. One simply needs to surrender.

And then it comes to him. The far-off beating of drums.

CHAPTER SEVEN

M ud emerges in a small pond. The pond is in a peat bog. The night is moonless, the sky milky with starlight. He listens to the croaking of frogs and the chirping of crickets. A few fireflies flit near the shore of the pond. The water is cool. It drips from the curls of the thick fur hanging from his face and skull. Warm air. Deep breaths. The earthy smell of the bog pleases him. He knows this place. He's home.

**

He remembers following the faerie through the black depths, the orb between his palms pulling him ever deeper. The orb was drawn to the faerie as if it was a part of her refusing to be forgotten. Light emanated from the sphere as they delved ever deeper and soon it shone like a candle burning in a forever night.

Mud knew, but he knew not how he knew that the darkness had been created from the light and rebelled against it. The darkness desired revenge. Dark desire struggled to crush the light in the pressure of its unbearable deepness. But the light held. Mud descended, the faerie always just ahead, her green jumpsuit the twinkle of a single star in an endless cosmos. Mud gripped the orb. The light was warm. The light was good. When the orb exploded, shards of light scattered through the void and shone like diamonds in moonlight.

***

Mud finds himself alone—the is faerie gone—but he isn't afraid. He made it through the deep and emerged on the far side. Wherever he is, he's happy. He exists. He is Mud.

The mud on the shore of the pond squishes between Mud's toes as he climbs out of the water. A smile stretches the corners of his mouth. The light of a billion stars mingles in the sky above, creating a luminous veil hanging over the land like a canopy. Mud sits on the shore of the pond and places his feet in the water. He wiggles his toes to wash the dirt away. His legs are covered with fur. As are his arms. His body. His face. That's why he isn't cold. But he's hungry.

He feels the fur near his belly and finds the familiar leather pouch strapped to a belt. Inside the pouch is a square of buffalo hide. Mud unfolds the skin and finds the remains of the buffalo tongue he cut from the beast before burning the meat, organs, and bones in the bonfire in the desert. He knows now that the buffalo wasn't poisoned. It died of a broken heart. It was the last of its kind.

Mud takes a bite out of the tongue. It tastes like blood and sunshine mixed with sage and dust. The meat is tough and dry but, as he continues to chew, the muscle softens. Mud is the last of his kind. A blend of blood and emotion, instinct and intellect. He swallows the meat.

By the time he finishes eating, the eastern horizon is the color of a ripe peach. A cool breeze whisks through the green grasses growing on the bog. The air smells of compost. Mud gets to his feet and rubs his belly. The buffalo will be forever part of him now, a slice of its spirit sheltered inside of his heart. Mountains loom on the western horizon. Soon, he will journey towards them. Not now. The faerie led him to the bog for a purpose. He trusts her. She didn't lead him here for no reason at all.

Mud walks through the bog. The ground squishes under his feet. He feels as light as a bird and fancies he could launch himself into the air and fly. Anything is possible. The fact that he exists is a miracle. He isn't the same as when he snuck out of the System as a fugitive on the run. He's different. New. But he can't fly. He can't create reality. He's no god. Yet, he exists. That's enough.

Mud doesn't know what he's looking for. But he knows he'll find it. He walks through the bog while whistling a tune. He can't remember how he knows the song, but it's as familiar to him as the bog. The sky is clear and blue. The sun shines dandelion yellow. The air now smells slightly of smoke, a rich aroma of tangled mosses, bog myrtle, and heather. A scent spun by water and time. Mud walks. He's happy.

He thought about ending it all while trapped in the System. Dark thoughts. He couldn't take the routine. The only purpose of life, it seemed, was to get through it comfortably. Perform an assigned task to keep the System running and then retire to an apartment filled with electronic screens. That was it. Nothing else. In return, the System promised a smooth transition to the peace of oblivion. No pain. No fear. There was nothing else. Nothing. Accept the inevitable. Play your part and be at peace.

The price of admission to the guaranteed peace was the sacrifice of spirit. Where there is no spirit, there is no longing. Ordinariness becomes its own reward. Where there is no drive, there is no hope. Where there is no hope, there can be no joy. Security stifles being.

System athletes no longer longed for victory. They merely avoided defeat. Artists composed paintings and symphonies based on algorithms. Live events were outlawed on the grounds they were dangerous. Contagions might spread. Thieves and scam artists would be encouraged to ply their trades. Prostitutes and drug dealers would prowl for new victims. Too dangerous. Everything took place within the confines of a screen.

No crowds to cheer on the performers. No rivalry. Stadiums full of empty seats.

Mud remembers his days with Uncle Sammy. They had been free for a time. He believes his uncle's death served a purpose. It planted in his nephew a seed of hope. Mud risked everything to find out if the seed would germinate and it did. The faerie had helped him. She is his uncle's faerie. He sent her. The faerie is gone now, but the seed has sprouted.

He drinks bog water that tastes like green beans mixed with dirt. The breeze blows, steady and cool. He continues south. Seagulls squawk overhead, alarmed by the sudden appearance of a red-tailed hawk. Mud comes upon a flutter of yellow butterflies. Muskrats plop into ponds bristling with cattails. He watches as a red fox disappears over a rise.

The thought of living in the bog pleases Mud. He'll build a hut out of squares of turf and make a roof of cattail stalks, grass, and mud. His fur will keep him warm during the cold months. He needs no fire. There's plenty of water and he'll eat frogs and snails. He might snare a muskrat or two. He'll harvest watercress, bog blueberries, and water chestnuts. He'll be at peace. He doesn't desire the company of men. Never again. Human drama is poison. Men fell into despair long ago. At the very beginning. Not his problem. Not anymore.

"Exactly."

The faerie stands looking at Mud from the stump of an ancient oak at the edge of the bog. She wears a blue jumpsuit. Her hair is as white as bleached wool.

Mud isn't startled by the faerie's appearance. The fact that she looks different doesn't bother him at all. She is the same. Uncle Sammy's faerie.

"Exactly what?" he grunts.

"Control. That's where it came from."

"Where what came from?"

"Despair."

Mud walks to the edge of the bog and sits on the stump. The faerie flits into the air to avoid being crushed by Mud's hairy rump. She hovers above his head.

"You will stop it," says the faerie. "That's why you're here."

"Stop what?" asks Mud.

"Despair."

Mud laughs and watches a seagull fly through the sky. "Is there an ocean around here?"

The faerie alights on Mud's shoulder. "They don't need oceans. Like you don't need men. But they're built for water. It's natural to them. Like you're built for earth."

"This here feels natural to me."

"Yes. But it won't last."

"Nothing does."

"They'll try to control it."

"Who?"

"You'll stop them."

"How? I'm not a man. Not really. Not anymore."

"Yes," chuckles the faerie. "You're something else." She jumps from Mud's shoulder and hovers in front of his brow. "You're the last of your kind, older than men and closer to death."

Mud stares into the faerie's eyes. They're the color of chestnuts. He stands from the stump and scratches his head. "Don't know what that means."

"But you do. Or you will. Follow me." She flies a few feet to the south and hovers. "Well?"

Mud stands, takes a step, and then stops. "Where?"

"To show you a secret."

Mud bends low and pinches some peat from the earth at his feet. He tucks it between his cheek and gum. "Secret?"

The faerie smiles. "The Secret of the Bog."

***

The house had been built before the System was conceived.
To acknowledge this is to conjure ghosts.

***

The grandfather sits in a reclining chair next to a peat-burning potbelly stove. The stove sits in the living room of a Victorian-style house. His beard is long and white, his head bald and polished. He plucks a wad of tobacco from a pouch strung around his neck by a leather cord and stuffs it into his cheek with the tip of his tongue. After a few chews, he spits a stream of tobacco juice into a big brass spittoon on the floor beside the chair.

The grandmother, holding a pot of steaming stew, steps into the living room from the kitchen. Her hair is as white as the grandfather's beard. She wears a dress hewn from gunny sacks. "I don't know why you bother with that. It don't do nothin'."

"I remember how it tastes," says the grandfather. "I aim to keep rememberin' too."

"May as well stuff your mouth with dirt."

"Dirt don't taste the same." The grandfather sits erect in the chair. "Don't know why you're hauntin' me about it anyways. Look at you cookin' that stew. Tryin' to remember what stew tastes like, are ya?"

"Don't be a fool, old man. I made it for him."

"For who?"

"Him. The one we've been waiting for."

The grandfather stands. "He's here?"

"He will be. Now go and get yourself presentable. Don't want to scare the poor thing to death."

"If it's him, he ain't gonna be scared of a couple of old goats like us."

***

One of the cottonwoods, the biggest, stood majestically on the west side of the house. It was struck by lightning long before the grandmother was born. Yew's mother studied the black scar on the trunk of the tree the night she followed her brother into the barn. The scar was round and smooth. Strange. Yew's mother kissed the scar and watched her brother do the same.

***

Mud walks through the day into twilight. He comes to an ancient cottonwood growing in the back of a Victorian-style house. He fancies he can smell mutton stew, though he can't recall ever tasting such a thing. His stomach growls. The sky was clear and blue during the day, but a rumble of thunder now rolls overhead. Lightning flashes on the western horizon. The faint smell of rain hangs in the air.

Mud notices a scar on the trunk of the cottonwood. It reminds him of the orb that had cured his blindness and guided him through the deep. He misses the orb and turns to ask the faerie where he can find it. She's nowhere to be seen.

"None of this is real," Mud says to the tree. "It's all in my head. I'm the same as I ever was. Crazy as a shithouse rat all drugged up and stuffed in a padded cell somewhere." He pats the scar on the tree with the palm of his hand.

"Don't be a bitty witty baby," chirps the faerie.

Mud looks up to find the faerie sitting on a cottonwood branch. She wears a red jumpsuit. Her hair is black, her eyes like polished coal.

"You're not real," says Mud. "It's a dream. All in my head. I ain't playing along no more. I know who I am."

"*Do* you?" asks the faerie. "And who is *that?*"

"Prisoner 767251. Convicted of sedition. I'm in prison. They're experimenting on me. That's why I can see you. I get it now. I've seen the light."

The faerie giggles.

Mud looks at the scar on the trunk of the tree. "Fun while it lasted. That orb was really something else."

***

The brother did not return from the barn.

***

The grandmother calls out from the back porch of the house, "Come inside. Come on in out of the dark."

***

The mother named the baby Yew.

***

"Can't you hear her?" asks the faerie. She jumps from the limb of the cottonwood and hovers between Mud and the house.

"Yeah," says Mud. "I hear. It don't mean nothing. I hear you too."

The faerie's laugh sounds like a chorus of birds. "But I'm not real, right?"

"Inside my head."

"Come on now," calls the grandmother. "It's warm inside. You're safe here."

The faerie lands on the ground and kneels before Mud.

"What are you doing?"

"Oh, great and mighty Mud," the faerie giggles. "You are the creator of reality. You are a god, and I will forever praise your name."

The grandfather steps out of the house and onto the porch. He stands next to the grandmother. "You comin' in?" he yells. "Been waitin' for a time, and the wife here's gone to a lot of trouble."

The faerie rises into the air until she floats before Mud's eyes.

"I ain't no god," says Mud.

The faerie smiles. Her teeth are perfect. "Then you should go on in out of the cold."

"I'm not cold."

"*I* am," says the faerie. "Hungry too."

***

"Is the baby safe?"
"She lives in Red Canyon."

***

"Yes. He gets it now." The grandfather sits in a chair hewn from a pine trunk at the head of a long pine table. "Yew's our granddaughter from way back down a long line of granddaughters."

The table is loaded with fresh loaves of bread, a cast iron pot full of steaming mutton stew, and tubs of fresh butter. In the center of the table, a silver candlestick sports four candles, the wicks burning golden. The glow of a peat fire warms the potbelly stove in a corner of the rectangular room.

The grandmother sits at the opposite end of the table. She pours a coffee cup full of red wine, corks the bottle, and takes a drink.

"I don't know why you bother with it," complains the grandfather. "Can't get a buzz no more, so why put on the show?"

"I remember the taste," says the grandmother. "And I aim to keep remembering." She holds the cup high in a salute. "To our guest! Go ahead, son. Drink up. Reap the gifts of the grape."

Mud sits in a pine chair in the middle of the table. He looks at the flames on the tops of the candles in the candlestick sitting between him and the faerie. The faerie is busy spooning tiny spoons of stew into her tiny mouth. Mud drinks from his coffee cup and wipes his mouth with his hairy arm.

"It's in the barn," says the grandfather. "Right where she left it."

The wine settles warm in Mud's belly. He smiles. "Okay. I got nothing better to do, so's I'll play along. Let me make sure I get it first. Games are more fun when everybody plays by the same rules."

"This ain't no game," says the grandfather.

"Leave him be," says the grandmother. "What's it matter if he thinks it's a game or not?"

"Don't, I guess," says the grandfather. "Long as he gets that we're playing for keeps."

"My soul to keep," sings the faerie. She puts down her spoon, floats into the air, and lands next to the grandmother's bowl of stew. "Can I have a sip of wine?"

The grandmother's brow furrows. "Don't know about that. Probably not a good idea."

"No spirits for spirits," says the grandfather. "That's the rules."

The faerie sits down on the tabletop next to the grandmother's bowl. "No fair. What's the difference between a spirit and an old ghost?"

"Remember what happened last time?" asks the grandmother. "You were sick for a week."

The faerie folds her tiny arms over her tiny chest and pouts a tiny pout.

"How old are you two?" asks Mud.

"Not as old as you might think," answers the grandfather. He scoots his chair away from the table and takes a dip of tobacco from the pouch at his neck. "They made us look old, that's all. They could've made us look any way they wanted but they made me look old." The grandfather leans to one side and spits a stream of tobacco juice into a gourd spittoon on the floor.

"Who made you look old?" asks Mud.

"Don't know," says the grandfather. "They was older than us. *Way* older. They were looking for some fella named Aengus."

***

Yew's mother stashed the secret in a metal lockbox in the barn behind the Victorian-style home. Then, she walked into boglands.

The mother had removed her daughter from the Victorian-style home, and the two of them lived for years in a small apartment at the System's center, hiding more than living, the mother working as a waitress in a café that sold soy burgers and hot dogs made from worms. She saved as many of her tips as she could because she never saw her wages. They were taken by the System in exchange for the apartment and a ration of food. She enrolled Yew in a System school as required and the child attended classes over the computer in her room. In the evenings, her mother told her about her grandparents. She told her about her uncle, how he had found something in the bog and given it to her as a gift. How the gift would become Yew's in her own time. She told her daughter where to find it when the time came.

She would find the secret stashed in a metal lockbox in the barn behind the Victorian-style house.

***

"The System brainwashed her into believing everything her mother told her about us," said the grandmother. "About this house. All lies. They taught her that the imagination—human imagination—was destructive and responsible for the murder of countless innocents. They showed her computer simulations of slaves building pyramids for Egyptian pharaohs, Genghis Khan's slaughtering hordes, Hitler's Final Solution, Stalin's gulags, and all kinds of crimes committed by man upon man. Inquisitions. Atomic bombs. Genocides. They blamed it all on imagination."

"How do you know all this stuff?"

The grandfather perks up. "What?"

"Did Yew come back and tell you?" asks Mud.

"She did come back," said the grandmother. "But never for long."

The grandfather spits in the spittoon. "Should a stayed here. Would've saved us a lot of grief."

"We rarely saw her," continues the grandmother.

"Then how'd you come to know all this? Who told you? Her mother?"

"She never came back," says the grandmother.

"The ones way older than us," says the grandfather. "Whoever they were. Said she'd come back someday. Said it was you who would be leadin' her."

"What?" says Mud.

The faerie stretches out on the tabletop, places a tiny elbow on the wooden surface, and plops her tiny head on her tiny palm. She stares at Mud.

"I don't mean no disrespect," says Mud, "but it don't sound like nobody saw nothin' at all. Just a story. Might be true. Might not be."

"They were with her," says the grandmother.

"They're everywhere," adds the grandfather.

"Who?" asks Mud.

"Listen," scolds the grandfather. "If you'd just listen, you'd dadgum find out. Stop with the cotton-pickin' questions!"

The stew in Mud's stomach is warm with spice. He burps.

"Bless you," says the faerie, her red jumpsuit bright in the candlelight.

"I'm listenin'," says Mud. "But I ain't hearin' much. You want me to believe who's everywhere? From what I seen, there ain't nobody out here. It's like I'm in someone else's story—like you're made up and don't really exist. All in my head."

"We're not who you think we are," says the grandmother.

Mud stands. "Seems like *nothing's* what I think it is." He looks at the faerie. "Why'd you bring me here? It was better in the bog. I'm happy there. Alone."

The faerie yawns.

"You got a part to play too," says the grandmother.

"A part to play? Seems like I've been hearin' that my whole life. A part to play. I want to be left alone. That's what I want. I'm goin' back out to the bog. Things make sense out there. The bog makes sense. If I've gotta be in the System prison the rest of my life, I'll serve the time out there. Otherwise, I'm gonna lose my mind."

"Maybe he *isn't* who we've been waiting for," says the grandfather. "His name may as well be Bog the way he's carryin' on."

"He's the one," says the faerie.

"If you say so," says the grandfather.

"He's the secret," chirps the faerie, and with that, she rises into the air and flies out of the room.

"The secret's gotta be spoken," says the grandmother. "Please. Please, sit down. I'll help you to understand."

"Sorry," says Mud. "Too many voices telling too many stories. It's quiet in the bog. It's home." Nodding at the grandfather, he adds, "It's like he said. I'm Bog. That's my name now. Bog."

"He's the one," says the grandfather. "That proves it. He is Bog."

"Yes," says the grandmother. "Hear me out and then do as you please."

The faerie zips back into the room and floats over the table. "You cheated! No fair! You told him before it was time!" She then zips back out of the room.

The grandfather motions for Bog to sit at the table. "Don't be rude. Just sit a spell. It's the least you can do with all the stew you scarfed down."

"Did you cut the tongue from a dying buffalo?" asks the grandmother.

The grandmother sees worry on Bog's face. "Don't worry about her. She'll be back."

"Yes," says Bog.

"Did you eat it?" asks the grandfather.

Bog burps and sits in his chair.

"There you have it. Just like they said."

"Who?" asks Bog.

***

They knocked on the front door of the Victorian-style home. Night. Full moon. They were dressed in black capes and hoods.

The door opened. The grandfather, the hair on his head thick and long, the beard short and dark, stepped onto the porch, holding a kerosene lantern. Crickets chirped in the darkness.

"You lost?"

"No," said a woman. She pulled the hood from her head. She was young and fair. Her eyes were the kaleidoscopic colors of spring. "We've come to tell you of the Yewberry Way."

***

"We knew by then that Yew was studying neuroconsciousness," says the grandmother.

"We didn't have a clue what neuroconsciousness was. Still don't. Just that she was studying it," adds the grandfather. "That's how everything went wrong—people studyin' things that shouldn't be studied."

The candles burn in the candleholder in the center of the pine table. A single red moth flits about the flames.

"We hadn't seen her in a long while," continues the grandmother. "We didn't know her—not really. Her mother had filled her head with lies. She told her that I murdered her uncle."

Bog stares at the candles as if he's back in the bog and away from the world of men.

"I didn't kill him. My own son. How could I? I tracked him down in the bog and found him living in a hut he had built with squares of turf. He had a peat fire and a bed of leaves. His hair had grown. It was strange because it had grown all over his body. He looked like an animal. He looked like . . . you."

Bog looks at the grandmother and then back to the flames.

"I told him what happened. That his sister had given birth to a baby girl. He didn't seem surprised."

***

It's neither night nor day. A thick fog mutes light and sound. It's as if they, mother and son, are lost in a cloud of smoke.

The son sits on his haunches next to a smoldering fire. He stares into a glow of embers. He appears to be more beast than man. Wild. The air smells of musk and smoke.

"I know," says the son. "I'm Yew's father, and you're here to kill me for what I did."

"You know the baby's name?" asks the mother. "How?"

"She told me," says the son. "She said, 'I'll name her Yew.'"

The son removes a knife from a sheath attached to his belt and offers the hilt to his mother. The blade is long and thin. The hilt is made of bone. "You need to know that I didn't force her. I had no choice. Neither did she."

"You're saying she seduced you?" asks the mother.

"Did she tell you she did?"

"She won't say."

"We had to. There wasn't any other way. It's what we were made for. If we didn't do it—if we refused—we would have been cursed forever. All of us."

"Refused? Refused who?"

"The Old One. In the bog where I found Him."

"I've heard the old stories. The myths."

"It's not a myth, Mother. It's true. All of it. And now I must sacrifice her."

"Who?"

"Yew."

"But why would you sacrifice your own child?"

"Out of love," says the son. He adds a few twigs to the smolder, and the smoke thickens.

The mother coughs. "I don't understand."

"Because you can't."

"Help me."

"It's beyond understanding, yours or anyone else."

"You're not making sense. You're crazy."

"We all must suffer."

"I can't let you do this."

"I know."

The son stares into the smolder.

"What if she can bear the suffering?" asks the mother. "Why does she have to die?"

"She will bear it." The son stands. He positions the blade of the knife in his palms and offers the hilt to his mother. "She will suffer for you."

The mother coughs.

"I'll kill her," says the son.

The mother takes the knife by the bone handle hilt. "She's just a baby."

The son kneels before his mother. "The baby's not safe."

The mother steps behind her son.

The son says, "People will sing of you."

The mother gently places a hand on her son's shoulder. "I'm sorry." The mother slices her son's throat with the blade of the knife. "Forgive me."

***

"But I didn't murder him," says the grandmother. "It was a sacrifice."

Bog looks at the flames on the tips of the candles in the center of the table. "Are you a ghost?"

"No more than I am," says the grandfather. He spits a stream of tobacco juice into the spittoon. "It ain't so bad once you get used to it. It's like you're a story that's waitin' to be read. Until somebody reads it, you ain't really there."

"Are you reading *me*?" asks Bog.

"We're reading each other," says the grandmother.

The grandfather chuckles. "As long as somebody's still tellin' the story, we'll all be just fine."

"Did you like the stew?" asks the grandmother.

Bog looks at her. "I couldn't taste it but it was warm."

"But you remember how it tasted, don't you?" asks the grandfather.

Bog nods and looks at the flames on the tips of the candles. He remembers the taste of the buffalo tongue. The red moth flies close to the flames and is singed.

"I am Bog."

"We've been waiting for you," says the grandmother.

Bog looks at the grandmother. "Am I your son?"

"Maybe," says the grandmother. "I don't know. Do *you*?"

"It was them people," says the grandfather. "They told us you'd come. That's what we been waitin' for. All this time. Seems like a dadgum eternity. Now you've come. Good. I'm tired."

"You're to take it to her," says the grandmother.

"What?"

"The knife."

"Where is it?"

The faerie, her jumpsuit as yellow as a daffodil in sunshine, whizzes into the room. Her hair is rose-petal pink. "In the barn."

Bog stands. "Where is she?"

"On the other side," says the faerie.

"Other side of what?"

"The bog, silly. On the far side of the bog."

"I *am* the bog."

The faerie pulls a tiny orb from her nest of hair. She tosses it to Bog. The orb grows as it sails through the air. It's as large as an emu egg when Bog catches it.

"Follow me," sings the faerie. And she flies away.

The orb glows yellow. Bog turns to follow the faerie, pauses, and turns back. "Thanks for the stew. Best mutton I ever had. Go and get some rest now. Go and sleep."

Bog walks away from the house. The orb pulls him toward the faerie's yellow jumpsuit pulsating in the distance. The darkness surrounding her is as vast. If the darkness managed to swallow the faerie, Bog muses, there would be no hope of getting her back.

He hurries to catch up.

CHAPTER EIGHT

The light of the full moon fails to penetrate the clouds that have gathered over the canyon. The desert stretching to the horizons on either side of the canyon is bathed in a silky glow.

Drumbeats guide Doc Waters through the darkness. He is night blind. The drumbeats ricochet from the cloud bank back to the canyon floor. Doc shuffles up the arroyo like a man drunk on wine.

Large droplets of rain—one here, one there—strike the parched earth. The thumping of droplets punctuates the drumming. Doc Waters steps slowly—one foot, then the other—each footfall kicking up a puff of dust. The night smells of creosote. Doc Waters moves steadily, the combination of drumbeats, rain, and footfalls propelling him into a trance. A dormant instinct rises from his belly into his spine. He knows this place. He's been here before. His heart quickens.

He touches a dead branch of a scrub oak with his bare foot. He's forgotten about shoes. Taking the branch in hand, he finds that it matches the length of his leg from foot to hip. One end of the branch is forked. Each tip of each fork has been sharpened. It's the staff of a Cactus Eater.

Doc Waters sniffs the air. He senses something behind him before he hears the growl. It sounds like the wolf, but he has been with the Cactus Eaters long enough to know it's not. A wolf wouldn't come into the canyon. Too smart. No way out. Doc Waters sniffs the air.

"Why have you forsaken me?" he asks the darkness. "What have I done?"

Thunder rolls through the sky. The drumbeats cease. The night breathes.

"Keep moving." It's the voice of the woman.

"I can't see."

"Use your stick," says the smaller man. He's invisible in the night.

"Is it mine?"

"What?" asks the woman.

"The staff."

"Use it," says the small man.

"Now." The voice of the big man comes from everywhere and nowhere at once.

Doc Waters takes the fork handles of the staff in hand and raises the shaft until it's like an antenna pointing up the canyon. He takes a step forward.

"No," says the big man.

"Up," says the smaller one.

"From where rain comes," says the woman.

Doc Waters points the stick at the sky.

"Walk," says the smaller man.

"Yes," says the woman.

Doc Waters takes a step. The tip of the staff pulls downward until it rests on the sand. Doc Waters tightens his grip but he cannot raise the staff.

"Walk," says the big man.

"Follow," says the woman.

Doc Waters loosens his grip. The end of the staff rises. Doc Waters allows himself to be drawn forward. He does not control the staff; it controls him.

"Yes," says the smaller one. "Walk."

Drumbeats, slow and steady, begin bouncing once more from the canyon walls.

***

Thump.

Thump. Thump.

***

Doc Waters walks.

***

Thump.

Thump. Thump.

***

He walks.

***

Thump.

Thump. Thump.

***

Doc Waters walks to the rhythm of the drums.

***

The Queen of the Cactus Eaters is a round woman with a double chin. Her hair is as gray as fire smoke, her skin the color of mesquite bark. She wears a dress fashioned from wolf hides, the fur turned toward her skin. Four-legged stick figures beaded in red and black cover the surface of the dress. The four-legged figures are forever running from two-legged black stick figures carrying spears. The Queen wears a headdress fashioned from raven feathers. She sits on a throne of stone that has been carved into the canyon wall.

Thunder rolls.

Yew sits next to the Queen on a smaller throne. She wears a dress of white buckskin. Her hair, the color of pinecones, is piled on top of her head. She wears a headdress of white egret feathers. She smells of sweetwood.

Four massive bonfires burn on the floor of the canyon. Stomp dancers dressed in wolf pelts, their dark hair wild and long, circle the flames. Drummers drumming buffalo-hide drums encircle the dancers. The drums vary in size and tone. The dancers stomp to the cadence of the biggest drums, knees pumping, arms flapping like the wings of birds. They dance the Dance of the Snake-Killer Bird. Their bodies are earthbound. Their spirits soar.

Gangs of Cactus Eaters mingle outside the ring of drummers. Some drink cactus wine from gourd cups—others from mugs of fired clay. Some watch the dancers stomp around the bonfires. Others mingle in the shadows beyond the reach of light.

The rhythm of the beating drums sinks into Yew's bones, leaks into her blood. Pressure builds at her temples.

***

Thump.
Thump. Thump.

***

Sweat blurs her vision. Light blossoms behind her eyes.

***

Yellow sun.

***

Her gut buzzes.

***

Thump.
Thump. Thump.

***

She remembers the Outpost Man propped against the bank of the arroyo in the desert. Blue Sky. Brown earth. The sound of a raven's caw.

***

Thump.
Thump. Thump.

***

She remembers the smell of buffalo guts and a humming cloud of black flies.

The drums cease. The dancers stop stomping. The shadow minglers at the edge of the light move closer to the flames. The drinkers of cactus wine drink from their cups. They stare into the darkness to the east of the canyon.

The Queen rises from her throne. She takes up a staff leaning against the red wall. It's aspen-hewn. It's not forked. The Queen glances at Yew before striking the base of the staff on the rock ledge at her feet.

"Time!" shouts the Queen. Her voice is too big for her body—too deep. It's steady and thick like a warm current in deep waters.

The Cactus Eaters, as one, look up to the Queen.

"Time for song," calls the Queen.

Her voice falls over the Cactus Eaters like summer rain.

"*Time,*" chant the Cactus Eaters. "*It is time. Time. We are time. Time. Song time.*"

"The Song of Sacrifice." The Queen glances at Yew, who sits next to her. "Stand," she whispers.

Yew stands. The white feathers of her headdress fall over her shoulders to cover her shoulders and chest.

The cloud cover cracks, and the light of the full moon falls over the canyon.

The drummers begin drumming buffalo drums.

A man stumbles out of the darkness into the light. Following behind are three Cactus Eaters, two me—one big, one small—and a woman. They point the sharp ends of their forked staffs at the man's back. The prisoner wears no shoes, but the remnants of his clothes betray the fact that he's an outsider.

"Doc Waters," whispers Yew.

"System man," hisses the Queen. Moonlight slides from the raven feathers of her headdress onto her shoulders. Firelight dances in her eyes.

"He helped me," says Yew. "I wouldn't be here if he hadn't helped me."

"He will betray you," says the Queen. "Betray *us.* He would be rid of us all." She points her staff at Doc Waters. "Bring him."

Doc Waters recognizes the voice. He looks up at the woman on the rock ledge. "Crow?" he yells. "Is that you?" He smiles. "It's me. Doc." He recognizes Yew. She looks majestic in the white buckskins and the egret headdress. Beautiful.

"I know you not," shouts the Queen. "You speak of Bav Catha. She has gone to Red Canyon. She goes to the Cave of the Snake-Killer Bird." Her voice rolls over the people below like a sudden storm. "I am Queen of People. But I am not one with them. I'm older. *Much* older. People sing the sung song to keep the song alive. You, System man—you have come to silence the singing. You have come to kill beauty. You lie. You are Erasure Chief." She strikes the base of the staff on the ledge. "The song must remain. The song must be sung."

The Cactus Eaters, as one, sing to the cadence of the drums:

Hózhó náhásdlíí'

Hózhó náhásdlíí'

Hózhó náhásdlíí'

Hózhó náhásdlíí'

Yew recognizes the language. A dialect of Athabascan. Something about beauty. Something about hope. Her belly burns.

"Bind him," shouts the Queen. "The final offering has presented itself to the gathering as the sung song sings. We will sing to Silence and we will hear the song without singing."

"Stop!" cries a voice from below.

The singers stop singing. The drummers stop drumming buffalo drums.

The Queen looks down at People.

A woman steps forward and stands at the base of the canyon wall. She looks up at the Queen. It is the woman who brought in Yew, the woman who is rumored to have driven System soldiers berserk until they slaughtered their own. It's said that she cut out their tongues and hid them in Red Canyon. It's said she buried the tongues in a cave.

"Speak, sister," says the Queen.

Thunder rumbles. The crack in the clouds closes as quickly as it opened and the blessing of moonlight is gone. A big drop of rain strikes Doc Waters on the top of his skull.

"Bav Catha has gone to Red Canyon?" asks the woman.

The woman's name flows through the crowd like a breeze: "Nemain."

"Yes," calls down the Queen. "Our sister has gone to take back the silence that was stolen. She fulfills her part. We must do the same, You and I. We must sacrifice the offering that has come to us of his free will. We shall eat of his flesh. So the sung song sings."

Yew stands. "I remember." She looks down at the woman on the canyon floor. "Nemain. My grandmother told me the story." She looks to the Queen. "And you are Macha. With Bav Catha, you are the One and Three."

"Yes," says Nemain. "One and Three."

The Queen looks first at Nemain and then at Yew as if she has just woken up from a dream. "And I remember *you*. You search for the Praying Man. You will find him by weaving the songs into one. The Weaver of Songs."

"You are the Phantom Queen," whispers Yew. "One and Three."

The Queen looks down on People. "Prepare him. He will roast. We will eat."

The two males from Doc Water's gang—one small, one large—step forward and seize him by the arms. They drag him toward the fires.

"You would kill a man who comes in peace?" shouts Nemain.

The two men dragging Doc Waters stop. They turn and look at the Queen.

The remaining Cactus Eaters look first to the Queen and then to Nemain.

"Where he goes, the System follows," says the Queen. "He is the System. He must be sacrificed as the sung song sings."

"Am I dreaming?" asks Yew.

"We will eat the flesh of the System," continues the Queen. "It will be woven into the song."

"And she will weave it?" asks Nemain, pointing up at Yew.

"Yes," says the Queen.

Yew closes her eyes. She remembers.

***

Listen.

***

"Aengus," whispers Yew. She sits on the throne next to the Queen.

***

Understand.

***

"Do *you* understand?" shouts Nemain.

The Queen, looking at Yew, whispers, "Awake."

Yew opens her eyes. "If it's not my dream," Yew says, "whose?"

"She has forgotten the Way of the Weaver" shouts Nemain. "The predictability of the System has leaked into her mind and strangled the vision. She does not know the One."

The Queen hears the distant rumbling before the others, steady like machines. She points her staff at Doc Waters. "His part has already been played. He has betrayed us. They come. He is no longer fit for sacrifice."

***

Remember.

***

Doc Waters stands between the two gang members holding his arms. The bonfires burn bright behind him. He has nowhere to go. The back of his neck aches. The MIU.

***

There is no mercy here.

***

A large drop of rain hits the ground in front of Nemain and explodes. A tiny cloud of dust rises and then settles at her feet.

"Then who?" asks Nemain. "Who is worthy?"

Yew remembers. "The Outpost Man," she whispers.

"Yes," shouts the Queen. "The Outpost Man. Only he can save us now."

"Where is he?" asks Nemain.

"In the Cave of the Snake-Killer Bird," says the Queen. "Our sister has trapped him in Silence."

A clap of close thunder blasts in the night. Doc Waters jerks as if jolted by a Snake Stick. He looks at Nemain and then at Yew. Blood oozes from a wound in his gut.

Another blast.

"Snipers!" yells a Cactus Eater. "Run!"

The Cactus Eaters scramble. The skull of the big man standing next to Doc Waters explodes. Doc Waters jerks. He's hit in the chest. The small Cactus Eater turns Doc Waters loose and runs. Doc Waters falls dead.

A mechanical war dog emerges from the darkness. It lurches forward on metal legs, its gait stiff and measured. It's followed by another of its kind. And another. The machines move quickly over the canyon floor. The war dogs latch onto their prey with teeth of polished steel. The victims of the machines are dead in seconds—throats ripped away, faces slashed, mouths torn agape. The dogs tune in to the fear. They move to the next victim. And the next. And more.

The clouds open, and rain falls in sheets. Dead and dying Cactus Eaters sprawl in the mud. Blood mixes with earth. Thunder rolls.

Four gangs of four Cactus Eaters surround one of the war dogs. They beat the machine with their forked staffs and probe it with the points of the spears. Eight Cactus Eaters are dead on the ground when a wolf charges silently out of the darkness. The wolf bites the neck of a machine dog with long canine teeth as bright as the moon. The wolf's teeth snap against metal. The war dog rips the wolf in half with a single chomp of its steel teeth. A Cactus Eater thrusts his spear between the shoulder blade and the neck of the war dog. The red glow in the mechanical eyes of the monster goes dark. The machine dog collapses into the sand.

A rumble of engines mixes with thunder. Dune buggies roll into the canyon like columns of ants into war. Each of the buggies carries two men—a driver and a gunner. The gunner stands behind the driver in the rear of the buggy. He grips the handle of the machine gun mounted on the roll bar. The men are decked out in combat gear.

Tinny and Rachet lead the invasion. The white orb hovering above their buggy throbs light. Rachet drives. It was he who took the orb from the basket of datura leaves. The orb is under his command. Tinny stands in the passenger seat, gripping the roll bar. The light of the orb cuts through the darkness, pulsing white light. Red mud splashing.

"Now!" yells Rachet. He grips the steering wheel of the buggy in both hands. The light of the orb has given him clarity. He is no longer a boy who feels like a girl. He is a man who once loved a woman and was betrayed. He no longer feels love. He is free. He is hate. He is Mean Eyes risen from the grave. "I am fire!" he screams.

"What?" shouts Tinny.

"Fire!" cries Rachet. The scent of blood and earth fuels his rage. The whites of his eyes bulge. "Kill them all! No one escapes!"

***

No hope.

***

Tinny takes a hand from the roll bar and places it on the machine gun.

"Hurry!" yells Rachet. "The bastards'll blend into the night, and we'll never find them. DO IT NOW!"

Tinny takes hold of the gun with both hands and yanks the trigger. Bullets pepper the canyon walls, the barrel of the gun rising from repeated concussions.

"Hold it down!" screams Rachet. "You're shooting air!"

Rachet's voice is lost in the cacophony of gunfire that erupts from the columns of buggies. The canyon lights up like a fireworks show.

Rain falls.

Nemain appears on the ledge of the canyon wall. She stands to one side of Yew. Three women watch the slaughter.

"Do something," pleads Yew. "They're dying."

"Not all," says Nemain. "Some will live."

Scores of lizards as large as wolves materialize out of the canyon floor. Some are yellow-headed with red bodies. Others are redheaded with yellow bodies. Their eyes are black.

"Not many," says the Queen. "Some."

The lizards engage the war dogs and jump into buggies, biting drivers and gunners with needle-sharp teeth. The lizards slash with razor-sharp tails.

"Some is enough," says Nemain. "Their dying is the sacrifice."

A bullet strikes the canyon wall above the Queen.

"We must go," says Nemain.

"Where?" asks the Queen. She looks at her sister.

"To the Praying Man," says Yew, standing between them. "He calls. He calls for me."

The Queen looks at Yew. "Are you the Bird Who Stole Silence? The Snake-Killer Bird?"

"No," says Nemain. "She is the voice of the One."

A tear slides down Yew's cheek.

"She will lead us to Aengus," says Nemain.

Another bullet strikes the wall of the canyon. Fragments of stone fall onto the Queen's throne.

"Not all People will die," says the Queen. "I will lead the survivors. I will lead them back to Red Canyon."

"Come," says Nemain. "Take my hand."

Nemain takes Yew by one hand and the Queen by the other. The sisters start to sing. Their voices sound like the synchronized flapping of a murder of crows.

CHAPTER NINE

Bav Catha hears the song. She feels the wind on her face. She searches for Silence in a cave. The walls of the cave are filled with runes, stick figures of men with bows and spears chasing buffalo and deer, the X-shaped tracks of the Snake-Killer Bird, shadows of buzzards skating over outlines of clouds forever hanging over the scene.

She sits on a buffalo-hide rug in the center of the cave. She takes a pipe fashioned from red clay from a pouch at her neck. She then picks up a stick of fatwood from the floor and ignites the tip in a small fire at the edge of the buffalo hide. She holds the flame of the fatwood over the bowl of the pipe and takes a puff from the stem. Blue smoke rises. The smoke smells of cat piss.

The pipe is sacred, handed down by a long line of grandmothers. It's said to have been carved by the Old Ones. The lines etched into the stem represent words of a forgotten tongue. Bav Catha cannot read the script. She cannot plumb the mystery of making. Bav Catha smokes and dreams. But she doesn't understand.

***

Jack-the-Bartender. A purple Harley Sportster.
Cody Lannard. The Lazy M Ranch.
Hopi Kachinas: Bear, Clown, Crow Mother.
The Puerto Rican. The Orchard.
Emily and Francisco.
The body of a raccoon beaten to death.
Red Canyon.
Snake-Killer Bird.
Old Ones.

***

Bav Catha dreams the dream of Aengus as her sisters sing his song.

***

Bog steps out of the darkness and into the cave. He is covered in a shaggy coat of brown fur. The points of two curved horns protrude from the sides of his skull. He smells of damp peat and carries an orb in one of his hands. The orb glows green.

A leather belt encircles Bog's torso. A sheath made from raccoon hide hangs from the belt. In the sheath is the bone handle knife.

Bog grunts.

***

They kissed the scar on the lightning-struck tree.

***

Bav Catha sings the song with her sisters.

***

I step out of the darkness on the opposite side of the cave. There is a rattle of six buffalo hooves tied to the rib bone of a deer in my hand. I don't know where it came from, but it's familiar as a phantom limb.

A woman sits in the center of a buffalo rug. She is singing.

I remember riding a horse with a foaming neck as it galloped under a sky the color of rust. The rust turned to darkness—no stars, no moon—and the foam on the horse's neck glowed with an unearthly light. The horse ran.

The memory isn't mine. A story told to me. A dream.

I recognize Bav Catha. I've seen her before. Tasted her. In the cave. I loved her once. She doesn't belong here. She wants me to love her the way I used to—the dreamy love of the otherworld. I would if I could but I can't.

Bav Catha falls silent. She takes a pinch of powder from a pouch around her neck and places it in the bowl of her red pipe. Looking at me, she says, "I've been forever waiting."

I say, "I've come through the darkness."

"On a horse?" she asks.

"Yes," I answer. "On a horse."

***

The horse was the color of rust and wild as the wind.

***

"I cried for that raccoon," says Bav Catha. "I cried for the boy who killed it. Was it you?"

"I don't know," I say. "It was a story. I was in it. Does that make it real?"

"Who?" asks Bav Catha. "Who told the story?"

"A man I found. At the Outpost. He was praying. Was he part of the story too?"

"No." Bav Catha takes a sliver of fatwood from a small stack at the edge of the rug. She lights it in the fire, touches it to the bowl of the pipe, and smokes. "What did he say, this Praying Man?"

"He told me that galloping horses please God."

Bog grunts and steps forward into the glow of the fire. The orb glows green in his hand.

"Mud?" I ask. "Is that you?"

My hand moves of its own volition, shaking the deer rib so the buffalo hooves clack.

Bog's orb glows brighter. Bog turns green. He grunts, "I am Bog. Where she?"

"Who?"

"Sister."

"I don't know."

"Search."

"For forever," says Bav Catha.

Bog lowers into a crouch and stares into the orb.

"What's her name?" asks Bav Catha. "Say it."

"She sings light," says Bog.

"Yes," says Bav Catha. "She sings the soul into the song sung."

Bog stands. His palm drops over the hilt of his bone-handle knife. He pulls the blade from the sheath. The green light of the orb swims over the surface of the metal. Bog grunts.

Bav Catha smokes from the pipe and offers it to me.

"What is it?" I ask.

"Secret things."

"No more secrets."

"No mystery, no life."

"No." For a moment I know who I'm supposed to be—the character I've been assigned. An Outpost Man. A System Man. "There is no mystery. It's a myth made up to cheat the void. It isn't real."

"And you?" asks Bav Catha. "A character in a story? What is real?"

"The dream," grunts Bog. "It shines."

"The System," I say. "The System is real. There is nothing else."

"No? Nothing?"

I can't think of anything to say.

Bog holds the blade of the knife next to the orb as if to charge it with the green light. He takes a step forward.

"No," says Bav Catha. "Not him." She takes a puff from the pipe and offers it once more to me.

"Why do you smoke it?"

"To find my way back."

"Smoke," orders Bog.

I take the pipe and puff.

The hint of a grin twitches at a corner of Bav Catha's flaking lips.

The smoke is putrid. I hand the pipe back.

"It's made of yew berries," she says. "And other things. It restores the things that are forever, brings them back into the light."

"Time," says Bog.

"It's the Yewberry Way," says Bav Catha. "It's the way out of nowhere."

I can't keep my eyes open. "Where is she?"

"Who?" asks Bav Catha. "Say her name."

"Yew."

***

An eruption of earthworms.
A cloud of starlings.
A chorus of crows.

***

Breathe.

***

The Praying Man told me that he had once dreamed of a woman and then fell in love with her ghost. His heart became sick. He set out from an emerald isle in search of a phantom. The longing led him to Red Canyon, and it was there that he forgot who he was.

The Praying Man yearned. The yearning engulfed him.

He sought refuge in a cave high on a canyon wall. He was tormented by dreams of swans hissing, "Yew, yeeew, yeeeew."

He didn't belong in a world of sandstone and cacti, vultures and ravens, scorpions and snakes. He didn't belong in a world of death. Heatwaves shimmered over the sand. The illusion of water. His skin, white as ivory, burned red and then brown. His hair, once the color of sunset, paled. His eyes went from green to hazel to a hue of burnt amber. And then they went black. He was no longer himself.

So, he went searching.

He found me.

What is a man but a dream dreamed by ancestors into a future they will never know?

When I found him, he was praying. That's how I remembered him. By his prayer.

"Father," he said, "why have you sent me?"

***

The glare of the sun on the sand causes him to wonder if a blind man might see light rather than darkness. He wants to weep but cannot.

***

"Did you find him, or did he find you?"

"Who am I?"

"The one he found."

Bog grunts.

"He could not find her without you," says Bav Catha.

"Yew?"

"Yes. You. There would be no story without Yew."

"She sings light," grunts Bog.

***

I didn't tell the System bastards about the Praying Man. Even with the way they prodded and drugged me, I still didn't tell them. I fell in love with Yew. I don't know why. Maybe because he loved her too.

Yew meant something to the Praying Man. She was the key to the lock that would set him free. She could save him. The only one who could save him. He sensed I knew her, and he hoped she had told me the story. He was in love with a story he had never heard, a rumor whispered, religion turned into myth. He remembered how to pray, it's all he could remember, and he found her in rhythm of prayer.

I needed her to love me like she loved him. I needed to take his place.

Yew kept asking me his name. I couldn't remember. I couldn't remember anything. Not at first. And then it started to come back. A memory carried on a scent. Sweetwood.

I remembered.

Aengus.

And he remembered me.

***

Understand.

***

"She's here," says Bav Catha.

"Yew?"

The faerie flits out of the darkness and hovers at Bog's shoulder. Her pantsuit glows, kaleidoscopic. She smiles. "Miss me?"

Bog grunts.

"Bring me the orb," says Bav Catha.

The faerie flits down and lands on the orb in Bog's hand. The orb goes dark.

"Bring it," repeats Bav Catha.

Bog steps forward.

"No. Not you. Her. Starglow will bring it."

The faerie takes flight, swoops under Bog's hairy hand, and squeezes through two of his fingers. She stands on Bog's palm holding the orb above her head.

"Bring it to me."

"It's not yours," says the faerie. "You think it is but it's not."

"Then whose? Yours?" asks Bav Catha.

"You don't understand," says the faerie. She rises from Bog's palm and hovers in the air, the orb above her head. "We're not supposed to be here. It's not our story. It's theirs."

"There's only one story," says Bav Catha. "One truth. Now bring me the orb."

"The story is One and Three," says the faerie. "Three stories in one. This story is one but not ours." The orb shrinks to the size of a marble. "Anyways, you're not my boss." She pops the orb into her mouth and swallows.

Bog grunts.

I can't move. The rattle falls to the floor. The deer bone shatters. The hooves clippety-clop into the outer dark of the cave.

The faerie hovers at the edge of the buffalo hide. "They'll just keep coming, you know. They have to get rid of us. We're ruining their story."

"*Our* story," says Bav Catha. "There is only one."

I say, "One and Three."

"Give me the orb," barks Bav Catha. "They can't find it. If they do, there will be no silence. Only the hum of machines."

The faerie says, "I'm Starglow. I take orbs from the darkness and return them to the light. There's only one left after this. I'll come back for it another day. Another time." The faerie winks at Bog before whizzing into the dark. When she's gone, Bog falls to his knees.

Bav Catha lights the pipe with a sliver of fatwood. She understands. "If she has to come back, the story goes on. Yew is of no use to us. Not now. Later."

I draw the dagger—the dagger Bav Catha used to torture Raggedy Man back in the cave—from my belt and grip the figure eights etched on either side of the hilt in my palm.

***

A cauldron of bats.
Electric hum.

***

"I smoke Silence," says Bav Catha. "I've heard the song without sound."

"It's a dream," I whisper.

"Just dream," says Bog. "A dream. Just a dream. Dream."

No," hisses Bav Catha. "Before the dream."

"Who am I?" I ask.

"You don't know? The day is getting late, the light fading. Time to choose."

I look to Bog. "And him?"

"The muck that feeds."

"The faerie?"

"His muse."

"Am I real?"

"What is real?"

"Love."

"Yes."

"Do you love me?"

"Another."

"Who?"

"Yew."

Bav Catha sets the pipe on the rug. "She's here."

Bog, knife in hand, circles the buffalo rug. His fur begins to vibrate.

***

Bav Catha sings but there is no sound.

***

Yew's mother told her the story that her grandmother should have, just as her mother heard the story from her grandmother before her.

Nemain, Macha, and Bav Catha were in the story. Three in One. There were other names, too. Bikeh Hozho and Cernnunos, Estanatlehi and Danu, Thelgeth and Balor. There were many names, including the names of the giants who had created Red Canyon. The last name in the story was Aengus. Yew's mother mentioned his name but gave him no place in the tale. It was as if she didn't know where he fit in. His was a name that named nothing.

When she met him in the hospital, she knew he was more than an Outpost Man. He had to be. He was at the heart of a story. She wanted his story to be hers.

***

Cauldron of bats.

***

"I was born of a tree," says Yew.

"Yes," says Macha, Queen of the Cactus Eaters. "You are of yew."

"And you are born of faeries," Yew says to Nemain.

"Sister Crow, we have found you," says Nemain.

"And I you," says the Queen. "The washerwoman of the dead."

"Remember," says Macha.

"Yes," I say. "I remember. But I don't understand."

"It is beyond understanding," says Nemain.

"Faith in the beyond," whispers Bav Catha. "Choose."

***

Behold.

***

I choose Yew.

***

The glow of a small fire. A crow sitting in the center of a buffalo hide rug takes to the wing. Two birds follow after, one a raven, the other a vulture.

***

Bear.
Clown.
Crow Mother.
Eototo.
Behold the dream of making.

***

Bog grunts.

When she appears, it seems like she was always here. Always watching. Always waiting. And now the moment has arrived.

I don't recognize her at first—can't remember what she looked like the last time I saw her. But I know it's her. Beautiful. She smells of sweet-wood. Hair the color of pinecones. She wears a white buffalo dress and a crown of egret feathers. Her eyes are hazel. She looks at me. I stand in the center of the buffalo rug. She takes a step forward.

"No," says Bog.

Yew looks at Bog. "Father? "

"I am Bog. I take you home."

"Where have they gone? The Queen and Nemain?"

"Gone," grunts Bog. "Gone with Crow."

"How will you get her home?" I ask. "You know the way?"

Bog grunts.

The fire at the edge of the rug burns blue. All is quiet but for the hissing of flames.

Yew looks at me, "Are we dreaming?"

The buffalo hide vibrates under my feet.

Yew takes a step forward.

"No," grunts Bog.

The faerie flits into the chamber. Her pantsuit is the color of fire, and her hair is an angry blush. "They're coming."

"Who?" asks Yew.

"Men," squeaks the faerie.

"System men," I say. "They're coming for me."

"Why?"

"He taught me how to pray."

"Who?"

"Aengus."

"Do you remember the words?"

"Yes. I remember."

"Whisper the words to me."

Mummified tongues fall from the darkness above. They are the tongues of men driven berserk into battle, men who killed their own brothers. The tongues were hidden in the cave by One of the Three. They are hidden no more. The tongues tremble on the stone floor.

"I will never forget."

I say, "Stay with me."

"We go now," says Bog. "Take home."

The blue flames of the fire at the edge of the buffalo rug grow brighter. The rug vibrates. Bog looks at me.

The hilt of the dagger grows warm in my palm.

"Come," I say.

Yew stands still.

The hum of machines vibrates the walls of the cave. A thrumming of diesel engines shakes loose the runes from the walls. Stick figures of men with bows and spears chasing buffalo and deer, the X-shaped tracks of the Snake-Killer Bird, and shadows of buzzards skating over outlines of clouds—all of it crumbles onto the floor of the cave. The rubble of runes covers the trembling tongues.

***

The faerie flies to the center of the rug and hovers over my head. "Come, Bog. Onto the rug."

Yew takes a step forward.

"Not you," says the faerie. "Not now. Later."

Bog shuffles to Yew and holds out the bone-handled knife. "For you. Not me. Not Bog. Yew."

Yew looks at the knife but doesn't take it. She shakes her head. "I can't."

"Youuuio, youuuuio, youuuuioooo," trills the faerie.

Yew takes another step toward the buffalo hide and stands at the edge.

Stepping to the edge of the rug I stand face to face with Yew. "Who am I?"

"The man who remembered how to pray."

"Yes. And you are the prayer."

The sound of machines grows louder. The thrum is throaty and deep, the sound of holes being bored into the walls of the cave. It is the sound of stories being erased.

"They won't forget," says Yew. "I won't let them."

The hair on the buffalo hide smolders.

"As it was sung," hums the faerie. "As the sung song sings."

The buffalo hide erupts into flames.

***

Hózhó náhásdlíí'
Is í an fhírinne áilleacht
Hózhó náhásdlíí'
Is í an fhírinne áilleacht
Hózhó náhásdlíí'
Is í an fhírinne áilleacht
Hózhó náhásdlíí'
Is í an fhírinne áilleacht

***

The thrumming of machines eats Silence. The walls of the cave collapse. All that remains are the sounds of war.

***

EPILOGUE

*S*unlight slices through the space between the curtains on the bedroom window. Dust floats in light. Yew lies asleep on the bed, a
stripe of sunlight slashing her forehead like a wound.

She awakens from a dream. She sits up. She reaches out and opens the
drapes. The sun is a golden circle outside the window. Yew realizes she
is in her grandmother's room. She is in the attic of the old Victorian-style
house.

She sees the big cottonwood standing outside the window. It was struck
by lightning before her grandmother was born. When Yew spots the familiar scar on the trunk of the tree— round and smooth like a black orb—
something strange and light and wonderful leaps in her belly. She smiles.
She is hungry.

She wonders what her grandmother has cooked for breakfast.
She wonders what new stories her grandmother will tell her this day.
She wanders down the stairs to the kitchen
As she wonders
If her grandmother will finish the Aengus' tale.

THE END

www.ingramcontent.com/pod-product-compliance
Lightning Source LLC
Chambersburg PA
CBHW061327050726
47504CB00013B/1030